ALPHA'S SECRET

A BEAR SHIFTER MMA ROMANCE

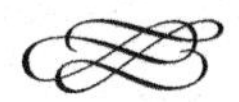

RENEE ROSE

LEE SAVINO

ALPHA'S SECRET

SHE BELONGS TO MY ENEMY. I WON'T STOP UNTIL SHE'S MINE.

I'm the ultimate predator. I live by a code. Hunt or be hunted. Kill or be killed.

Then I meet her. The second I catch her scent, I know she was meant for me. She was born to wear my mark, and I was born to protect her.

She belonged to my enemy until I took her. He wants her back. He'll wage war to get her, but no one's taking her from me.

She's mine, and I'm not letting her go.

Published in the United States of America

Renee Rose Romance and Silverwood Press

Editor: Celeste Jones

❀ Created with Vellum

ACKNOWLEDGMENTS

A huge thank you to Aubrey Cara, who is without a doubt, the best beta reader on Earth.

Huge smooches to Celeste Jones for the last minute edit job when our plans shifted, and to Jane, for her proofread.

Thank you to Lee's Goddess Group and Renee's Romper Room for your support and love. Thanks to our ARC readers and to Ardent Prose PR and the bloggers who support our releases. You are all amazing!

CHAPTER 1

rizz

Fucking twisted vampires.

Toxic, the vampires' BDSM club, is half lounge, half medieval dungeon: all heavy wooden furniture, red velvet, and dark corners a guy can get lost in. At one end, a small bar serves only top shelf liquor and rare wine. Glasses clink, a civilized sound that will soon be drowned out by the darker ones coming from the dungeon.

Above our heads, music starts to pulse, throbbing through the ceiling. Not long now before couples start to descend from the nightclub on the first floor.

I thread my way through the stations, careful not to touch any of the implements of torture, the custom-built furniture that looms like nightmarish monsters in the dim light. The sight of spanking benches and St. Andrew's crosses is enough to make a submissive quake. Pant with desire. Makes no damn sense to me, but I watch it happen every night.

I wait in the shadows as the first of them enter, pairs of people slipping down the stairs. Some head straight for their favorite area or private alcove, others freeze at the foot of the stairs, staring into the dungeon with a mixture of fear and desire.

The vampires keep it dark down here, maybe to hide what they are. That might work on frail human senses, but I smell 'em at every turn. Here's one tying a lovely blonde to the wall. There's another seated in the lounge with a slender man on his lap. The vampire whispers in his submissive's ear and the man's eyes grow wide, locked on a lighted display of implements. Torture tools, I call them, even though the submissives seem to love them. Hell, arousal pours off the male sub as his vampire master tugs him to a spanking bench. The human can't wait to get his ass smacked.

I don't get it. It's a mystery to me, a mating ritual that makes no sense.

The vampire snaps his fingers and a lovely redheaded woman joins the male couple. She goes to the wall and selects a black flogger before returning to the vampire who's making a big show of tying his partner down. The redhead is a little slip of a thing wearing a skimpy white robe, her white thong clearly visible under the thin fabric. A white leather collar is buckled around her neck. Head bowed, she offers the flogger to her master, holding a serving pose for as long as it takes for him to grab it. At his dismissive gesture, she retreats to wait for his next order. A few people gather to watch the vampire flog his male sub, but I only want to watch the redhead. A breeze stirs in the club, cool air blowing from the air conditioning vents. The little redhead's skin breaks out in goosebumps and her nipples harden. She's cold, dammit. I don't know why I care, but I do.

I don't get the point of all this pomp and ceremony. It's the worst sort of foreplay, unnecessary and complicated. No wonder the vampires love it. Half of these fuckers grew up in the Victorian era.

Now the redhead, I get the appeal of her. She's got a delicate spray of freckles across her face, and bare feet. She stands on the edge of the scene, quiet and unobtrusive as her master scenes with another. If I was her master, I wouldn't ignore her. I sure as hell wouldn't scene with another. I'd keep her close, tie her up until she knew she belonged to me. Train her to greet me, tug me to the couch with eager hands, get on her knees between my feet and give me a proper welcome.

And now my dick is hard. I turn away from the redhead. Watching her riles up my bear, and I need a cool head tonight. I took this gig because it's low key, but more importantly, it gets me closer to my ultimate prey.

My heavy boots beat a familiar rhythm as I make my rounds of the club. I can move silently, but better that they see a big lumbering oaf, a bear employed by vampires, a shifter servant of the king. Most couples ignore me. This vampire BDSM club takes some getting used to, but it's quiet, unlike the shifter Fight Club where

I used to work. Here, most patrons are polite and do their thing.

A blonde slinks by, naked but for a tiny red lace thong and black collar. There's a leash hanging from her collar, between her bare breasts. She smiles as she passes me, flicking the leash over her shoulder so it hangs between the reddened globes of her perfect ass.

Yep, bouncing at the vampire BDSM club is a nice gig if you can get it. Some nights are nicer than others.

I round the corner and there she is—the little redhead—naked with her arms stretched over her head. The vampire demonstrates some sort of rope bondage thing, using the redhead sub as his model. Her white robe pooled at her feet, she obeys with a calm, almost blissed out expression. There's a smattering of freckles on her arms and shoulders. Her chest rises and falls with deep even breaths as the rope constricts her chest. Her eyelashes flutter.

The vampire finishes the demonstration and unties the girl, directing her to put away the rope and sending her off with a smack on her ass. A growl lodges in my throat. Fuck, I've been standing here staring for far too long.

"Like what you see, shifter?" a vampire lisps at my side. "Maybe you should try it."

I wait until the redhead disappears into a private alcove before murmuring to my unwanted conversation partner, "Sure, Benny. How 'bout on your dead body?"

The vampire Benny draws his teeth back, showing fangs. "The name's Benedict."

"I know." I tilt my head to the side, already bored.

Benedict is one of the younger vampires, turned only a century ago, pale and thin like he's dying of fucking consumption. Maybe he was when he was turned. "I gave you a nickname. If I was unfortunate enough to be named Benedict, I'd fucking embrace an alternative."

Benny's eyebrows shoot up. I'm careful not to look in his eyes, but I can tell he's upset by the way his chest rises and falls like bellows.

"Careful, bear. You may have the king's favor, but you're no match for a vampire."

"That's what you think," I mutter, and shake my head when he snarls. "Get outta here, fangs."

"Why you—" he huffs.

I curl my lip and give him my back for a solid second before walking away. The worst insult to a vampire: turning your back like he's not a threat. Most shifters would never do it.

I'm not most shifters. The vampires have no idea. They talk down and taunt me, completely clueless. They don't know what I am, what I'm capable of. And when the time comes for me to hunt them, they won't understand what's happening. Not until too late.

I head back towards the bar.

"The king wants you," the bartender tells me and nods to the throne in the middle of the room. So Frangelico has decided to grace us with his presence. I pivot and trudge back to see the boss.

The throne is on a raised platform. It's an actual medieval throne, imported from Italy or some shit. Frangelico's old stomping ground. You can take the vampire outta the Middle Ages but you can't take the Middle Ages outta the vampire.

A slender young waiter in black tuxedo pants, red cumberbund, a black velvet choker and nothing else, beats me to the throne. He bows at the waist to offer up his tray of beverages. Frangelico extends his hand beyond the throne and browses among the glasses, selecting one and motioning the waiter to move on. The waiter backs away, still bowing.

Oh for fuck's sake. I roll my eyes. So much pomp and circumstance. I guess if you're practically immortal you have time to indulge in all the ceremony you like.

The waiter turns and leaps out of his skin at the sight of me. His face pales, his Adam's apple bobbing under his collar. The black velvet chokers are part of the uniform here, but I'd kill any vampire who made me wear one. I'm a bouncer for contract, not a fucking slave. Maybe it's time to remind the king of that.

I saunter around the giant wooden chair and meet Frangelico's amused glance. No sneaking up on the king.

"Grizz. So nice of you to join us." He waves a hand and two men in chokers arrive with another ornate chair for me—smaller than the throne, of course. Sitting in it would put my head a full two feet lower than the vampire king. So I don't sit. Instead, I prop my boot on the seat. Frangelico sighs.

"Must you put your feet on the furniture? I'm sure we can find you a footstool if you like." Frangelico snaps his fingers and motions to one of the servants. I catch the man's shoulder before he kneels down on all fours in front of my chair.

"No," I growl. "Stop it. You know I'm not into this shit."

"Of course." A flick of the king's fingers and the men disappear. Frangelico leans forward. "I forgot how much you dislike our little power games. But what is sex about if not power?"

I shake my head. I don't have time for this. "You wanted to see me?"

Frangelico sits back and studies me. Even with him seated and me standing, he's still slightly taller. The vampire is bigger than you'd expect, and for all his fancy talk, he's not stupid. Power isn't a little game to him. It's the only game, and he plays to win.

"I did, my friend."

I flinch at that. Fuck, are we friends? I contracted with him to watch his club at night and keep an eye on a few of his operations. In exchange, he gives me what I need to do what I gotta do.

"You take offense at me calling you *friend*?" the king asks. Can't hide a thing from a fucking vampire.

"I'm not here to braid your hair and wear bead bracelets or some shit. You and I have a contract."

"We do," the king confirms. "But surely we can renegotiate. There must be other needs you wish filled. Desires. And surely we can fill them here, in this pleasure paradise." He spreads his hands to encompass the whole club, then motions. The blonde I saw earlier slinks by me, heading toward the master vampire. At his invitation, she sits on the arm of the throne, angling her body to best show off her breasts and thighs. Frangelico slides a hand up her supple calf. "Surrounded by such delights, surely you have been tempted."

I ignore the blonde smiling at me. Creeps me out the way Frangelico handles her like a slab of meat. I guess to him, all humans are food. "You know what I want. You've known from the beginning."

"Ah, yes." The vampire's long finger taps the submissive woman's knee, as if she was a part of the furniture. "Are you any closer to getting what you want?"

"I play the long game." Frangelico is the best chance I got at getting what I want. If it takes the rest of my life, fuck, so be it.

"So you do play games?" The finger stops tapping.

I sigh. "What the fuck is this about?"

Frangelico releases the blonde and waves her away. "I'm wondering what happens if neither of us get what we want."

I shrug. "We go our separate ways." Not like there's anything keeping me in Tucson.

"And if I don't want you to go?"

"That would be unfortunate."

I don't look the vampire in the eye—I'm not a fucking idiot—but I do level a glare at his chin. I haven't challenged or threatened the king—yet—but he gets the message and sighs, settling back in the throne. His velvet dressing robe flops off one shoulder, revealing powerful muscles. He may act like a lazy playboy, but he'd be no slouch in a fight. Even if he didn't have super vampire reflexes and powers.

"So you see why I called you here. I wish to explore alternatives to our arrangement."

Fuck. "There's only one thing I want." And if

Frangelico can't give it to me, I don't know how I'm going to get it.

"Surely there's something else you want. Or, perhaps, someone."

The redhead. The image of her pops into my head before I can squelch it. The sweet freckled face greeting me when I come home, angling up for a kiss.

I force the fantasy away. "No. Nothing. I told you in the beginning. It's all or nothing." My course was set long ago.

A woman shrieks. I stiffen, but don't turn. I don't like that sounds of people's pain have become routine. Then the auburn color catches my eye and I whirl.

Benny has the redhead—my redhead—strung up on a rope dangling from the ceiling. He's painting her back with a heavy flogger, each snap of the leather leaving marks. She's naked, dancing on tiptoes, twisting away from the blows. The leather strands wrap around her hip and flick her breasts. She screams and I hear fear in the pitch, not the lower notes of pleasure.

Before I know it, I'm across the room and in the vampire's face. The flogger's on the floor between us, in two pieces.

Benedict registers surprise before stuffing it down and sneering at me. He turns back to the trembling redhead, and I clamp a hand on his arm.

"No. You don't get to hurt her."

"I have permission," he snarls. I snarl back and he blurs away, ending up across the club. Fucking coward.

I turn back to the redhead only to find another vampire has taken Benny's place. A tall, patrician-faced vampire who was giving the redhead orders earlier. There's no sign of his male sub.

"What is the meaning of this?" he barks, looking down his nose at me, even though I'm almost his height. "Benedict had my permission."

"Show's over. Cut her down. She's done."

"She's mine, and I'll say when she's done." The vampire takes a step towards a table full of implements and I block him.

"Call off your dog," he says to the king.

Frangelico raises a brow. You don't give orders to the king.

"I'm not a dog," I growl. "I'm a bear." My grizzly's about to burst from my skin and brawl in the middle of the club. We'll see how sturdy the furniture actually is.

"Augustine," Frangelico drawls with mild disapproval. I tense up. I've never seen him before, but I know Augustine is one of Frangelico's lieutenants. "You know as well as I, I do not give him orders. Which is why I hired him. He's here to make sure you're following the rules." And with that, the vampire king turns away, effectively dismissing us.

Augustine's lip curves up, showing a fang. "I didn't break the rules."

"You loaned your girl out to a vampire who was hurting her." Beside us, the redhead slowly spins from the rope noose around her wrists. Fuck, is that good for her circulation? Welts mar her skin, as numerous as her freckles. Some of them even show spots of blood. Benny really worked her over.

"If she wanted to stop, she'd safe out." The vampire

motions impatiently, and a waiter offers him a drink. Augustine drinks greedily, wiping water from his lips. He doesn't offer any to his punished submissive.

The redhead is limp, her eyes half closed. I peer into her face, gently raise an eyelid to check her blown pupils. "She's too far gone to give a safe word." I may not be into this stuff, but I know how endorphins work. Load after load drops until the submissive is too drugged to even speak.

"She likes it." The vampire goes to a table and picks up a riding crop. I step between him and the redhead. Between the vampire and his prey. It's probably the first time anyone's told this vampire no.

Augustine looks shocked. It's a good look for him.

"I said stop."

"Very well. It's time to eat, anyway." With a flick of his fingers, he orders another club servant to come forward and loosen the rope around the young woman's wrists.

She slumps, a cascade of red hair falling over her freckled face. Her head rolls on her neck. She's totally blissed out from endorphins. Another sweetblood. A submissive, willing vampire victim.

It's not my business. I shouldn't get involved. But the redhead's lips part and she turns toward me and I catch her scent…

And suddenly I know why she caught my interest.

I lean forward. This one is a shifter. Not a wolf or bear, but something close. Fox, maybe. That would match her red hair. I glance between her thighs. She's mostly shaved but for a small groomed patch. Natural redhead. Definitely a fox.

How did I not notice her animal before? Probably because it's shy, submissive. Plus all the cloying smells of vampires in the club. Prey animals don't make themselves known like dominant ones. And this one is sweet as can be. My bear is fighting to burst forth and carry her off to a safe, dark place where he can protect her.

My instincts war a moment. But I have to remember why I'm here. I swallow and step back and act disinterested. A bouncer more concerned with the club's reputation than protecting a willing sweetblood. "Frangelico know you're feasting on a shifter?"

"She belongs to me."

"Shifters don't belong to vampires."

"Says the king's guard bear."

Technically the vampire king and I have a partnership, but I don't correct the vampire.

With a wicked smile, Augustine snaps his fingers. A minute later, club servants have provided a seat and handed over Augustine's submissive. He shifts her in his arms, almost tenderly arranging her limp body as I watch. My fists clench as Augustine's fingers spear the auburn hair, tugging the woman's head back to bare her neck. Without ceremony or gentleness, he strikes like a viper, burying his fangs in her neck. Her body convulses but the blissed out look on her face turns to ecstasy.

Fuck this. I pivot and head back to the throne in the center of the room.

"We can make them like it, you know," Frangelico says. He's holding a goblet filled with a red liquid. A nice show, but it's just wine.

A gasp makes me turn again. The redhead thrashes in

her vampire master's arms, ecstasy turning to anguish. Augustine shoots me a nasty look. He's making it hurt on purpose. The redhead's hands beat at his suit. Her blood stains her pale skin, his shirt collar. He's making a mess.

Her cries sharpen, growing frantic.

"Leave her alone," I growl.

"Augustine," Frangelico calls softly before I can stomp back over there. The younger vampire turns with a snarl, but lowers his eyes. "Enough," orders the king, and Augustine bows his head and motions to a club employee to take her away.

"You can't save them all from my sired's sadism," Frangelico murmurs as I watch the redhead disappear behind a curtain of a private alcove. She's safe now. For the next hour, she'll be wrapped in a blanket, given orange juice and chocolate and whatever else she needs to come safely down. For a moment, I toy with the idea of shoving aside the curtain, kicking out the club employee, and caring for her myself. I reject the thought as soon as it surfaces. The redhead is cute, but she's none of my business.

My bear bellows in protest.

When I turn back, the vampire king is watching me closely. I shake my head. "Not gonna save them. Like you said, they like it."

The king regards me over steepled fingers. "This club caters to all sorts of desires. Some desire pleasure mixed with pain. We have a word for them. Sweetbloods."

"Yeah, I know." The vampires love masochists. The pain releases endorphins that make the blood taste sweeter, or some shit. I'm about to tell Frangelico where he can shove his sadism, when a new scent hits my nose. Wolf.

"Frangelico," a female voice calls. A leather clad she-wolf strides forward, followed by a huge wolf with a pierced eyebrow. Sheridan and Trey. I give Trey my full attention. He and I don't get along. I used to be a bouncer at his Fight Club but when he found out I also work here, things went sour. Fast.

As soon as Trey sees me, he shows his teeth. His woman puts a hand on his arm and mutters, "Behave."

"Ah, my dear Sheridan," Frangelico purrs. "How nice of you to come with your wolf guard."

"My mate," she corrects. Her hand automatically goes to her shoulder, covering where he must have marked her. Shit, she and Trey are mated? I open my mouth to congratulate them. Trey glares at me. After what I did, he won't accept anything from me. I close my mouth.

"What brings you to our little club?" Frangelico asks. "Business or pleasure?"

"Business," Sheridan answers, though she casts a longing look about the club. I don't get the attraction of this place, but it's none of my business.

"Come then," Frangelico motions for more chairs to be brought close. Waiters appear and offer drinks.

"We're here because we've heard rumors. Shifters are disappearing from this area."

"Wolves?"

"Not wolves. Other types of shifters. Ones that don't have the protection of a pack."

"What sort of shifters might those be? Forgive me, I am not as well versed in the animal kingdom as I should be," Frangelico says. He's lying, of course. He makes it his business to know everything.

Sheridan swallows and glances at Trey, who nods at her. "A few loner cats who didn't have a clan. Leopard, tiger. But also rarer shifters—owls, ravens, eagles."

"Really? There are shifter birds?" Frangelico bluffs really well. Not even I can smell anything but his interest.

Sheridan nods. "They keep quiet because they're not as plentiful as wolves or big cats. That, and they're prey animals."

"And someone is kidnapping them? Didn't that happen before, when a company was capturing shifters to experiment on?"

"That company is gone. We destroyed their facilities, rooted out the people who were doing it. But there's still a black market for kidnapped shifters, and we think the shifter traders have found new customers. Vampires."

Frangelico's long fingers steeple. He doesn't move when Sheridan drops this bombshell. Instead, he waits a moment as if making sure she's finished talking, then stirs. "And what would vampires want with kidnapped shifters?"

"We don't know. That's why we're here." Before Sheridan can continue, her mate steps forward, tall, tattooed, and intimidating.

"It would be wise for you to look into it, unless you want the pack knocking on your door," Trey says. Sheridan grabs his arm again.

"What my mate means," she says with a fixed smile, "is that given the Tucson pack's alliance with you and your vampires, it would be wise to join forces to look into the shifter disappearances. For the sake of keeping the peace."

"Indeed." Frangelico flicks a glance at Trey, then turns back to Sheridan. "You do have a flair for diplomacy, my dear," Frangelico tells her.

"Thank you," she answers levelly. "But I'm not your dear."

Frangelico ignores her growl. "We will look into it." He glances at me. I nod back. By *we* the king means *me*. And I'm okay with hunting down vampires who have bought kidnapped shifters. I know just where I'll start—Augustine and his little redheaded sub.

"That's settled," Frangelico announces. "Now that your business is concluded you are welcome to make use of my club. Will you stay and scene tonight?"

Sheridan hesitates, her gaze darting around the dimly lit club with poorly hidden interest.

"Yes." Trey steps between her and the vampire king. "As long as everyone remains on their best behavior."

"I'm sure my vampires will," Frangelico offers with a glint of fang.

"And your pet shifters?" Trey looks at me.

"I have no pets shifters. Only friends and...playmates," Frangelico says.

"Which one is he?" Trey asks, still staring at me.

"A business partner," I offer.

"I'm sure Grizz will also respect the rules of the club, and all its members." Frangelico raises an eyebrow at me.

I hold my hands up. "I got no problems with these wolves." Last I checked, I didn't have a problem with the wolves. It's not my fault the wolves have a problem with me.

"Good," Frangelico claps his hands and Sheridan jumps. Trey puts his hands on her shoulders, steadying her. He leans in and whispers something in her ear. She flushes. Trey turns her and gives her a gentle push towards a free table. He watches her strut away. I have to admit, if I had a mate as fine as Sheridan, I'd watch her coming and going as long as possible, too.

Trey turns back to me and Frangelico. His eyes narrow on me.

"Hey, Grizz," his voice drips bitterness. "You still on to fight Friday?"

"Last I checked, I was still on the schedule." I quit working at the Fight Club as a bouncer a few weeks ago, but fighting is good for my bear.

"Good." Trey shows his teeth in a macabre grin. "We have a special guest ready to fight you. Be ready."

I watch him stride away. He's a big, bad wolf, but not as dangerous as I am. Not alone, anyway. Wolves are never alone. That's always their advantage. Strength of the pack.

"If that's all, I'll head out," I say to Frangelico.

He nods. "You're off bouncer duty the rest of the night. Ask Peter to call in a replacement. In the meantime, I'll make the rounds."

"Right." Time to go on the hunt.

I head to the rope where Augustine tied up his shifter sub, where the white robe she wore lies crumpled on the floor. I pick it up and give it a good sniff. The scent is spicy, with a touch of floral. Fox. Definitely. If I can't track the vampire by his scent, I can at least find the fox.

A few discreet questions later, and I learn the redhead left with Augustine. Her *master* they called him. Not sure if that means he owns her, or if it's just a game they play, but I plan to find out. I can get his address from the records Frangelico keeps—I'm one of the few people he gives access to. He knows I'll never betray him. I need him too much.

Halfway up the stairs to the main floor, I pause and survey the vast club. Trey and Sheridan have already claimed a table under one of the spotlights. Trey has opened a black duffel bag and is laying out implements. Sheridan stands beside him, her bare skin glowing in a fancy leather harness, swaying a little with excitement.

Trey finishes and turns towards her. He snaps his fingers and she falls to her knees, gazing up at her mate. I don't need to see her face to know that her eyes are shining. Trey's face softens as he looks down at her. Another couple stealing a moment before they engage in the complicated mating dance of submission and dominance. I've seen it a million times before, but somehow it's not as grotesque on shifters. That still doesn't mean I get it.

I climb the rest of the stairs and hit the door with my fist to escape.

CHAPTER 2

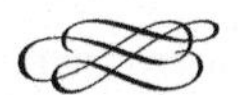

rizz

AUGUSTINE LIVES in a fancy neighborhood in Oro Valley, up against the Catalina Mountain range. I park my motorcycle, climb the wall, and scan the backyard. Huge pool, fancy patio. But beyond the stone bar and grill and deck furniture, there's a regular door. It'll be easy enough to kick it in.

I take a moment to slip past the cameras. No flood lights on the lawn—vampires can see in the dark. Luckily, so can shifters. I hunker down into the bushes and wait.

Vampires are at their strongest at night and I find they're a bit sluggish closer to daybreak. Not Frangelico—he's old enough that he can stay awake until the first ray of dawn. But even his oldest sired are well inside by the dark hour before sunrise.

So I crouch until soft light glows in the sky just beyond the mountains. After taking a swig from my flask, I amble to the back door and let myself in. It's unlocked—you'd have to be crazy to steal from a vampire. Most save all their defenses and booby traps for their sleeping lairs, which is why I want to catch Augustine here awake. He won't expect it. After a life of hunting vampires, I know what brings them down. Hubris. They're the biggest, baddest predator on Earth, and they know it. They don't realize otherwise—until I'm standing over them with a stake.

Of course, I don't have orders to kill Augustine. Just question him. He might live if Frangelico likes his answers. Frangelico hates killing his sired because, according to him, it's difficult to make new ones.

The house is cool, clean, and scented like lemon. I search the rooms, but they're unused. Perfectly decorated but they smell empty. I open the fridge—a few decanters of blood, and a half drunk bottle of wine, but nothing else.

The vampire isn't here. He probably sleeps elsewhere. Unless I want to catch him partying or fully awake, this is a dead end. Not that I expected it to be easy.

Beside the fridge is a bag of dog food. An expensive type—real wild caught meat or something. I take a moment and tune into the scent below the cold stone smell of the vampire. That's when I catch the familiar musk.

Dog. Or something close. Not wolf.

Skin prickling, I head to the tiled pantry. In the corner,

a colorful Mexican blanket covers a large structure. A cage.

The monster bear in my chest starts to rumble. Not a growl, but a low soothing sound.

I flip up the serape and there's my little fox. Crumpled, still in human form. Naked but for the white collar. She's shivering.

My bear rumbles louder.

I open the cage. She winces at the loud metal scrape, her eyes squeezing shut, her body contracting into the smallest point possible. There are still a few marks on her pale skin, though most have faded. Thank fuck she's a shifter not a human. The dom really worked her over for her to still be healing.

And then he left her in a cage. My body shakes with my bear's grumbling. I rip the blanket off the cage and cover her with it.

"Master?" she asks in the softest whisper. Her quavering voice touches me light as fingers. Fuck, I'm hard.

"I'm not your master," I answer her gruffly. I'm so pissed, my bear is ready to burst from my skin and tear down this mansion room by room. What kind of asshole leaves his sub to go through sub drop alone? Not just alone, but *trembling in a cage?* With nothing but *dog food* to feed her?

"Come here," I order. She responds instantly, crawling closer.

"Closer," I encourage before I can think about what I'm doing. "Come to me. All the way, kit. Out of the cage."

Eyes still closed, she crawls out of the cage, straight

into my arms. "That's it." I automatically cradle her close. As soon as her small body tucks against my chest, my bear's angry commentary quiets into a low bass note. He's purring. I didn't know he could do that.

The woman rubs her face against my t-shirt, burrowing. Still on autopilot, I rest a palm on her head, guiding her to settle.

With a sigh, the little submissive relaxes.

"Good girl," I murmur. The words are right there on the tip of my tongue. I've watched enough scenes at the club to know what to say, but I spoke them easily, without thinking. Her breathing slows, her mouth grows lax. Her eyes are still closed, so I don't know the exact moment she falls asleep.

All I know is I'm standing inside a mansion I broke into, my arms full of a vampire's pet, and I can't let go. For the first time in a long time, my bear has found someone to hold.

Jordy

THE RUMBLING under my ears fills my world. Cool air hits my face and then I'm tucked into a seat and strapped in. Two doors slam, one after another, and a big presence fills the space beside me.

I say the first word that's usually on my lips. "Master?"

"I'm not your master," the voice growls and my eyes fly open.

A scarred face greets me. He's glowering at me and I lower my eyes.

"I'm sorry."

"Don't apologize," he snarls and I duck my head. "No, fuck, don't do that."

I peer at him.

He's rubbing his chest. "You're all right. You're safe with me." He puts the truck in gear and pulls from the curb.

My fingers creep up and check for my collar. It's still buckled snug around my throat. I sigh, sinking further into the passenger seat.

I do what I do best and stay meek and quiet for the first few minutes of the ride. I should be frantic leaving my master's neighborhood with a strange shifter. A huge, angry shifter who hasn't stopped growling since he unlocked my cage, scooped me into his arms and carried me from the house to the truck.

The road flies by before I have the courage to speak up. "Are you okay?"

"What?" He looks startled.

I shrink deeper into my seat. "You're growling."

He grimaces and rubs his chest. "Yeah. My bear didn't like how you were being kept."

I almost agree with him out loud, but a twinge of guilt keeps me from speaking against my master.

"Did my master send you to get me?"

The big guy looks away and I know his answer before he tells me. "No."

I chew on this for the next few miles. I'm pretty calm, all things considered. But then, I've always rolled with life's punches. When you're a submissive shifter, there's not much else you can do. The world is big and bad and the animal inside me likes to hide.

Now she's alert, taking stock of our surroundings without the usual fearful edge. The truck is big and loud but doesn't smell like the big shifter bear beside me.

"This is a nice truck," I say.

"Not mine," he grunts. After changing lanes, he offers more. "I stole it. I only had my bike and didn't want to wake you."

I glance out the window at the exit signs flying by. "Where are you taking me?"

"Somewhere safe."

Safe. The magic word. My fox relaxes. She doesn't retreat, but I'm filled with the happy drowsiness that I rarely feel and always seek. My fox is usually on such high alert watching for predators, it takes the controlled pain to quiet her, to let me sleep. Even in subspace, she's silently watching and waiting, filled with disappointment for a master that won't appear. A good master. Someone who will protect us and keep us safe.

The sun cresting over the mountains means it's morning.

"How long did I sleep?"

"Fuck if I know," he sounds angry, but my fox is tuned into the loud rumble in his chest, and she knows the anger isn't directed at her. "I arrived and you were alone. Why the fuck did your master leave you after a scene? Not just alone, but in a fucking cage?"

"My fox doesn't always do well when I'm asleep. She's scared." Scaredy fox, I call her.

"You don't belong in a fucking cage," the male says, his voice mixing with his bear's in a nearly unintelligible growl.

I bow my head and the rumbling in his chest subsides.

"I didn't mean to scare you," he mutters. He spares me a quick glance. His eyes are a mix of brown and gold, his bear making his presence known.

"You don't scare me," I assure him, my heart light and free when I realize it's true.

"Here." The bear hands me a bottle of water. "You need to drink something."

I recognize the bottle as one of Augustine's fancy imported waters. My vampire master wouldn't waste something so fancy on me. I don't know if I can tell the bear that.

With a grunt, the bear pushes the water on me, and I don't protest. I'm parched. The water is cool, almost sweet, and I drain the whole bottle.

"He shouldn't have left you," the big man mutters. I gnaw my lip, studying him out of the corner of my eye so he won't notice. He's a big guy with a battered face and scars like I've never seen on a shifter before. His scent is large and in charge—a sign his bear is close to the surface, and super dominant.

Despite the tension in his giant body, he smells…safe. My fox leans into the smell, savors it. Either she's clueless, or she's reading him as someone who will protect us. I really, really hope it's the latter.

"Is that why you took me?" I venture. "Because I was in the cage?"

He glares at the road. Yellow eyes, glowing with his

bear. "I'm taking you somewhere to clean you up and let you heal and rest."

I swallow. Not sanctioned then. Augustine won't be pleased. I'll be lucky if he doesn't blame me, or take out his displeasure on my ass.

My captor gives me a sharp look as if he knows my thoughts. "You know Frangelico?"

"Yes," I whisper, shrinking in my seat at the name of the vampire king.

"I work with him. He wants me to look into your master."

This doesn't reassure me a bit, but I know better than to ask about the affairs of vampires. "Don't you mean *for him*? You work *for* the vampire king?"

"That's what I said."

"You said *with*." Implying they were equals.

"*For, with*, what the fuck difference does it make?" He shrugs. I should be frightened out of my mind that I've annoyed him, but instead I want to giggle. I duck my head to hide my grin behind the thin fall of my hair.

If he notices my amusement, he doesn't comment on it. Instead he brushes a big hand over my hair. I still, letting him pet me.

"Red," he says.

"What?" I never question dominants, but I can't help it. His tone was deep and growly, with a touch of something more. Reverence. Or longing.

He doesn't explain the 'red' comment. Instead he says, "I watched you last night."

"Oh." I scan my memory of the past night's events. My fox helpfully supplies what she noticed—a dark, brown gold shape just outside of the spotlight, waiting in the shadows. A big, strong presence. Safe. "I remember you. Or at least, my fox does. She likes you."

Something in his shoulders relaxes. "Good. I'm glad."

I want to ask where we're going, but instead I yawn.

"Sleep, kit," he says. I love that he calls me by the name for a baby fox. It makes me feel babied. Protected. There's a dominant push in his voice that's impossible to disobey, even if I wanted to.

"Okay." I snuggle against the seat. The last thing I see is his big hand checking to make sure the heat vents are on and directing them toward me, then dropping to tug the blanket tighter around me.

"Thank you," I murmur. "Feels nice."

His bear rumbles again. *Go to sleep.* It says. *I'm going to take care of you. Just relax and let go.*

So I do.

~

Grizz

STUPID. So fucking stupid.

I'm not in the business of collecting liabilities. I'm a hunter. I learned my lessons young. A hunter never leaves tracks. Not if he's hunting a predator, and I hunt the most dangerous predators in existence.

But the second she dragged herself from the cage into my arms, she became too important to leave behind.

Besides, she's my best link to Augustine. At least, that's

what I'm telling myself, although how the hell I'm going to hunt a vampire when I have to babysit his pet fox, I have no idea. I wasn't thinking when I stole her from the vampire's home. Not with my head at least.

The blanket slips off her shoulder and I can't concentrate. I wonder how that creamy skin would feel under my lips. I'll bet it's so damn soft. I brush the back of my knuckles over it.

Fuck—she's chilly! I tug the blanket back over her. The heat is on full force in the cab, but the poor female's body is small and frail. Damn vampire locking her up like that. She's too fragile to handle that sort of neglect. Too pale, too thin.

While I fiddle with the blanket like a girl with her dolly, the truck drifts outta its lane into the path of an eighteen wheeler. The driver honks and I bite back a roar. Don't wanna wake my sleeping beauty. Instead, I glare at the driver with mad bear eyes.

Fates, the kit isn't even awake and the bear is fighting to protect her. Keep it up and she's gonna think I'm her knight in shining armor. That'll be a mistake. I'm no one's hero.

I don't sit easy until I pull into my hidden drive. My den is tucked into the side of a mountain. Nothing fancy, one of those nuclear bunker type places, except the side sticking outta the hill has a few windows. I don't sleep exposed. Too dangerous. I learned that the hard way a couple hunts ago.

When I crack open the truck door, my little fox doesn't stir. The walk to the house is easy with such a light bundle. I stash her in my bedroom and my bear finally relaxes, seeing her tucked up tight in the dark, warm cave of my bed. She curls right up like she's in animal form, her little fist resting against her lips. She wasn't sleeping so deeply when I opened her cage, but then I remember—I gave her an order. A dominant push, without meaning to. I'm so used to being the biggest, baddest alpha around other dominant predators, I forgot to temper my power. She took my order to heart, like a good little submissive.

What will she need when she wakes up?

I head back into the kitchen. My last grocery run, I grabbed a couple bottles of orange juice. Must have been trying to look normal, add some basic items to my cart full of meat. I don't really drink the stuff.

A few minutes later, there's a glass of juice waiting on the bedside table for when my guest wakes up. I unscrew two of the three light bulbs outta my bedside lamp and click it on, a sorta makeshift night light. In case she wakes up and gets scared.

I stand at the foot of the bed and watch her sleep, barely daring to breathe. Her red hair fans out on the pillow, copper lashes rest on her porcelain skin. The beautiful fox looks good in my bed. Feels right.

Her little nose scrunches. A toe twitches, dislodging the blanket. Immediately, I tuck the comforter more tightly around her.

Fuck. I am so fucked.

I get the hell outta there before I spend a half hour sitting beside her, watching her sleep. I knew my bear would fall for a girl one day. Never figured it'd be this bad.

Back in the kitchen, I pull out a couple packs of meat from the freezer so they'll be ready for breakfast. Or at the rate she's sleeping, lunch. No worries, it does me good to see her resting like that.

I could use some shut-eye, in a minute I'm gonna slip back in there and join her. First I gotta tie up some loose ends. I pull out my burner phone and dial a memorized number.

"Jay-sus, Grizz, it's before seven in the mornin'." The chipper Irish accent has a murderous edge.

I glance at the clock. "Seven's not that early."

"It is if ya went tae bed three hours ago. We had a fight last night. Nix the Kid against this big bruisin' gorilla brawler. Not as good as ya, but still, went twelve rounds—"

I clear my throat as a signal that I'm interrupting. Declan will go on forever when he's worked up, and his accent gets so thick I can't understand him anyway. "Gotta job for you."

"What am I, a handyman?"

"A favor then."

The Irishman sighs. "All right then." He owes me more than a few.

"I was on a job this morning, and I had to stash my bike and 'borrow' a truck. Need you to pick up my bike and meet me."

"Let me guess, we'll take the truck in trade, while it's hot."

"I'll put new plates on it. You can take them off before you leave it for the cops."

"I know, I know, this isn't my first rodeo. Fine. How soon do ya need it done?"

Another glance at the clock to calculate sleeping time, waking time, making breakfast. "Four-thirty. Fight Club."

Declan sucks in a breath. "Is that wise? Word on the street is the wolves consider you their enemy."

The wolves. Sooner or later I'm going to have to deal with them. "I'm not. Not unless they make one of me. And they don't wanna do that." Trey might, but his alpha, Garrett, is smarter.

"Word on the street is you're working for the vampires. Not just any vampire. The king of the vampires."

I growl in answer. I don't like people knowing my business.

"Is it true? You're employed by the king?"

"The king and I have an arrangement," I tell him. I don't know why—I don't answer to him. But I need Declan as an ally.

"The wolves aren't likin' it," Declan goes on lecturing me about vampire/shifter politics. "The treaty's still new but some shifters feel you've chosen sides. And anyone sidin' with the vampires isn't tae be trusted—"

"You gonna meet me at the Fight Club or not?"

Silence.

"Declan…"

"Sure, sure. I'll see ya then. Keep your panties on."

I growl again and hang up. Head to the door to lock up and check my security system. Vampires don't hunt during the day, but they have money and money buys lackeys. When I'm satisfied everything's locked down tight, I head back to bed. Day's shaping up to be full, even without dealing with my rescue. The thought of her makes me soften, and I tread lighter so I won't wake her. I'm not gonna touch her, just lie beside her.

But when I get to my bedroom, the blankets are on the floor. The glass of juice is drained, empty like my bed. My fox is gone.

CHAPTER 3

ordy

I CROUCH behind the blue truck, holding my breath. When I woke, I was so disoriented, I thought I had crawled out of my cage and lain down on a bed in my master's house. I was up and out from under the covers like they burned me. No telling what Augustine would do if he caught me taking luxuries he didn't dole out. He's not bad as far as masters go, but he definitely likes complete control.

The big male who took me away on the other hand…I don't know what he wants. He was there in the club. And later, in the house, his footsteps approached slowly while I shivered in the cage. The heat of his anger washed over me and my fox reacted the opposite of how she felt when faced with other angry dominants. Submissive, not fearful, but free and easy, as if his anger was a warm den I could curl up in and hide.

Then I literally woke up in his den. Master Augustine will loan me out, share me, send me as a package to stay overnight with someone he wants to reward—but all those times were with vampires. Even the time when—

Don't think about that.

Master Augustine never loaned me out to a shifter before. As far as I know, he disdains shifters, even though he owns one as his submissive. I shouldn't be here. The longer I stay, the angrier my master will be. I have to go, no matter how good the bear makes me feel.

I'm not just worried about punishment at the hands of my master now. I'm worried about my life. Augustine is to be feared, especially when he believes he's been betrayed.

And then there's what the big bear said on the phone a second before I snuck past: *The king and I have an arrangement.* That should be enough reason to leave. No shifter tangles with a vampire and wins, but this guy sounds like he's struck a bargain with one. If there ever was a sign I should skedaddle, that'd be it. I can't get involved with vampire turf wars. My master won't like it. I've got to get back to him and explain what happened. I'm not even sure what happened, but maybe on my way back I can think of something.

I peer over the truck bed back at the house. It looks like a long box, one half stuck in the mountain and dark as a basement, the other half—the kitchen and large living room sticking out of the red rock. Big picture windows and a stunning view. Light, lots of it. I noticed as I was leaving. I even thought I wouldn't mind claiming it as a den.

My fox is stalling.

I just have to take off down the long drive, except that'd be the most obvious escape route.

Maybe I can climb down the mountain. I go to the edge and look over all the red stone. My fox might blend right in.

I take a step and a big hand closes on my nape.

"Gotcha," the bear growls. He moves quiet for such a big guy.

My body jerks once, my feet scrambling uselessly. The big man turns me to face him, clamping me to his hard body and I go limp. All the fight goes out of me, submission so programmed into me I hardly know how to resist. But if truth be told, I'm relieved to be caught. I'd rather be enslaved to this grizzly bear than with a cold, punitive Augustine any day. Not that I think he's enslaving me. There's way too much kindness in him for that. He believes he's protecting me, helping me. He just doesn't know how ruthless Augustine can be. What he'll do when he gets me back.

"That's right," his deep, delicious voice rumbles in my ears. "No running. Not from me."

He throws me over his shoulder and I remain limp, arms hang down as he strides away from the overlook's edge. I'm eye level with his behind, and boy, is it a nice one. I probably shouldn't be checking out my captor, but his backside and thighs fill out his ripped up jeans perfectly.

He carries me across the parking lot, past his big shiny

truck and into his house. "No use trying to escape. You're gonna be with me awhile."

Okay, maybe I am his slave now. And that shouldn't make me so terribly excited.

I wait for him to drop me to the floor and punish me, but he doesn't. Instead, he tromps down the hall, stopping a moment. A thud and his boots hit the floor. He took the time to toe them off. He strides to the room where I woke up and lays me on the bed.

He leaves a moment and I lie there, blinking at the low ceiling. I realize I'm toying with my collar, and I lower my hand.

A few minutes and he returns, shutting the door to close us in a warm, dark cocoon. Automatically my head tips back and I show my throat, acknowledging him as dominant. It's always nerve-wracking to expose my throat to an apex predator, but I have to do it. Instinct is a bitch. With any luck this will appease him. In a perfect world, the submissive act is one of ultimate trust. I expose my neck, the ultimate show of faith. Offering my life if he wants to take it. I should be more afraid than I am, but something about him soothes my fox. In a perfect world, a dominant protects the weak. Maybe this one will protect me.

A hiss of indrawn breath and strong fingers wrap around my chin. "What is this?" A rough thumb traces my shivering pulse. His anger vibrates through me, but somehow my fox knows it's not directed at me. I lie docile in his grip, obedient when he tips my face up to meet his blazing eyes. He's close to shifting.

I put my hand to my neck. As soon as my fingers touch

the seam running up my neck under the white leather, I remember. "It's nothing," I tell him. "A bite."

"That's not a bite," the bear growls. "He fucking gnawed on you."

I can only nod. My vampire master usually fed neatly from the artery, but that night he'd wanted to punish me.

Rough fingers fumble with the strip of leather. I realize he's trying to unbuckle the collar and I panic, grabbing his wrist. He growls and I lie flat again, closing my eyes and pressing my hand to the bed. The leather tightens as he tugs, and when the buckle doesn't yield he snarls again. A claw slides against my neck, close to my beating pulse, then a flick and the collar flies away. I grip the blanket, my breath coming faster.

Then my captor does something I'd never expect in a million years. Both his big hands settle around my head, gently angling it back to study the old wound.

"Shhhh, easy, kit."

I blow out a long breath, willing myself to calm.

"That's it. Good girl."

When I open my eyes, he's studying my neck, his hands cradling my head.

"Scarred," he murmurs. "Takes a lot for a shifter to scar. There's only one way for sure to do it."

I nod. I know how shifters scar. The marks on my neck are like a brand, signalling my weakness. Telling any shifter who knows the signs that I'm vampire food. I'm scarred like a human.

I close my stinging eyes. I'm so sick of being a victim.

"Hey." His thumb strokes my chin. "It's okay. The scars aren't so bad. I didn't even notice them before."

My face crumples further, and he tugs me close, saying gruffly, "Didn't mean to hurt you." His voice is gravelly but his arms around me are gentle. "Now," he sets me back an inch so I can see his face, "we're gonna lie down and sleep. It's been a long night and you need it. No more running."

I bite my lip. I can't agree to that.

An avalanche-like rumble comes from his rock-hard chest. "You run, I won't like it. There'll be consequences. Understand?" His thick fingers squeeze my nape, not choking, but hard enough to make my spine go limp, signalling submission.

"Yes," I answer. "I understand." I understand consequences real well. I grew up in a clan of crazy, paranoid, in-bred fox shifters. The kind who sell their own to slavers because there are too many mouths to feed.

I wait but he doesn't move, doesn't change his grip. I'm beginning to think he's going to hold me like this all day when he kneads my neck a little and tips my head back to meet his gaze. His eyes are light, his bear still close, but he looks calm, thoughtful. The rough stubble and jagged scar make him look rugged, not ugly.

That's when it really hits me: he's scarred, like me.

"Name?" he asks.

I blink at him, still wondering about the scar. Shifters don't scar easy, as he said. How did he get his?

"Name, kit. What do I call you?"

"Me? Oh. Jordy."

He grunts in acknowledgement and drops his hand. I immediately miss its comforting weight. I catch his hand before he can pull away. He stills as if my soft touch freezes him. Which I know it might—my hands are always cold. But I'm no match for a shifter, any shifter really, much less one of this bear's size and weight.

"What's your name?" I ask. A part of me is shocked by my brazenness. Another part of me is too curious to keep from asking, too eager to get to know him to let him go.

"Grizz. Short for Grizzly."

I cock my head to the side. "That your real name?"

"Nope." He moves away as if to underscore the point that his nickname is all I'm gonna get. I wipe my face of disappointment as he gets up from the bed.

"Here." He's back, shoving a carton of orange juice in my face. "You need to drink."

He watches as I drain half the carton. "You need the bathroom?" he asks as I hand it back.

"No."

He sits and turns off the light. In the darkness, my senses go on alert. Grizz is a big shape next to me, warm and golden. My fox sees the world through scent, and to her the grizzly is a softly glowing sun. He smells comforting and familiar, like sugar cookies or gingerbread.

The bed creaks as he sits down and I push back to the wall. "What are you doing?" I squeak. Not because I'm frightened of him, but because I'm excited, and my eagerness frightens me.

"Gonna get some shuteye. You too. We have a long day after this after an even longer night."

I lick my lips, considering. "You're keeping me here?"

"For now. No more roaming." He gives me a dominant push. "No sneaking out."

"What are you gonna do with me?"

"Nothing bad. Just sleep." His voice drops an octave. "Do I have to order you?"

If he does, I won't be able to wake up and try to get out of here. Until the order wears off, I won't be able to get up at all.

"No, no," I say. "I'll sleep." I burrow deeper into the covers, curling around a pillow. After a moment, the bed creaks as he does the same.

We both settle in side by side, back to back, and even though we're not touching, I can feel him close to me.

I squeeze my eyes shut, and just like that, I fall under into the darkness of my dreams. There's someone waiting for me there—a huge black presence with fangs and talons, reaching for me, watching with a single glowing eye.

"Jordy," someone calls from far away. "Jordy, wake up."

I come to with a gasp, my limbs thrashing. Someone's holding me tight, almost crushing me. I wheeze and the grip loosens.

"You're okay," Grizz croons, one arm wrapped around my shoulders, the other at my waist. His body surrounds me completely. As soon as I realize that, I go limp. I can't help crying a little, rubbing my face in Grizz's soft t-shirt. My fingers dig into the fabric, curling into fists resting against his firm, muscled chest.

"I'm sorry."

His big arms flex around me a second before relaxing. "It's okay."

"I had a bad dream," I whimper. I sound pathetic, even for me.

"Shh, you're safe here. It was just a dream." Calloused fingertips brush my forehead.

"It wasn't, though. It really happened. It was a memory." Waiting for me. As if my body knew I was safe so my mind served up the memory of that night, delivering it to my consciousness so I could process it.

"It's okay, kit." He keeps stroking my face and hair and I close my eyes against the delicious sensation. "No one can get you here."

"What about—"

"Vampires?" he answers for me and rearranges me in his arms so my head is tucked under his chin. "They can't get in. This is my den. They'd need an invitation."

I shiver. "They can send in other forces."

I feel his grin as his jaw moves against my head. "They can try. Anyone finds this place, and enters, I'll eat them."

A giggle escapes me and I cut it off, unsure if he meant to make me laugh. His chuckle echoes around me and I relax again, a smile curling deep inside me. His light mood gives me courage to ask what I've been wondering since I got here.

"Why did you bring me here?"

Instead of answering he adjusts his hold on me again, this time so he can rub my back.

"It wasn't locked," he says gruffly after a while.

"What?"

"The cage wasn't locked. You told me your master put you there, but the cage wasn't locked."

"Oh," is all I can think to say.

"You could've left at any time, but you didn't. Why?"

"To please my master."

"He's a shitty master."

"He saved me. He provides for me and protects me." I swallow anything else I would say. Augustine isn't perfect, but he's delivered on everything he promised. That's all I can ask for. I owe him my loyalty, and my life.

"He loaned you out, beat you, fed from you. Then threw you in a cage."

"The cage is my home."

He sighs as if he understands but wishes he didn't. "You going to be okay without it?"

"I'll be good," I promise in a whisper.

"That's not what I meant. Does your fox need the cage to feel safe?"

"No." I lick my lips, wanting to explain that I already feel safe with him. "The cage…it was more for my master's benefit. My master doesn't know how to handle my fox. Once, she bit him."

"Your master, Augustine. A vampire." His tone is dry.

"Right."

"He should be able to fucking handle it. In any case, turnabout's fair play." He mumbles the last part.

"What?"

"I mean, *he's* biting *you*." The big guy strokes the scar on my neck. "Maybe your fox doesn't like it. Maybe she thought to give him his own taste of fangs."

I giggle, even though it's not funny. My master was so angry when my fox acted out. He didn't let me out of the cage for a week.

When I explain this, the big man's face gets dark. Scary dark. My fox pokes up her head, fascinated. I'm smarter. I sit quietly.

"Maybe you need a new master."

Yes, I want to agree, but I don't. I already feel guilty betraying Augustine like this.

"You need to sleep." He settles us back on the bed, my back to his front. He takes time to lift my hair away from my face and neck, so my skin rests directly on the pillowcase's smooth surface. I hold my breath the whole time, waiting for him to pull away.

"Will you…" I stop my question in its tracks. I'm not supposed to ask for anything. I'm so relaxed around Grizz I've forgotten the rules.

But he growls, "Will I what?"

"Will you keep holding me?" I can barely hear myself, but he hears me just fine.

"Sure, Kit. No problem. Sleep now." It's not an order but I'm out.

CHAPTER 4

rizz

I'M up a little after one p.m., closing the door to the bedroom softly and growling at the bright light. I could've stayed in bed and held Jordy for hours, but we've got a lot to do, starting with meeting Declan and friends at the Fight Club. Almost twelve hours, and I'm no closer to figuring out why vampires are risking the peace treaty to take shifters than before. And now I have a captive, a complication I didn't foresee.

Augustine is gonna shit his pants when he notices she's gone. He might not care about her too much, but vampires don't like other people playing with their toys without their permission. Control thing.

Augustine can kiss my werebear ass. Still, no need for

him to know if he doesn't have to. I took her telling myself I'd return her as soon as I got the info I need. She's my only lead, the only shifter I know who services a vampire.

The fact that my heart flips when I see her standing in the entrance to the kitchen, sleepy-eyed and wearing nothing but one of my flannels has nothing to do with the reason I'm keeping her. She's part of the job, nothing more.

I can't describe how much I like the sight of her in my shirt and the pair of socks I left out for her. My cock is so hard it's about to split in two.

I turn back to the counter to hide it. No sense scaring her.

"Sit down," I tell her as she hesitates, blinking in the bright light. I dish up the meat I've been cooking, confident that she'll obey. "Did you sleep well?"

"Yes, sir," she answers softly. I've heard submissives call their doms 'sir' countless times, but the word never made my cock stir like it does on Jordy's lips. Fates, what's that about?

I turn, ready to tell her to just call me *Grizz* but she looks so small, so heart-wrenchingly fragile sitting at my kitchen table with her legs dangling, I don't have the heart to correct her. So what if she calls me *sir*. Maybe it makes her feel more comfortable. I can sacrifice my comfort to make her happy.

The fact that I hope she'll say it again means nothing. For some reason my bear is into her. Doesn't have to mean anything.

I get back to cooking, asking over my shoulder, "Did you have any more dreams?"

She doesn't answer right away. Her hand strokes her neck where her collar used to be, her gaze faraway.

I raise my voice over the bacon's sizzle. "Jordy, did you hear? I asked if you dreamed again."

"I heard."

I raise a brow. Is she playing games, trying to resist me? This is the opposite of *sir*. Is she pushing for punishment? "And?"

"I had them again." She keeps her eyes on the table. Her reluctance only makes me want to push more. I need to question her, anyway. With any other witness, I'd have done it long ago, instead of coddling her and letting her sleep. Fates, she has me off my game.

"Were they bad dreams?" I'm not letting her off so easily.

Her forehead creases. "Yes."

"Was it about Augustine?

"No. Another vampire."

"A vampire Augustine loaned you out to?"

She shrugs. Not a direct answer but I don't push it. I set the bacon aside and start on the eggs and sausage. For all her reluctance to answer my questions, she's at ease. Her fingers fiddle with items on my table—a pen, a stack of old junk mail.

Maybe I don't have to do this the hard way. "How'd you get to be with Augustine anyway?"

She mumbles something. I set a cover on the frying pan, go to her and tip her chin up. "Tell me."

"My family sold me." She doesn't look in my eyes. Her cheeks grow pink.

I swallow my anger and release her, but don't move away. "Why?"

"Too many mouths to feed. My clan was getting too big, harder to hide. Foxes have to hide."

I grunt in understanding. Prey animals usually survive by hiding.

"I also broke the rules," she offers after a moment.

"How?"

"I helped a stranger. Someone outside of the clan, but a blood relative. She was searching for my older brother, and I gave her information to help her. But it put the clan in danger, so when there was a chance to get rid of me, they took it."

"That's fucked up," I growl. Her face falls.

"How did they sell you to Augustine?"

She shrugs, looking miserable. "There were these men in dark masks. They smelled blank, like their scent was wiped away. Then there was an auction, and I ended up with Augustine."

I should be focused on this information and be relentless about asking her follow-up questions to find out as much as I can about the shifter slavers, but I can't. All I can focus on is Jordy. Her shoulders are up by her ears, her scent sad and ashamed. No wonder she doesn't want questions about her past. She's probably toning down the horrible way she's been treated, letting the memories fade. If I'd been through all that, I'd have nightmares too.

I grip her shoulder. I want to comfort her, but what

am I gonna say? "It's okay." Is it me or does she lean into my hand a little before I remove it?

I go back to making breakfast. We fall into silence, but Jordy doesn't seem to mind. She's comfortable sitting where I told her to sit, sifting through things on the table. She even picks up a pen and starts doodling in the corners of an old coupon flyer.

"Why do you think he wanted you?"

Still drawing with the pen, she answers readily. "I'm a submissive."

"So?"

"Sweetblood. That's what they call us."

"I thought sweetbloods were all human."

"No. There are human submissives." She's got her head down, still doodling. "But Augustine says they take work."

I lean back on the counter as I think about this. "Humans submissives need to be seduced and coddled. And you can't just make them disappear. But buy a prey shifter at an auction and you can do what you want."

"Right."

"You were already off the radar in hiding with your clan. To the world, you don't exist."

She shrinks a little more. The pen in her hand stills.

"Jordy." I wait until her gaze flicks to me. "I'm not asking about this because I want to. It's part of my job."

A pause and she gives a short nod. It's not much, but it makes my bear feel better.

Jordy

. . .

GRIZZ BENDS OVER THE STOVE, his corded biceps bunching as he stirs the sizzling meat. He covers the pan and heads to the fridge, rummaging around there for another package wrapped in butcher's paper. He moves fluidly for such a big guy. His powerful bulk flows from the fridge to the stove and the controlled grace of his movements makes my breath flutter in my chest.

My fox is fascinated by him. I have to admit, she has a point. He's so large and rugged, he belongs on a mountain, chopping down trees. On a construction site, working with his hands. Or in a war zone, unleashing the violence I sense inside him. Watching him cook in the kitchen is like having Godzilla knit you a sweater. The great and powerful executing the mundane. Every little domestic thing he does is a miracle.

"What did Augustine do once he had you?" he asks. I focus on my hands and the point where the pen touches the paper. The ink leaks out easily and I doodle swoops and swirls. A flowered vine grows in the margin of the faded newspaper.

"Nothing too bad. He told me he was my master. I was supposed to obey. If I didn't he'd punish me. I was rewarded for my obedience with sexual pleasure."

Grizz growls a little at that—I'm not sure if it's the punishment or reward he objects to. "And he'd loan you out."

"Yeah. I liked that less. Most of those doms respected his boundaries, though." I shiver and clutch the pen tighter in my left hand, while my right presses to my chest and rubs the itchy skin over my heart. I jolt when I realize Grizz is watching me, eyes narrow. His gaze follows my hand and I drop it in my lap. I wait for him to say something, but he grabs a plate and loads it up for me, setting it down with a decisive clunk.

"Eat. Need to get some meat on your bones."

I stare at the piled plate, my mouth watering. I haven't eaten this well in months. Certainly not this much food. I've trained myself not to think bad things about Augustine—otherwise I never would've been able to endure my life in his lair—but being with Grizz makes all the bad stuff come into focus.

"Jordy," he puts a hand on the back of my neck as he returns with his own plate. "Eat. That's an order."

I snatch up my fork and begin shoveling food in, chewing as fast as I can. My stomach cramps against the sudden onslaught.

"Whoa, whoa," Grizz says, his hand still resting on my bare neck. "Slow down."

Instantly I put down the fork and focus on my full mouth.

"Sorry about that," he murmurs. "I need to watch the orders."

"It's all right," I swallow. "I'm used to them."

"I want you to be okay. And healthy. Did Augustine really feed you dog food?"

I nod.

He growls and I startle. "Shhh, it's okay." His big hand squeezes mine. "I'm not mad at you."

"I know." I lift my eyes to his, taking comfort in the yellow blaze of his bear.

"You need to eat well. You're not a dog."

"I'm a fox. That's close enough."

"You're a shifter. A lovely young woman. You need real food."

My cheeks warm. He called me *lovely*. "Augustine didn't want me to eat too much. He liked me thin."

"Liked having you weak and dependent, probably."

I press my lips together. He's right, though I feel guilty even agreeing with him. I should be loyal to my master.

Grizz's face gets tight when I tell him this. "Why? He didn't treat you well."

I set my fork down. "He treated me better than the clan did."

The big man grunts at that. He plows through his food while I pretend to look at my plate, sneaking glances at him whenever I'm sure he's not looking. The scar on his face isn't ugly, I decide. The seam makes him look dangerous, not weak. His nose is crooked, like it's been broken and set badly, but that only adds to his violent aura. Combined with the tattoos, rough stubble and shoulder length golden locks, he looks like a badass biker. The type to live free or die.

I'm confident I've gotten away with studying him without him noticing when he reaches out and grips my knee. Instant arousal gushes through me, a flood filling the cup of my sex. I squeeze my legs together to keep from overflowing. I know what it's like to get turned on—Augustine took delight in making me desire his bite and beg for it as much as he enjoyed hurting me—but I've never felt anything like this.

Grizz raises his head, his nostrils flaring. He turns

bright eyes to me, high beams in the dark. His fingers give me one more squeeze.

"You finished eating?"

I nod, unable to speak.

He forks the rest of my food into his mouth, eating with his hand on me like it's the most natural thing in the world. Like he can't tell my breathing has quickened and the air is filled with my scent.

"You called me *sir*, earlier," he says casually. "Why did you stop?"

"You didn't like it," I whisper before I can stop myself. He doesn't need to know how closely I watch him, how I saw his lips press together in the start of a frown when I said it the first time. How I pushed to see how far I could push before his dominance kicked in. Testing limits is just something I do naturally.

He grunts and I feel a second of panic. "You didn't want me to keep calling you *sir*, did you?" Did I read the signs right? The thought that I might have disappointed him squeezes my chest.

"No, no," he soothes, catching my hand. "Relax, Kit. You can be yourself. I want you to be yourself around me."

"Okay." I lower my eyes. How can I explain that submissive is just what I am?

"Good girl," he rumbles and in an instant I'm content. Maybe he knows what I am. At least, on some level. Even if he doesn't want to admit it.

With one final squeeze, he rises and clears the table.

"Time to go, Kit. You wanna wrap up in that blanket?"

"What?"

"You need clothes. You can wear my flannel, but wrap up in that blanket so I can take you out."

~

Grizz

JORDY BLINKS AT ME.

"Kit, let's get a move on."

It's bad enough that she's looking at me with big baby doll eyes. Her scent surrounds me, sweet as fuck, and I'm thinking about my fantasy in the club last night. A sexy little piece who will trot around my home in a shirt and no panties, drop to her knees whenever I want. Here she is, but I can't touch her. She belongs to a vampire.

She plucks at the shirt that swallows her small body. "I can borrow this?"

"Yeah, seeing as you got nothing else to wear. We'll get you clothes first thing."

With a sassy smile, she slips it off.

"Kit..." My mouth is dry. I saw her naked in the club and this morning when she tried to run away, but somehow, having her in my den is different. Her pale body is freckled, her torso slender and thighs sturdy. She looks like she belongs here. My mouth waters.

Before I can ask what she's doing, she pulls my shirt around her, leaving her arms free, and buttons it up almost all the way. The middle button ends up between her breasts and the shirt clings to her. She takes the arms and wraps them around her like a belt. "There," she smiles, pleased. The shirt dress ends about mid thigh and leaves her shoulders bare, but it's enough coverage to hit the surplus store.

"Good enough," I say, and it comes out a growl. Not surprising, I'm pretty close to tossing her over my shoulder and taking her back into the bedroom. 'Cause that'll teach her to trust me.

I shrug on my jacket as Jordy sticks her feet into my extra pair of Timberlands. The boots are enormous but she stuffs paper around the socks.

I check my pocket for my flask and weapons, taking care to hide what I'm packing from Jordy. "Let's go."

Outside she waits and watches me switch out the license plates on the truck.

"This truck is hot," I explain.

"Hot?"

"Stolen."

She cocks her head to the side. "Why did you steal it?"

"Couldn't take you on the bike."

A sigh escapes her. She's gnawing on her lip, staring out over the valley.

"What is it?" I ask.

"Grizz, seriously, why am I here? Augustine isn't gonna like it."

"You call him *master* and sometimes Augustine."

She flushes, her eyes meeting the ground.

"It's not a judgment. I'm just curious about it. The dom submissive stuff is a game."

"It isn't," she insists.

I raise a brow at her as I haul my tool box back to the shed.

"It is, and it isn't," she falters. "You know how important dominance and submission is to shifters. We live and die by it."

"Yeah, but the sexual part. I don't get it."

She gnaws her lip, staring up at me. I'm about to order her to stop biting her lip before she chaps it, when she blurts, "Haven't you ever wanted to give someone everything? Prove how much you love them?"

She presses forward, laying a hand on my chest, right over my heart. Her touch hits me like a Taser. I jerk but she doesn't notice. Her eyes are wide, rapt, and words rush from her like she's been holding them in all her life. "Haven't you wanted to love someone so much you'd do anything, even let them drag you beyond the boundaries of normal, into forbidden territory? And you go with them, just to show how much you trust them. You'd do anything for them. You'd give your life, your heart, your pain, and it'd be a pleasure."

The air leaves my lungs. "Jordy—"

"Don't you want a love like that?" She has both hands on me now, her little fingers fisting in my leather jacket. "If you found it, wouldn't you do anything to hold on to it?"

I take her wrists. "Kit—"

"Wouldn't you?"

I stare at her. She's got a clear blue ring around her eyes but it fades to brown close to the pupil. Her lips are plump and soft. She's up on tiptoe, her whole body thrown into convincing me of what she's saying, hoping I'll understand.

I hate to disappoint her. "No, Kit. I can't say that I would."

It hurts watching the light fade from her face. She starts to pull away and I grip her wrists tighter.

"Did you love Augustine?" My words come out a growl.

She bites her lip and looks away. I take hold of her chin and turn her face back to mine. "Answer me." My bear is clawing my insides, roaring to break free.

"No, okay. I don't. But I like what we have. My fox is… I need to be protected. All I ever wanted was that." Her shoulders slump at the admission. It's a half lie. She wanted more, but she settled for protection. I want to say something, comfort her, but what? We don't see the world the same way. For me, there's only predator and prey, and I've made damn sure I'm a predator. Jordy is weak. At worst, she's prey, a pawn to those more powerful than her. At best, she's collateral damage. But I can't say that. On some level, she already knows it. Despite her hope for something better. A love to be all, end all.

"I guess it sounds silly to you," she whispers. She won't meet my eyes.

I drop her chin. I've done enough damage.

"Get in the truck, Kit. We need to go."

CHAPTER 5

rizz

On the ride, Jordy is quiet.

I keep thinking about what she said. She laid it all out for me. Fates, this kit needs someone to protect her. The first guy to come along and treat her decent and she spills her guts to him. As if I'm her soulmate. Her one true love. I've seen enough to know that shit doesn't exist. I might want to fuck her, my bear might want to keep her, but that's just biology. She makes love something noble. She has a whole manifesto. Love is something to live and die for, something to believe in.

The only thing I believe in is revenge. Revenge: that's what I live and die for. The only reason I met her in the first place is this job for Frangelico. A job I took because he can give me what I want.

I gotta find more leads. More proof that the reason the vampires are taking shifters is to use them as sweet-bloods. Nail down the location of the shifter slavers Jordy mentioned. If there's a black market for shifters operating in Frangelico's territory, we need to shut it down.

Then I can continue on my original hunt.

The only wild card is Jordy. There's no way I'm sending her back to Augustine, but I can't keep her. Snatching her was just part of the job. If I'm not careful, she'll become a distraction.

In my line of work, distractions will get a bear killed.

Jordy's just a clue to the mystery. She's nothing but a means to an end. As much as my bear wants her to be more, it's not safe for her, or fair to me.

Bottom line: I can't get involved. No more fantasizing about keeping her forever. I'm going to use her to complete my mission. If she lets me in, I'll take a taste, but I'll make it clear it means nothing.

She thinks love is forever—she's wrong. Everything ends. And when the time comes, I'll be ready to say goodbye.

Now I just need to harden myself to the disappointed look on her face. It kills my bear when she hurts. I can't think too hard about that.

She makes a small noise when I park in front of the surplus store.

"Stop number one. Get you some clothes."

I hop out and scan the street as I head around to open her door. She exits more slowly, probably because she's wearing a shirt and too-big boots and nothing else. She doesn't have panties on under my shirt. Better forget that fact, or I'll get too hard to walk.

"Come on, Kit." I steer her towards the women's clothes. Her big eyes blink up at me. Her little nipples show through the thick flannel of her shirt dress.

I grit my teeth. Think of baseball. Baseball…nice and boring. Jordy in a jersey and nothing else, kissing the ball, handling the bat… No!

"What do you want me to wear?" she asks, oblivious. Her scent rises, thick and sweet. Her body responding to me. On some level, she's not so oblivious.

"Doesn't matter."

"Do you want certain outfits? For any special events?"

"Not going to attend any fancy balls, Kit. You just need clothes. Stuff for going around town. Clothes to keep you warm and cover you. Nothing to draw attention. Shoes too."

A nod, and she disappears. Slowly the cart fills with shirts and shorts, a pair of canvas shoes, a light sweater.

I catch her arm as she comes by again. "Grab some dresses."

"What type?" she asks. She looks up at me, so sweet and trusting. If only she knew what I want to do to her.

"Fuck if I know. Dresses. I like these." I turn her away from me, towards a rack of floral, flouncy outfits.

She fingers them. "They're pretty."

I grab a few, including the ones she touched longingly.

Blushing, she swaps them out. "I'm not an extra small."

"You're extra small to me."

She flushes. "I'll need to try them on."

"Go ahead. I'll wait. You got everything you need?"

"I think so." She bites her lip as I sift through the tank tops and shorts she picked out.

Before she can leave to try on the dresses, I stop her. "Panties too. Did you forget?"

"No," she flushes. "I don't usually wear them."

I growl. "Out here you wear them. In the house you can go bare."

"Is that an order?" she asks. I'm about to pull her into a dressing room and bend her over when I realize she's teasing.

Growling, I stomp off, pushing the cart so no one can see my raging hard on. She takes a moment to change, so I've barely got myself under control before she finds me.

"Is this okay?" she calls. She's in a little dress, a floral thing with straps that leave her arms bare. It hugs her body, showing off her slight curves. She looks sweet and wholesome and innocent, and I'm just a big old grumpy bear.

"Yes. Good. Get a few of those. And some sweaters." It still gets cold at night.

"Do you want me to wear it today?"

Yes. I want you to wear it while I drive us back to my den, your head in my lap. I'll carry you to my bed, rip the dress off and fuck you until you cum.

"Not today," I manage to growl. "Got shit to do. Something practical."

"Okay, Grizz." She skips off.

I hide behind a display of jackets and adjust my jeans. Dress shopping with Jordy—not happening again. I'm turning into a fucking pervert. There's an easy solution: get her home, tie her to my bed.

But that's not why I took her. I've got a job to do.

I pay for everything and stop her from carrying the bags. I was raised to treat women like ladies. I open the doors and I carry the bags. Jordy is obviously uncomfortable with me doing things for her. She bites her lip but obeys.

I escort her out with my hand on her back. In a pair of overall shorts and t-shirt, she looks like a tomboy sent out to play at recess. Fresh-faced and young. She shouldn't be around me.

We stop at a drugstore next. I park the truck and point to the doors. "Girly shit. Get it."

"What?"

"Kit, I'm on a job. You got intel I might need. Until I figure out what I need, you're with me.

She pales. "But my master—"

"Forget him. You're with me."

"When it's over, will you send me back?"

"Cross that bridge when we come to it," I say, even though I have no intention of sending Jordy back to the likes of Augustine. Ever. Augustine will be pissed, but he doesn't have to know how she escaped. And after a while, he will forget about her and I can find her a new master. I'll screen doms for her myself if I have to. Maybe Trey knows a good wolf who would accept a sub, even if she's a fox.

But as I think of handing Jordy off, my bear growls. Jordy shrinks smaller in her chair.

"Out," I tell her. "Grab anything you need. Hairbrush... girly shit. I don't know what you need."

She gnaws her lip again.

"Stop that," I growl and she does, straightening to attention. Fuck, now I'm giving her orders.

I tear out of the truck and let her out, slamming the doors a little harder than necessary. "Come on." I prowl into the drugstore and grab a shopping basket, handing it to her.

She looks lost.

"Go, get what you need. Just for a week or so."

She faces the store. "I don't know what I need."

I stare into her wide eyes and realize I'm asking her to think of herself. But if she thinks I'm going to pick her shampoo out for her, she's got another think coming. "While you're with me, I want you to look good. Not makeup, but take care of yourself. If I find out you went without because you didn't want me to have to buy it, I'll go buy twelve of them for you." I dip my head closer, making sure the cashier can't over hear us. "And then I'll punish you."

Her pupils dilate, like that excites her, but she nods and scrambles down an aisle. I follow, grabbing a handful of chapstick and throwing them into her basket.

I shake my head. For someone who hates the dom/sub power games, I sure like getting my way.

"Sir?" she asks. She's poised at the entrance to the brightly lit makeup aisle. Cardboard cutouts with celebrities' painted faces greet me at every turn. Fucking clown house.

"No make up—" I start to say when she whispers,

"Just some foundation. To cover up the scar."

Shit. Can't say no to that.

"All right. Cover up, or whatever. And..." I glance at the painted faces with disgust. "Whatever else you want. But nothing too crazy."

"Thank you," she skips up to me and kisses my cheek.

"Don't mention it," I mumble, and turn away, stomping down another aisle. I saw some things I want for her.

A few minutes later, the cashier's ringing everything up while Jordy crouches nearby, fingering a candy bar longingly.

I grab the candy bar and add it to the pile then jerk my head to the junk food aisle. "Go get us some snacks."

"What do you like?"

"Meat."

I send her off with a gentle pat on her butt. While she's gone, I pull out the stuff I found for her, and get the cashier to ring it up and hide it in a bag before she returns. A little surprise.

Back in the car, I toss the bags onto the back seat and roll into traffic.

"Get what you need, Kit?"

She nods.

She's happy, I can tell. Her cheeks are flushed, and she's braiding and re-braiding her hair, using the hair shit I just bought her. She finally settles on two auburn pigtails.

I stop at a fastfood joint and order twenty burgers. Jordy's eyes go round when I hand her the bags.

"Um, Grizz? I'm not really hungry. Breakfast was really big." She looks guilty.

"Not for us, babe." I roll up to a stoplight and put my hand on her knee, giving her my full attention. "You get hungry later, I'll get you whatever you like. This is for someone else."

She's silent. Content to let me take her wherever I need to go. I head to the Fight Club and try to ignore how great it feels to have a willing woman riding shotgun.

We stop at a light and I look over. She's leaning her head against the window, the reflection showing a lightly freckled face and faraway gaze. Her expression is thoughtful, but a smile isn't far away. It hits me then, she's content with me.

I shouldn't encourage it. I really shouldn't. But I can't help it. When it comes to her, I just can't help myself.

"Here." I reach behind me and pull out another bag from the pile on the backseat. "I almost forgot. I grabbed these while you were in getting dresses." I hand her a pack of colored pencils and an adult coloring book. Her eyes go wide but she takes them before the light turns green and I hit the gas.

"Saw you doodling on my stuff." I keep my eyes on the road.

"I'm sorry—"

"Don't apologize. It looked really good. I figured you'd like to do it, if you're grabbing pieces of trash to doodle on."

"I do." She holds the book and pencils to her like an award for best submissive in Club Toxic. Like it's a treasure.

"Well, now you don't have to use trash. I'll get you a sketch pad, too, if you want."

Her face lights up. She practically bounces in her seat, so sweet and beautiful my chest tightens.

"Thank you, thank you," she breathes and before I can stop her, she leans in to give me a peck on my scarred cheek. My cock perks up and I'm a second away from letting her know how she can show her gratitude when she pulls away and looks up at me adoringly. Fates, just the expression on her face is enough to get me off. No good. I gotta shut this down.

"It doesn't mean anything." I announce and she pulls back, still glowing.

"I know," she says, but she's lying. But, when it all comes down to it, so am I.

~

Jordy

GRIZZ GLARES AT THE ROAD, growling when a dark blue Jetta gets too close to our truck. The Jetta driver glances up and turns white, immediately throwing on the brakes. The dark blue car drops behind us and Grizz's body rumbles as his bear claims victory. Any other shifter, I'd be cowering in my seat, but I sit up straight, watching Grizz scare off human drivers, feeling totally contented. My fox perks her head up, studying our captor with rapt attention. She's enamored with him. Totally.

For a second he softened. He tried to hide it, but I felt it. His walls came down. He's trying hard to keep his walls high and not to get involved with me, but he already is.

He took me out of the cage, he helped me. He says I'm his captive, but I'm sitting free, surrounded by stuff he bought me. Actions speak louder than words. Augustine said he'd provide and protect me. But Grizz actually does it. Better than Augustine, if I'm allowed to think that.

I should hate being Grizz's captive and want to get back to my master, but I don't. If this was a loan, I'd have to crawl back to my master and beg him to forgive me, to punish me for being disloyal. But this isn't a loan. Grizz saw me, he wanted me, he took me. He might deny it, but it's the truth. It's dangerous, for both of us. But most of all for me. I'm the one who will live with the consequences, but in the moment, here with Grizz, I can't think of the pain coming down the road. The longer I'm with Grizz, the less my master, my training, my future matters.

As soon as we pull into the industrial area, Grizz changes. His face hardens, his eyes locking on a nondescript warehouse on one side of a long chain link fence. A few cars are parked close to it, but he parks far away.

"What is this place?"

"No man's land. Not shifter, not vampire. They both claim it, though. But everyone knows what happens here is off the radar. Doesn't count. No retaliation allowed."

My eyes trail back to the building. "Retaliation for what?"

"You'll see. Here"—he shrugs out of his jacket— "Put this on." He continues as I scramble to obey, "When you're here, you're my property."

The statement sends zings straight to my things, and he notices it. "Not like that. I'm not collaring you."

I put my hand to my neck. The vampire's scar is a clear

enough mark of ownership. Grizz thinks so too, his face turns dark. "You don't belong to him." His hand surrounds my neck, a living collar. His fingers are rough against my skin. His face dips to mine and he growls. "He mistreated you, and I stepped in. Shoulda done it sooner. Would've, if I'd known. Now you're in my care. That means when we're here, stay close, stay quiet, follow my lead. You understand?"

"Yeah. Like high protocol."

His brow wrinkles. "Not sure what that means, Kit."

"It means you want me to behave a certain way, and if I don't, there'll be consequences. High alert for both of us."

His fingers gentle, stroke my scar. "High alert is right. In my den, it's safer, we don't need protocols. Here, one false move could be dangerous. I wouldn't bring you here, but didn't want to leave you alone. So stick with me, I'll get you through. Got it?"

"Got it. Grizz—" I catch his hand. "I know you told me not to run. It's nothing personal. I'm bound to Augustine. I…owe him."

"You owe him nothing. Not that I can see." Now he strokes my cheek and I find it hard to breathe. "It's okay. It's the way you're wired, I'm getting that. I'm going to work on it, though. Maybe if you owe me more than him, you'll forget him, yeah?"

I nod, swallowing on a dry throat. I like the sound of that. Way, way too much. He's declared at every turn that this is just a job for him. I can't lean on him more than I have to.

He gets out and heads around to my door again. It

feels like he's serving me and I don't like it. I've been trained to serve, not to be serviced.

But when I open my door ahead of him, he growls. "You wait for me, Kit."

Okay, right. Follow his lead.

He holds out his hand, I take it and wait while he grabs the fast food bags and drops them into the bed of the truck. We head across the parking lot, attached at the hand. Biting my lip, I race to keep up, taking two strides to his one. The place smells like shifters, all sorts. My fox isn't scared though, walking in Grizz's shadow.

As we wait a white Camaro rolls up with a dark-haired guy and a second, better dressed one with silver hair. By his young face he's prematurely grey. The dark-haired guy has a cigarette sticking out of his mouth, unlit. He looks a little like James Dean. I don't realize I'm staring at him until he winks at me. Flushing, I look at the ground.

"Well, well," the black haired guy puts out his hands as if he's going to hug us. His accented English is mocking. "The prodigal son returns."

"Declan." Grizz nods to the black haired guy. "Parker." The grey headed dude nods back and Grizz plants his boots in the pavement. "Where the fuck is my bike?"

Declan cocks his head. "It's coming. Any minute now. Ya ready for your fight? You know the wolves are mad at ya? Gonna try to set ya up." Irish, I realize as he keeps talking. He has an Irish accent.

"Not here to talk about the fight," Grizz grumbles.

Grumpy Grizz, I tag him silently. I have the feeling that most people know Grumpy Grizz. I'm the only one who sees his other side. That makes me smile, deep down, but I don't let it show. Not to these strangers. I can't glare at them, like Grizz, but I blank my face. I'm pretty good at not showing what I'm feeling. Augustine got mad when I expressed too many emotions.

"I want my bike and then I got a proposition."

"A proposition? I haven't been propositioned in a parking lot since—"

"Shut up, Dec." The grey haired guy, Parker, elbows him. "Grizz, the bike's coming. In fact"—he turns to the entrance—"here it is."

Sure enough, a guy riding a big ole Harley roars up to us.

"Who's that ridin'?" Grizz growls. His body's all hard. I angle close to him and he puts a hand on my back. Soothing me without taking his eyes off his bike.

"That's Laurie," Declan says. "No worries. He's our boy."

"Why the fuck is he riding my bike?"

"Ya told us to pick it up. He's the only one who could handle that monster." Declan rolls his eyes like it's obvious.

The tall, skinny guy rolls the bike near us and puts the kickstand down, staggering a little under the bike's weight. He wobbles as he gets off and Grizz gets tense like he's going to run and catch his bike before it crashes to the pavement. I put my hand on his back to soothe him as the ungainly rider manages to extricate himself from Grizz's bike and walk away with the Harley upright.

"He got it here safe and sound," Parker says smoothly. He's got a lighter out and is flicking it on and off.

"Besides," Declan adds, speaking around the unlit cigarette. "He has his own helmet."

The thin guy named Laurie heads our way, he removes his glasses, pulls off the helmet and replaces the glasses. His hair sticks out everywhere. I swallow a giggle. These guys are like the Three Stooges, only they're all skinny. And shifters. But strange shifters—I can't tell what species they are, and each one is different.

"Here." Grizz tosses something to Parker, who catches it without looking. "Take the truck, clean it up and ditch it. Plates in the back. Wipe the prints."

"Yeah, yeah," Declan mutters. "We know the drill. Weren't born yesterday."

"You mentioned another bit of business?" Parker asks.

"Yeah." Grizz still has his eyes on the bike. He dips his head, whispers, "Get the burgers," to me and gives me a push. I'll have to walk away from Grizz, back to the truck. Part of me wants to stick close to him.

Grizz looks down and sees this.

"You'll be okay," he murmurs. "I've got you."

Grizz

RELUCTANTLY, Jordy turns and trots to the truck. I keep my eyes on her as I tell Declan, Parker and Laurie, "I need info."

"Who's that?" Parker asks after a cursory glance. He's smart enough not to gawk at Jordy while I'm present.

Declan isn't so circumspect. "She looks like Anne of Green Gables."

"How would you know?" Parker asks.

"I saw the movie." The Irishman shrugs. "It was on cable."

"You're a dork." Parker shakes his head.

"Feck ya. It's a classic."

"Guys," I interject before they start fighting. Fucking weirdo shifters. But they have ears everywhere. And I need them. "Focus. I've got a job for you, and I'll pay."

Jordy returns with the giant white bags.

"Thank you, baby," I say and she glows.

I hold up the bag of burgers.

"Jackpot," Declan whoops. Laurie reaches for the bag and I hold it out of range. "First, we discuss terms."

"You can't buy us with burgers," Parker says.

I hand over the burgers to Laurie, who retreats behind his two friends. "There's payment in it too. Couple grand. Maybe more, if I get what I want."

"And what's that?"

"Vampires are grabbing shifters, using them for food. I want to know who's supplying them, and why."

"Is that all?" Declan scoffs. "Why not ask for the moon?"

"Frangelico know about this?" Parker asks, his eyes narrowing.

"Frangelico sanctioned my search. I'm digging into the vampires. I need help. Everything and anything you know about the slavers."

"You want us to talk to the shifters," Parker says. He

catches on quick. "And you know none of them will talk to you. Not after you sided with the vampires."

"I didn't side with the vampires—"

"The hell ya didnae," Declan snaps, his accent coming out thick.

"You need more than our help talking to shifters. If you're gonna be poking around here, you need amnesty. Time to go to Garrett and grovel," Parker says.

My answer is a growl.

"Come on, Grizz," Declan says. "You walked into wolf territory and pissed them off. They hate that. And even a big strong grizzly can't take on a whole wolf pack. Even if you do have vampire friends."

"Vampires aren't my friends."

"Just your employer," Parker points out.

"So I work with Frangelico," I shrug. "So what? I'm a fighter. I'm allowed to moonlight."

Parker shakes his head. "War is coming. You gotta pick a side. Wolves or vampires."

"Neither."

"Waste of a good fighter." Parker shakes his head.

"Look, I don't have time for this."

"Yeah, you're too busy doing the vampire king's bidding," Declan mutters.

I glare at him. I'm going to have to spill more than I want to. "I want to stop the deaths."

"The druggie deaths? The humans?" Parker asks.

"I think the vampires are involved in those as well as the shifter snatching."

"We know they are." Declan crosses his arms over his chest. "So what?"

"So something's up. Frangelico wants them stopped."

"He's gonna send you after his own people?"

"He already has. They're breaking the rules. Leaving out dead bodies. Kidnapping and keeping shifters for some reason. I'm gonna find out, if you help me, I'll find out faster. And we'll stop them."

"You think the shifter snatching and the humans' deaths are related?" Parker asks. "Why?"

I shrug. "Just got a feeling. I think the vamps were addicted to human sweetbloods and now they're switching to shifters. I wanna know why. Humans are easier prey. Why switch to shifters?"

"Who knows why vampires do anything?" Declan shakes his head.

Parker flicks his lighter thoughtfully. "Maybe shifter blood's more potent." His gaze focuses on Jordy. "Is this one of the shifter sweetbloods?"

I snarl and move in front of Jordy, blocking Parker and Declan's view of her. "Leave her out of this."

The two misfit shifters exchange glances, but say nothing. I don't like it. Motioning to Jordy, I pull her in front of me, presenting her to the guys.

"This is Kit," I say. I don't want to use her real name and put her at risk. "She's under my protection."

"You claiming her?" Declan asks. Jordy sucks in a breath.

"As far as you or any other shifter is concerned, yes. When she's here, she's with me. When she's not, forget she exists. Understand?"

They both mumble that they understand, but they don't look happy.

"You know something you're not telling us," Parker accuses.

"Maybe. Maybe not. Help me, get me intel, and I'll bring you in." I rest my hands on Jordy's shoulders. "You can refuse to help me. But there's more at stake than our pride."

Declan swears.

"All right, Grizz," Parker says. "We've got nothing, so nothing to lose. We'll help you. Finish this errand with the truck and poke around to figure out what we can about the shifter slavers. But watch your back. You go poking around Tucson, Garrett's pack is not gonna like it."

"I'll handle the wolves. Hell, I'll go talk to them right now." I wave a hand at the warehouse at the end of the lot.

"I wouldn't." Declan pulls the cigarette out of his mouth and pretends to blow out smoke. The whole smoking an unlit cigarette is fucking bizarre, but when you work with these three, weird is what you get. "You're *persona non gratin* right now."

"*Persona non grata,*" Laurie corrects softly from his spot beside the car.

"What?"

"*Non grata,*" Parker says. "You said *gratin*. Gratin is a cheese sauce."

"I'm hungry, all right." Declan throws up his hands. "Jaysus."

I clear my throat. "As I was saying, the wolves will take me back. I tell them I want to stop human deaths and shifter snatchings that bring our community law enforcement heat, and they'll welcome me with open arms."

"Go on then, make nice." Declan jerks his chin towards

the shifter Fight Club building. "I want tae see it." He hops up on the hood of the Camaro, tagging a greasy bag and pulling out a burger. "Dinner an' a show."

"You gonna eat with that cigarette in your mouth?" Parker snipes at him and Declan raises his eyebrows.

"So what if I am? What's it tae ya?"

They settle into their habitual bickering.

"All right," I mutter. As entertaining as the Declan-Parker-Laurie freak show is, I'm not gonna stick around to watch it. It's too long and got no intermission. In fact, it never ends.

I start walking towards the Fight Club building, ushering Jordy with me.

"Keep close, Kit," I tell her, my hand clamped on the back of her neck. It feels right to hold her. "Follow my lead."

She doesn't answer but her body moves and responds to mine, taking cues from me, molding to what I need her to be. Alert, attentive. Completely in tune. Fates, she's fucking perfect.

She stays one step behind me as I stride to the Fight Club door. I used to work here until the Tucson wolf pack found out that I work for the vampires. I didn't mean anything by it. Frangelico just offered me a better deal—a chance at actually completing my mission.

I slow as I approach the Fight Club door. It's new and sturdy looking. The last time I saw it, it had yellow tape over it. Someone's cleaned up the place since I've been here, but it feels familiar. My bear thinks of this place as home. Even if the wolves think I betrayed them, I belong here.

Jordy stays one step behind me as I approach, glancing right and left. A bunch of punk bikers have their rides parked alongside the chain link fence. They're talking and chilling before the bar opens. Cat shifters, from the smell of them. Even if I couldn't smell them, the way they fuss with their colored leather jackets and run combs through their hair constantly would tip me off that they're a bunch of pussies. They don't even ride real bikes, just crotch rockets, which probably makes them cheetahs. Cheetahs live for speed.

They barely glance my way as Jordy and I hit the Fight Club doorstep. Before I can grab the handle, the door opens and a giant shifter looms in front of me. Bright green eyes hit mine. This guy is big, and his animal is bigger—and ready to blow. Direct eye contact with a brawler bear like me is a straight up challenge. Red cape to a bull, gauntlet thrown.

"Hey." I stand my ground but don't offer offense. "Is Jared or Trey in?"

"Nope. Who the hell are you?"

"Someone who wants to talk to a wolf."

"No wolves in here." His feral eyes flick up and down, sizing me up. "At least, not for the likes of you."

Insults, great. "You got a beef with me? Bring it." My bear could use a fight.

Out of the corner of my eye, I catch a flash of auburn hair. Jordy. Fuck, I don't want her involved in this.

"Ready when you are." The guy folds his arms over his chest and the light in his eyes flares. Lots of muscle mass and a barely contained animal. Not sure what species, but he smells dangerous.

"Or you could just let me pass."

"Got orders. No bears allowed. In fact, the wolves said if you showed and The Bastard wanted a fight, I could take you down."

"The Bastard? Is that what you call your animal?" I shake my head in mock pity. Behind my back, I wave Jordy away. She paces back slowly, not drawing attention to herself. Good girl. "I'm a fighter and I got a booking tomorrow," I tell the bouncer. "You gonna stop me from walking in then? Got a right to be here."

He shakes his head and I get a whiff of his scent. Something fruity—bananas?

"Gorilla," I murmur and the green eyes narrow. "All right, monkey boy, you take dictation?"

"What?"

"Can you read and write? I'm gonna leave a message."

"Fuck off."

"You don't want to know the message?"

The gorilla starts to pull away to shut the door. Before he can, I punch him in the face.

He recovers in a split second and comes roaring after me. I dance backward.

"You want more of this? Sign up to face me in the cage. Animal to animal."

"They told me about you," he spits. "You're in league with the leeches. You fight for them."

"I fight for whoever pays me."

"Species traitor."

Fuck this. "You wanna go, banana eater? Let's go." He's big, but not the brightest bulb in the box. It'll be easy.

The gorilla stops in his tracks. I can practically read the moment he has an idea.

"Hey," he shouts to the cat shifters. "Didn't one of your females get bitten last week?"

Fuck.

The head cheetah, a guy with a face full of piercings and a black mohawk lopes forward. He's lean but not scrawny. "Not one of ours. We protect our own."

"She was a cat, though." Another pipes up. "A rare one. Lynx or something."

"Yeah. And a vampire bit her." The gorilla says.

"Yeah? So?" The cat's hackles are up. If he was in animal form his hair would be on end. Pissed.

"So this guy works with vampires." The gorilla points at me. I growl at him and he shows his teeth. Not blunt like a normal gorilla. Sharp like the predator he is.

"Asshole," I mutter as the cat shifters head from their bikes towards me.

"Not so brave when the odds are against you," the gorilla scoffs.

"Fifteen to one isn't a fair fight," I mutter and back up until I reach Jordy. "Kit, you get ready to run."

"Grizz," she grips me. The cheetah pack spreads out, starting to flank me. I can't let them circle until Jordy's outta here.

I reach into the jacket she's wearing, pull out my flask, unscrew the top and take a swig.

"Now. Head for the Camaro." I give her a push. Declan, Laurie and Parker are still a half a parking lot away, watching us. They'd have my back but they're smaller than most shifters. Their animals are messed up, broken.

Not exactly fighting material. Still, I know they'll protect Jordy.

I turn back to the lead cheetah and growl loud enough to set him back a step. "You know I can take you?"

"Not all of us." His eyes are lit. Fuck, I'm surrounded by crazy shifters. "You the grizzly?"

I straighten. "I'm a grizzly. One of them. We're apex predators. Not exactly endangered species. At least, not like cheetahs." I show my teeth.

"That's funny. There's a bunch of us and only one of you. Now who's the endangered species?"

One of the cheetahs breaks off from the pack and heads for Jordy. Fuck. No.

"Leave her alone," I snarl just as the cat blocks my Kit's path.

"You with him?" He bends down, getting in her face. "You with the grizzly?"

She looks at me, eyes wide.

"You smell like him." He grabs her and she squawks.

Aw, hell no.

"Get your hands off her." I head towards the guy tugging at Jordy. She's fighting, trying to free herself.

The pack closes in. I grab the first body in front of me and haul it out of the way. It goes flying, three more take its place. With a roar I push forward.

They push me back, but I got a secret weapon. I raise my flask and drain it. Power hits my cells. Before my vision turns black, I call my bear.

Jordy

A RUSHING SOUND like the wind and brown fur bursts from Grizz's skin. His animal explodes out of him, shredding his clothes. Cheetahs go flying as giant bear paws hit the pavement, sending a mini earthquake rippling through the parking lot. The black top cracks.

The cheetah holding me pauses, watching his friends rip their jackets off and shift. I bite him hard, and he snarls, gripping my throat and raising me above his head. I kick him in the crotch. He drops me and I twist away. Sucking air through my bruised neck, choking a little, I scuttle away from him as fast as I can. He doesn't follow.

All around, greasy bikers fall to their knees and contort, their cats emerging. They're bigger than any natural cheetah, with teeth like sabertooth tigers. They leap on Grizz.

"No," I shout when someone clutches my arm. I fight wildly and another hand clamps on my other arm.

"Lass, it's all right, it's us." Declan tugs me towards the Camaro. "We're on your side."

"No, I can't leave him." I try to dig my feet into the pavement.

"You're not. We just gotta get you safe."

Behind us, the grizzly bellows as cat after cat leaps on him while a huge gorilla hangs from the chain link fence, laughing.

"We gotta help him!"

"Not our fight, lass." Declan tugs me the final few feet to the bike and pushes me down. "Stay here."

I gnaw my lip, wishing I was stronger, faster, more dominant. So far Grizz has swatted most of the cats away. It's crazy. The bear's completely outnumbered…and he's winning.

"Never seen anything like it," Declan whispers beside me as Grizz whips around, smashing an attacking cheetah to the ground. Another move, too fast to track, and more cheetahs lay out on the blacktop, moaning. Grizz throws cats like they're hollow. And—

"He's moving so fast he blurs," Parker says.

The gorilla roars in frustration. More cheetahs fall.

"Uh oh," Declan murmurs and my heart seizes. Five cheetahs crouch behind Grizz, waiting to jump him. Two more run at the bear, who easily deflects them. But he takes a step back, right into the trap.

"No," I moan. Five cats jump Grizz at once. One gets on his back, claws dug in, head rearing back for a killing bite.

"They're killing him!" I shriek. "Do something."

"Feckin' hell," Declan mutters and shouts to Parker. "Wrap this up."

The grey-haired shifter is on top of the Camaro. "Cops are coming!" he hollers. The brawling animals don't notice.

A whistle pierces the air. The cats scream and I cover my ears, wishing Declan warned me he was going to whistle.

Parker repeats, "Cops are coming."

"Cops," one of the bikers takes up the cry. He lets out a scream and his buddies stop mauling Grizz.

"Cops!" Declan whoops. "Every animal for himself!"

The cheetahs turn tail and run.

Grizz picks himself up. His fur is red in patches and he's limping. But he's still alive.

The gorilla roars and leaps from his perch, landing a few feet away from Grizz.

"He's not gonna let Grizz leave without a fight," Parker says. "Don't got time for this. Cops are coming."

"Feck, did you actually call them?" Declan gasps.

"I did," Laurie says from the passenger seat of the Camaro.

The Irishman swears and grabs me. "Call him," he orders.

"What?" I gape.

"Call him," Declan repeats, and hands me something. A helmet—the one Laurie was wearing. "Call Grizz. Now!"

"Grizz," I scream. The big bear is pacing back and forth, waiting for the gorilla to charge. "Grizz the cops are coming! You gotta come! Come back to me."

Grizz turns and starts to shrink. The gorilla pounces, but at the last second, Grizz whirls. A blur and the gorilla's down on the ground, shrinking back into a human body.

"Come on," Declan shouts as sirens rise around us. "Now!"

The bear races towards us. Fur recedes from bloodied skin, and then it's just Grizz running up to me and the bike.

"You're naked, man, here," Declan hands him a pair of sweatpants. I pull off the leather jacket and wince as Grizz shrugs that on over his bloody torso. He shoves his feet into the Timberlands and swings a big leg over his bike.

"Hop on," he orders and my skin crackles with his dominance. Helmet secure on my head, I climb on behind Grizz and grab his jacket.

"Arms around me," he says, and growls when I hesitate. I don't want to hurt him but when I put my arms tentatively around his middle, he tugs me snug to his back.

"Tight, Kit," he orders and kicks the bike off. The engine blasts to life and we zoom away, following the white Camaro in a twisting, turning escape route out of the warehouse district.

We turn onto the main road a second before a firetruck screams past, flashing red and flying towards the Fight Club as we make our getaway in the opposite direction.

CHAPTER 6

rizz

THE BIKE GROWLS as I weave between cars, pushing it faster and faster. Jordy's fingers dig into me, but I don't slow. I gotta get her home, get her safe before the power drains from my veins, leaving me too weak to defend her. Coming off the juice is always hard.

At least we're not being followed. Just in case, I change lanes and turn onto a side street.

By the time my bike has climbed my mountain, the red hot rage simmering in my blood has cooled. I cut off the engine and slump forward, my limbs heavy and cold. My stomach a mass of knots. When I fight, I'm made of adrenaline. After the adrenaline leaves, nothing's left.

My vision goes black a moment. I fight through the

sludge of my own consciousness, back to reality, back to life. There was something I needed to do—

A slight weight moves behind me and I raise my head. Jordy. Gotta get her off the bike, get her safe.

"Grizz?" Jordy calls. She's standing beside me now. I'm losing seconds, losing time.

Blinking, I shake my head. "Inside. Now."

I haul my body off the bike, take a few steps and stagger.

"Grizz!" She presses to my side. Propping me up. Helping me walk. Not right. I should be helping her.

"Inside. Gotta get…safe…" My tongue is swollen, filling my mouth, making me mumble.

Keys clink and the door opens, the familiar scent of my den embracing me. Almost there. I power forward and fall to my knees before I reach my kitchen.

"Grizz, what's wrong?" Jordy's voice is high pitched. "What do you need?

"Coming off the fight. Be…fine." I don't know if I will be fine. It's never been this bad before.

"It's okay, just lie down." Her hands pat over my body. Something cushions my head. My boots come off. "Grizz, can you hear me? Can I get you something?"

"Meat," I groan and lick my lips. "Water."

A rushing sound and she's back, holding the cool rim of a glass to my lips. "Drink this." Her breath comes in frantic little pants. I pat her leg. I want her to know I'll be all right. The water rushes down my throat, clearing out my lungs. I can breathe. Yes, that's it. Replace the juice with something clean and pure.

"Here," Jordy says. Her voice is funny. Blood hits my

lips and I snarl, grabbing the hunk of meat she found. It's half frozen but my bear doesn't care. I rip and gnaw into it, slowly coming back to myself. I'm on the tiles, lying on my back, my leather jacket under my head. Jordy kneels close to me. She gives me more water when I ask, and another hunk of meat.

I raise my heavy arm, find her face with my hand. I cup her cheek, frowning at the wetness I find there.

"It's all right," I mumble around my swollen tongue. "Just give me a second. Be right back."

"Shhh." She holds my hand to her face. "It's okay. I'm here." Beyond her is my front door. She could easily walk out and leave, return to her master, but she doesn't.

"Stay with me," I murmur. I don't have the energy to order her.

"Of course," she whispers and I let my head roll back as I slide out of consciousness.

I COME TO IN STAGES. There's something soft under my head—softer than the leather jacket. A pillow. A slight body presses against my sore ribs. A lovely scent wafts up to my nose. Jordy. She's lying next to me and my bear loves it.

I'm warm, too warm. Something's draped over us and it smells of vampire. With a growl, I rip off the blanket I found on Jordy's cage and toss it across the room. It lands by the door. I'll burn it later. Don't want to smell that vampire again.

I'm on the floor halfway between the door and

kitchen, my jacket's hung on its hook and my boots are stacked neatly underneath. My body is a mass of fiery pain, the worst is a bite on my leg and another on my shoulder. Damn cats. As soon as I can move I'm gonna rinse these bites out real good.

In the meantime, I'm just gonna lie here and thank my lucky stars things went down like they did. That was the hardest I've come off the juice. And I'm healing slower, my body having to recover in more ways than one. Not a great sign. I'll have to be more careful in the future.

I'm the luckiest bear in the world. Not because I survived the fight, but because of the warm weight tucked against me. Jordy got me inside, fed and watered me. She made a bed on the tiles and lay down next to me.

I could lie here forever, sore ribs be damned.

A small noise and Jordy raises her head. Her eyes are worried under the tangle of her hair.

"Hey," she whispers. I grin and stroke back the auburn strands. "You doing okay?"

"Much better." My voice is deep as the grave.

"You were so out of it." She bites her lip. "I was worried."

"Didn't mean to scare you, Kit." Shit, was I out for a couple of hours? That's the worst by a long shot.

She holds still, snuggled into my side with her freckled face turned up to mine, as I brush her hair back. When I drop my hand, she stirs.

"Here." She gets up and heads to the sink, returning with a big glass of water. I sit up and drink while she crouches beside me.

"Thanks."

"You want to eat something?"

I nod. "That'd be good."

"You want some meat?"

"Nothing frozen."

She shoots me a tiny grin over her shoulder as she heads into the kitchen again. "I pulled a bunch out of the freezer, put it into the sink to thaw."

I sit up as she putters back and forth, handing me a slab of steak, refilling my water glass. She makes no comment when I find new strength and rise on wobbly legs. I look like a newborn fawn, and groan as I sink down like an old man. Silently, she serves me another plate of meat. I'm eating it raw but it goes down just right. Gotta replenish what the fighting took outta me. It feels like there's a hole in my middle.

The whole time I eat, I don't take my eyes off her. Jordy fixes another plate for me and heats up some cooked leftovers for herself. Every movement is fluid and graceful, as if she's in a choreographed dance. Did Augustine make her serve him and his friends like this? Probably. The thought makes me choke. Jordy whirls around, eyes wide and I quickly swig some water and swallow the mouthful. Only when I signal that all's well does she go back to what she's doing. So attentive, so well trained. I guess I should be thanking Augustine, but I just want to kill the bastard.

"Do you need anything else?" Jordy asks. She waits until I shake my head to set her plate down and slide into the chair next to me. She catches me staring at her and freezes. "Is this okay?" Her soft voice is musical, sweet.

"Yeah, Kit. You're good. Make yourself at home."

Biting her lip, she looks around the kitchen. "I kinda already did."

"Good," I say firmly, and pat her knee. I like her close to me. Hell, I want her in my lap, but my body's still knitting itself together.

It's been a long time since someone cared for me this way.

She finishes before I do, and waits with her eyes downcast. I follow the line of her gaze and realize my knuckles are bloody. Hell, my entire body is one raw mass of cuts and bruises. I feel it now that I've come down. The meat is helping though. I'm beginning to heal. One solid night sleeping and I'll be back on my feet.

Jordy rises and clears the table. She's still in those ridiculous overalls, but they don't hide the luscious curve of her ass.

"Hey, Kit." I catch her arm as she walks by. She stills but doesn't look at me. "I'm sorry. About passing out like that."

Something flickers on her face but disappears immediately. She wasn't expecting an apology. Hope she realizes how fucking rare it is. I don't usually act like I have someone to answer to.

She turns fully toward me. "Is it the fighting that makes you do that?"

I weigh the costs of telling her the truth for a crazy second and go with a partial lie. "Yes."

"You were amazing. So fast. Parker and Declan said they'd never seen anything like it." She bites her lip like she's not sure she should've told me.

"I did what I had to do."

"It was incredible," she says. "You went so fast, we couldn't even see half your movements. You didn't look real."

I shrug. "It was dark." Not really, but I gotta stop this line of thinking.

"You were faster than any shifter."

"You've seen a lot of shifters fight?" I scoff.

"Yes, tonight. You took on a whole pack and nearly won."

"Not really. It was touch and go at the end."

"Not really," she insists. "You could've beaten them."

"You don't know that," I dismiss.

"I know what I saw." Her voice gets soft as she figures it out. "You blurred. You were so fast you blurred. The only other creatures I know who can blur like that are..." She doesn't say it but I hear the end of the sentence, anyway. *The only creatures who can blur like that are vampires.*

"I'm just fast is all." Lie, lie, lie. From the look on her face, she knows it too. But she's not correcting me. Too well trained. By Augustine. I growl.

"Thanks for dinner." It's still dark out, so can't be breakfast yet.

"It's your food. I just served it up."

"You took care of me, Kit." I strip off my shirt and she gasps.

"You're hurt!"

"Yeah, Kit. Fought a pack of cats." I check the spot where the claw dug into me. It's not bleeding but not healing as quickly as usual. My system's still dealing with the effects of the juice.

"You need a bandage." Jordy leans close. My cock jumps as she inspects the wound, her breath light on my abs. I can't help reaching out and lifting her hair back to see her face.

That's when I see the purple mottling above her collarbone, around her neck.

"What the fuck," I growl. "You got bruises on your throat." I take her head in my hands to examine her.

She bites her lip but holds still. "Grizz, please. It's nothing."

"Doesn't look like nothing. Looks like someone tried to choke you out."

"It was one of the cats. He grabbed me and kinda…got his hand around my throat." She raises her hand to demonstrate.

My bear rumbles deep in my gut. I'll kill him. Gripping her hair, I turn her head this way and that, memorizing the placement of the bruises. The pattern. The cat will die with the same marks around his neck.

"It's been hours. Why aren't you healing faster?"

She hesitates. "Prey shifters heal slower."

I feel like a tool. She took care of me and all I notice is how hot she is. How much I want to bone her. I'm not taking care of her the way I should.

Time to rectify that. Right the fuck now.

"Shower." I let go of her hair so she can stand. "You go first."

"You're hurt worse," she murmurs. "Maybe you should—"

I shake my head. "Ladies first. My momma raised me right." I don't add that she would've smacked me for not taking better care of Jordy and offering sooner. "Come on." I head to the bathroom and turn on the shower. Jordy waits by the door and I motion her in.

"I can't," she says, her eyes downcast. "Please, let me serve you."

Serving me in the shower...now that's an idea.

No! Bad bear!

"Strip," I order.

Her hands fly to her t-shirt and pause, her eyes meeting mine.

"That's right," I tell her before turning my back to give her privacy. "Clothes off, then hop in the shower." I close my eyes at the sound of rustling of clothes. I remember every curve of her beautiful body. I want to touch all that alabaster skin. Find out where her sensitive spots are. Learn what makes her hum.

Too much fucking temptation.

"I'll get you clothes." I head out of the bathroom.

Jordy

I CLOSE my eyes and let the warm water cascade over my face. Showers are so good, but rare. Most of the time Augustine just had me hose off in the backyard. He really got off treating me like a pet.

It wasn't until I met Grizz that I realize how messed up my master was. Sure, I liked some of it. But he never treated me like an equal. To him I was an animal. A pet.

Or not even that—just a plaything, a food source, an object to be used and thrown away.

There was a time when he was kinder. When I thought we could be more. But then—

The scars on my chest itch at the memory. I wish I knew what happened that night. How I tried so hard but still displeased him. *Worthless,* he called me. He'd never been so cruel before.

A knock on the door breaks my thoughts. I jump.

"Clothes out here, Kit."

He calls me 'Kit'. I've never had a nice nickname before. I like it.

I turn the water off carefully. I didn't shave, but my legs are still pretty smooth.

I walk out and Grizz is playing messages on his home phone. It's on speaker, but even if it wasn't I could hear every word. Not because my shifter hearing is that good, but because the person who left the message is shouting.

"Of all the stupid fucking things to do—and then you call the fire department? We don't need this kinda publicity."

Grizz hits a button, and the message stops as I approach. I tried to be quiet but there's no sneaking up on him. Either that or he was waiting for me.

I flush as he looks me up and down. My hair is wet—he doesn't have a hair dryer, but I pulled it back as neatly as I could. I'm wearing an oversized t-shirt of his and a clean pair of underwear. Someone must have put the things we bought in the bike saddle bags. One of the silly shifters we met—Declan or Parker.

"I forgot to get pajamas," I say what he already knows.

His gaze sweeps over me, snagging at chest level. My nipples are hard, showing through.

"It's all right," he says thickly, and goes back to listening to the message.

"Garrett here," the voice recorder says, and crackles as Garrett immediately launches into a yelling rant about what happened in the shifter Fight Club parking lot. Grimacing, Grizz listens through. I sigh when the angry noise stops and Grizz's eyes crinkle at me.

"Made some waves tonight," he says.

"It wasn't your fault."

"Doesn't matter. Getting blamed for it. My phone is blowing up."

"Did the fire department really show up?" Exposing ourselves to humans like that would be a death sentence for my clan. Maybe it's different for predator shifters.

"No. Laurie's smarter than that. They reported a fire two warehouses over. It was just a firetruck that showed. The pack arrived on the scene fast, though, and cleaned up."

I wince. "There was a lot of blood."

"Blood, shredded clothes, fur…humans would definitely ask questions if they found it. The pack probably hosed off the parking lot. Garrett probably will have them scrubbing up blood all night. Still, it was a close call."

"Yeah."

"I understand why he's upset, I really do." He punches a button, and the machine announces *message deleted*. "The Fight Club is wolf run, but it's drawn attention and trouble before." He shakes his head. "Not a great time to be a shifter. It's getting harder and harder to hide from humans."

"Yeah." I murmur. "My clan used to say that all the time. That's why they sold me."

"Hey." He puts a finger under my chin and tips it up. "You didn't deserve that."

"Thank you for saying that," I whisper. He looks like he wants to say more, but he shakes his head and steps away. I wilt without his touch.

He sucks in a breath as he peels his black t-shirt off.

"Oh no," I whine. His body is a mess. That broken claw he pulled out was only the beginning.

I wave my hands in the air, not knowing where to start.

"First aid kit, bathroom," he says and I rush to get it.

He follows me, filling the small space with his bulk. I squeeze into a corner as he wipes steam from the small mirror and angles his body so he can assess the damage. It's no use—the mirror is small and dingy and his entire massive body is covered with cuts and gashes.

Grabbing a washcloth, he starts wiping like he's scrubbing a counter. Like his mangled body is concrete and not flesh. I know he's strong but I wince just watching.

"Please, let me help." I hover.

He hands me the rag, I rinse it out and dab at his skin. He sucks in a breath and I pause.

"Does it hurt?"

His head is bowed, his eyes gleaming through his hair. "No, Kit. Not that." He clears his throat. "You can be rougher with me, I can take it."

I continue cleaning. Every inch of him is hard with

muscle. It's crazy, like something out of an anatomy text-book, except there probably aren't words to describe all the muscles he has. Big ones, medium ones, small ones crammed in between the ones I recognize. He has a twelve pack, for crying out loud. I run my hand over the rugged contour and he makes a noise between a moan and a growl. A purr, I'd call it, if he was a cat.

"Good bear," I whisper, and duck my head so I don't see his expression.

When I reach his side, he lifts his arm. There's another claw stuck in his side and when I tell him he growls at me, "Pull it out. Make it fast."

I tug it out and wash the wound with plenty of water. Now that all the extra blood stains are gone, he looks a lot better. His healing has kicked in a little and some cuts have scabbed over. I'm going really slowly, making it thorough, trying not to hurt him. It's taking a lot of time but Grizz doesn't seem to mind.

"I do this sometimes," I say to fill the silence. Distract him a little from a particularly rough scrape. "Clean up subs after blood play."

"At Club Toxic."

"No. There's another place vampires play harder. Um." I raise my head and meet Grizz's bright eyes in the mirror. "Outside of the king's jurisdiction." My face burns; I've told a secret.

"He's not gonna like that," Grizz says. With his eyes bright he looks like a machine, a blond terminator sent to kill humanity.

I shake my head. "Don't tell him."

"Gotta tell him, Kit. I'm on this mission for him."

"I don't want to get anyone in trouble." I go back to cleaning him up. Why did I have to open my mouth? Augustine will kill me if he finds out what I spilled.

Grizz's hand closes over my neck. I still but he only strokes back my hair. "Won't be your fault if they are."

I swallow. "What will the king do if he doesn't approve of the secret club?"

"That's up to him. Not our business, Kit. Where is the club? Do you know?"

I close my eyes. "I can show you." I've already betrayed my master. In for a penny, in for a pound.

"Good girl," he murmurs, tearing me in two. I shouldn't feel good about helping my master's enemy, but I do.

I stay silent as I finish his back.

When I'm done, I wait as he takes the mirror down and checks out his back at all angles. "Thanks, Kit. Should heal faster now."

I wait on his bed as he showers. I should try to run and warn Augustine, but something makes me stay. I tell myself it's his orders, but he hasn't given me an order in a while. I wish he would, so I could turn off the thoughts buzzing like angry bees around in my head.

Grizz enters barefoot, wearing a soft-looking pair of sweatpants and nothing else. Even though I know it's a lot better, his chest still looks bad. I wince at the red marks.

"Like raw meat, huh?" he says. "Don't worry, I know my chances at a modeling career ended long ago."

He picks up the clothes on the bed—the ones we bought. I folded them but didn't know where to put them. With an arched eyebrow, he clears out a drawer in his dresser and drops my clothes in. I should comment on this, but I'm too tired. His movements are fluid and graceful but seem to fill the room.

The fighter returned home. The conquering hero. His presence saturates the air, making me aware of how small I am. How female. The perfect prize for a warrior.

I tuck my knees under my chin and hug my legs. "What now?" I ask.

He looks back at me, his eyes still bright. Oh yes. His bear's aware of how fragile this situation is. How he wants me. How right it would be. I belonged to Augustine, and he took me. The strong rule over the weak, and if you want something and you're strong enough to take it, it belongs to you. That's the way of the jungle. And when shifters and vampires are involved, everywhere's a jungle.

"Do you want me to take you to the secret club?" I ask, trying to diffuse some of the tension.

His eyes dim like a light switches off. "Not tonight. Tomorrow. Tonight we sleep."

Oh.

"Don't worry, Kit, I'm not gonna hurt you."

"I didn't think you would."

He prowls to the bed and lays his hand on my neck. A gentle move, but even a human would recognize it for what it is. *I can snap your neck, but I won't.* Another way to stake a claim. Being powerful enough to be violent, but being gentle instead.

I shiver.

"Sleep, Kit. That's all."

As I lie down and he turns out the lights, I don't know if I'm disappointed or relieved.

CHAPTER 7

ordy

THE DREAM STARTS AS SOON as I shut my eyes, like it was waiting for me. A dark monster in my head, snapping its jaws, swallowing me whole. I'm in the secret vampire club. Augustine is there, a menacing presence. That's not right—he should be a comfort. I strain to remember the times when he was a comfort before. But in this dream's time and place, Augustine is not benevolent. He's not my friend. He's just my master.

"This her?" another vampire asks. Augustine confirms yes. Their voices are muted in that dream state, but I know they're talking about me. Hands begin to crawl up my flesh, stroking and probing, taking liberties. I should lie still—Augustine orders me to—but I can't. I fight and get restrained for my trouble. Not with ropes. With hard hands.

"Feisty little thing," the other vampire comments.

"Not usually," Augustine grunts. His voice drips disgust. I know he despises shifters, and in this moment he makes no effort to hide his feelings. I feel small, inferior even as the hands on me dirty my skin. "Be still," my master hisses again.

"Let me." The strange vampire says and digs his fingers into my skin. I arch and try to cry out but my throat is a tomb. The aura of this predator is so strong, it's suffocating. The air's too thick to breathe. "That's it," the vampire says in mocking reassurance. "Be easy." His fingers are claws now, slicing my skin. The blood flows. "Be still and give me what we want." His lips find my chest. I jerk once, and still again. This isn't a dream. It really happened. "Good girl," the one-eyed vampire croons, and, lowering his head to my left breast, begins to feed.

Grizz

I LIE IN THE DARK, trying to rest. Jordy's breathing funny, soft puffs against my bare chest. It is not helping. Every time I try to relax, she whimpers and presses close to me, and it's all over. I'm sprung.

With a sigh, I roll to my back. My dick sticks up like a flagpole, tenting the sheet. Yeah, yeah. I'm hot for this chick, I get it. Enough already. I will my cock to go down.

A choking sound makes my eyes fly open. Jordy jerks against me, her little fingers digging into my raw chest. It hurts, but I don't fucking care.

Something's wrong. She's upset. Her face is screwed up tight, her mouth open like she's trying to scream.

"Kit." I thumb her cheek and she convulses so hard she nearly hits my chin. What the fuck?

"Kit. Come on, wake up. Jordy. Jordy!"

~

Jordy

Someone's calling my name. I follow the voice down the dark tunnel, stumbling towards the light.

"Jordy!"

My eyes fly open and I heave in a breath like I've been underwater.

"Fucking fates, Kit, what was that?"

"I had a dream," I whimper, and flinch as he cuts on the light. "A bad one."

"It'd have to be bad. You were thrashing and crying out." He cups my chin, examines my face. "Here." He reaches over and grabs the glass of water by the bedside table and hands it to me. "You wanna tell me what it's about?"

"No," I say honestly. I don't want to relive it. I don't want to talk about that night. I don't want to remember it. Ever.

He waits, expectant. I'm grateful for the reprieve, a chance to get my heartbeat back to normal.

I open my mouth. I could tell him. I've already spilled so much. But this would be the final betrayal. *Augustine took me to the one-eyed vampire and they—*

No. I can't.

Grizz frowns at me, his forehead puckered as if he's trying to read my thoughts. I lick my lips. He could order me to tell him.

But he doesn't. "Okay, Kit," he says, and switches the light back off. He's given me a choice.

"Come here." He tugs me down next to him.

I shrink away from his beat up chest. "No. I'll hurt you."

His chuckle fills my ears, a dark, velvety sound. "You could never hurt me. You're too little."

"I am not that small," I protest, but he just tugs me down.

"You are small," he settles me against him. "But perfect." His scarred lips caress my ear.

"I don't know if I can go back to sleep," I inform him, a bit breathlessly.

A pause. "You want me to help?"

Another choice. I revel in it. "Yes," I decide. Even if it's just an order, I want it. I chose.

But he doesn't give me an order. Instead, he shifts me in his arms so I'm lying fully against him, my hips cradled in his. My head doesn't quite reach his chin, but he must bow his head because his breath stirs my hair.

"Now, what should I do to help you sleep?" His hand

begins to drift upwards, creeping up my leg, taking the big shirt with it.

"Whatever you want," I whisper. Because it's true. My body lies against him, soft and compliant. My mind might still fight it, but he owns my body. My fox is ready for him to stake his claim.

"What do *you* want, little fox?" I love the deep rumble of his voice against my ear.

I fold one leg up, knee toward the ceiling to give him access.

He growls his approval and shoves down the covers. Heat flares everywhere—across my skin, between my legs. It's a different kind of heat than I'm used to. Submission always turns me on, but this is like arousal times twelve. My pussy turns molten, heart rate ramping. I'm itchy and feverish and he hasn't even touched me intimately yet. Knowing he's going to claim me—possibly roughly—thrills not just the submissive in me but also my fox. That's what's different. What makes it feel so right.

He crawls down and grips the thigh I have lifted. "You inviting me down here, Kit?"

I jerk at the first flick of his tongue. Fates, it's like a bolt of lightning shooting straight through my clit and out to every nerve ending in my body. My nipples turn hard as diamonds, nails sink into his empty pillow beside me.

He traces the inside of my labia, circles my clit. I squirm, pushing my knee against his head involuntarily. "Uh uh, Kit. You stay open for me while I lick this sweet pussy of yours."

I shiver, my pussy contracting at the order. No one's

ever licked me there. Augustine tortured my clit plenty of times, sure. He spanked it, pinched it, put clips on it. But he never put his own mouth on me. I've never felt the velvety smoothness of a tongue on my most sensitive bits before.

I don't mean to—it's not slave-like at all—but I reach down and grip his hair, tugging him into me again.

He chuckles. "That's right, little fox. Take your pleasure."

Take my pleasure.

What a wicked, terrible thought. But he told me to. It was an order, right?

I surrender to the sensations—of his tongue, his deep, dominant growls, the commanding grip of his huge hand on my thigh. I lift my core to his mouth, wriggle and undulate.

He flips me to my back and pushes my other knee back, too, spreading me wide. I cry out when he licks me from anus to clit. He returns to my opening, penetrating me with his tongue. It's not enough, and I don't mean to demand, but I do—fates help me, I do. I grip his head and push his mouth against me, lift my pussy. He releases one of my thighs and shoves two fingers into me, rough.

I yip with pleasure, my eyes rolling back in my head. "Grizz!" I cry out, the panic that comes before an orgasm flooding me.

"That's right, Kit. Who makes you scream?"

My mind can barely follow the question, I'm so close to coming. "Um...*you do!*" I scream as he repeatedly hits my G-spot with his huge fingers. "Grizz does! Oh please, Grizz."

"You don't have to beg, *just take it,*" he growls.

I come like an explosion. A bursting open. A simultaneous emptying and filling. My body rages beneath his skilled fingers and tongue, legs thrashing, pelvis jerking. My internal muscles squeeze and release, quake. He stops pumping, instead stroking my G-spot with his fingers as he sucks and licks my clit.

The earthquake passes and I whimper, falling limp. My knees splay open, body boneless.

Grizz lifts his head and licks my juices off his lips. "You taste like honey."

A shocked laugh falls from my lips and I reach for him, wind my arms around his neck. "Says the bear."

He nips my neck. "Bears love honey."

I attempt to push him to his back so I can return the favor, but it's an impossible feat when he's on top of me, pinning me to my back. I reach for his cock between our bodies. It's huge and thick and hard for me. I give it a squeeze, but his growl has censure in it.

I instantly let go, eyes wide.

"Shh." He strokes my cheek. "I'm helping you sleep."

"May I please suck your cock?" I almost said, *master's cock,* as I'd been trained, but caught myself in time.

Still, Grizz narrows his eyes. "No," he growls and settles beside me, pulling me in to spoon against him. His body is huge and warm and completely wraps my smaller one. My fox sighs in contentment. After a moment of silence in which I worry about what I did wrong, he murmurs against my ear. "Sleep, little fox. You're safe here. I won't let anyone hurt you. That's a promise."

Now I sigh, too.

He strokes my arm. "Everything's going to be all right. You're always safe with me, Kit."

Happiness—a dangerous feeling—descends over me and I sink into it. Let the contentment of my orgasm and the safety of Grizz's arms and words lull me into a deep, dreamless sleep.

CHAPTER 8

ordy

"MORNIN', Kit." Grizz's gravelly voice rumbles through me.

I press back into the warm wall of his giant body and his purring growl sends pleasant vibrations through me. I automatically arch my back, grinding my bottom into the taut frame of his hips. His growl deepens with frustration. Large hands force my legs apart. I hold my breath as his right hand begins to explore.

Outside the room, a harsh ringing sound breaks the silence. I jerk in Grizz's arms and his hold tightens.

"It's okay. Just the telephone."

"You should get it," I whisper as the phone keeps ringing.

He answers with a growl.

A beep and the answering machine picks up.

"Rise and shine, it's a beautiful day," an Irish brogue trills.

Grizz growls as Declan continues leaving a message. "I got news for ya, so call me maybe."

"Did you tell him—" another voice breaks into the message.

"Right, right, I'll tell him," Declan interrupts. "Jay-sus, calm your bits."

"I'm just sayin'—" the second voice says and the two start arguing until the machine beeps the end of time to leave the message.

A second later the phone starts ringing again.

"Oh for Fate's sake—" Grizz groans.

The phone rings until it beeps again and a new voice leaves a message. "This is Parker. We're at the burger joint. Stay away from the Fight Club."

"Give me the phone," Declan breaks in.

"No. I told him—" the two start arguing again and the phone cuts out.

Grizz heaves an aggrieved sigh while I tuck my face into Grizz's chest and giggle.

"Guess we gotta go meet with those idiots," Grizz huffs into my ear.

"You know, you're the only person in the world still with a landline," I say to him.

"I'm old school."

"Or just old." I wrinkle my nose at him.

In the next moment I find myself over his lap.

"I'll show you old school." He flips up the shirt and swats my bare bottom.

"No!" I kick, even though he barely spanked me. "I didn't mean it! I take it back!"

"Sure you do, now that you've earned a punishment," he says, and I clench my legs together, a thrill running down my spine. He's joking, but Grizz doling out playful punishment is enough to make me wet.

A second later, his hand slides between my legs and he feels my aroused state for himself.

"Fates," he mutters.

I relax, surrendering happily as he explores my sopping folds. He knows just how to touch me—light but firm. "You like having your ass smacked, don't you, Kit?"

"Yes," I admit.

"Why?"

"Don't ask why. There is no why. I've tried to understand this thing about myself my entire life. Why punishment turns me on. Why I like to be dominated. There's no answer for it. I was just born this way. That's the one good thing that came out of my enslavement to Augustine. I discovered a whole world of sexual satisfaction. And I also discovered I'm not alone in my desires. There are dozens of other sweetbloods even more into pain than I am who play at Toxic."

"You want more?" his voice is gruff and I hear concern in it, like he's unsure about even asking the question.

"Yes, please," I answer, as sweetly as I know how.

His huge palm claps down on my buttocks, spanking one side then the other a couple times. He tests my wetness again. I moan with pleasure. He clears his throat. "How hard?"

"Harder, please."

"You want me to hurt you?"

"Yes," I admit. I like the sensation of pain. The hot tingle that comes after it's been delivered. The build up to sex I require before I can find the satisfaction of release.

My shifter ears pick up the sound of his heart beating faster than normal. Is he excited? Or genuinely nervous about hurting me?

He tugs my wrists behind my back and pins them there with one hand. "Okay, little fox. You're going to get a spanking. And then you're going to show me your gratitude."

I smile into the covers because he's already such a natural dominant. He starts spanking me hard and fast and I writhe over his lap. It's a perfect spanking. His hand is huge like a paddle and he spanks with enough force to make it really burn. I count the slaps in my head to keep my mind busy, keep myself from squirming right off his lap from the intensity. He delivers thirty, then stops and strokes his calloused palm over my twitching ass.

"That good?" His voice is rough.

"Yes, Mas—Grizz." I remember in time not to call him Master.

He delivers another four smacks, concentrating on the backs of my thighs where it stings more. Yep, he's a total natural. "Now, what are we going to do about this?" he muses, sliding his fingers between my legs. I part my thighs and tilt my ass up, offering myself to him.

"Good girl," he murmurs, screwing two fingers into me.

I cry out with pleasure. He pumps them, his thumb burrowing between my asscheeks to rest over my anus. The moment he applies pressure there, I start to hump his lap wildly. It's embarrassing how little stimuli I require from this male to reach climax but I can't help it. My body's been primed for him since the moment I heard his deep growl.

"Fuck, Kit," he growls pumping his fingers in and out of me. I only last another thirty seconds and then I come all over his fingers, my walls tightening and releasing, my juices leaking onto my inner thighs.

"Well." He sounds almost shaken. "I still don't get it, but…"

I twist and look over my shoulder to seek his face. "But?"

"I sure as fates liked my end of it."

A smile tugs my cheeks so wide it almost hurts. "But I haven't even shown my appreciation yet." I crawl off his lap and rearrange my position to suck him off, but he groans and shakes his head.

"Gonna have to take a raincheck. Gotta big day today. Up and at 'em." And he rises, his big form taking all warmth from the bed.

I whimper but scramble to follow.

He disappears into the shower and I make myself ready and race to start breakfast. I only get as far as making the coffee before he tromps into the kitchen. I serve him coffee as he starts frying up some meat. I'm wearing a dress today, the one he picked out. It flutters around my knees and I prance around the kitchen, feeling pretty as I set the table.

As soon as Grizz drains his coffee, I'm at his elbow with the pot to fill his cup with a smile. I go to grab plates and suddenly Grizz is at my back, pressing me to the cabinets. His big arms come around me and he leans on the counter caging me in.

"You don't have to serve me," he mutters in my ear.

"I like to," I whisper back.

He grunts and the back of my neck prickles. I'm not sure if he's pleased or upset, so I wriggle around to face him. His eyes are bright and he moves his lower half against me. His hardness brushes against my stomach. He's not mad. Just frustrated. Well, it's his own fault.

"I can serve you," I say. "As much as you like." I'm not bold enough to take hold of his erection, but I lean into him.

"Got lots to do this morning," he says.

"So you said."

"Don't have time to take you back into the bedroom and deal with you."

"It doesn't have to take a lot of time," I offer.

"I think it does. I'd need at least a day. Maybe two."

I smile at him and he steps away, adjusting his jeans.

"Stop being cute," he orders with a grin. I duck my face.

His hand drops to my hip, caressing me through the thin floral fabric. "This the dress I picked out?"

"Yep. You like?" I ask, suddenly bold. I twirl. The skirt swirls out. Oops, too far. He definitely got a glimpse underneath. At least I'm wearing panties.

His eyes are bright. "Careful. Don't do that around anyone but me."

I nod.

"Go on, set the table," he orders gently, patting my hip.

I obey, biting back my smile.

After breakfast, he listens to all the messages again, and deletes them. His face is serious, all business.

"Ready to roll out?"

I nod and hold up a plastic bag. "I packed water bottles. There are no snacks left—I think the Stooges ate them."

"Stooges?" Grizz raises an eyebrow.

"The three shifters..." I drop my eyes. I've insulted his friends.

"Actually, that's a good name for them," Grizz grunts. "Shifter Stooges. There's three of them."

"I won't call them that to their face," I say anxiously.

"I will. They'll probably think it's funny." Grizz grabs the motorcycle helmet and motions to me. "Grab your coloring stuff. I've got errands to run, and you might get bored."

I want to protest that I won't get bored with him, but grab my stuff instead.

As the bike zooms down the mountain, I lean with Grizz into each turn. Three days since he stole me from Augustine, and it feels so natural to be with him. The time with my master seems further and further away. But Grizz hasn't told me what he plans to do with me. I can't get too comfortable with him.

Sure enough, we're sitting at a light when Grizz turns to me.

"Where's that secret club?"

I lick my lips, glancing at the light. It's still red, but could change at any second.

"Tell me quick, Kit," he orders.

I blurt the street name. "I'm not sure of the exact address, but there was a restaurant nearby with a blue sign." I describe the area.

He grunts and faces forward just before the light turns again.

I let out a sigh and hug his back as the motorcycle rolls through the intersection. Grizz is my master's enemy. I can't forget that. Even if he makes me feel good.

We pull into the parking lot of the burger place we hit up yesterday afternoon. The white Camaro is waiting.

I hop off the bike, pushing down my dress as Grizz dismounts and pulls my things out of the saddlebag.

"Wait here," Grizz says, handing me the coloring book and pencils. I hug them to my chest as he advances on the three Stooges. One of them is wearing an old fashioned pageboy hat, the type men wear in the old black and white movies I used to watch during the day, when Augustine let me. The three shifters all lean out of the car, eager to tell Grizz something.

I fidget with my skirt and rock from foot to foot until Grizz turns and waves me over.

He meets me halfway, just as the breeze catches the hem of my dress and flips it up around my thighs. I smooth it down and make a note to wear bike shorts underneath it next time. Although the look on Grizz's face as his eyes roam over me makes my almost-Marilyn Monroe moment worth it.

I halt in front of him. He puts a hand on my back, inching me closer and bending so his face arrives at my level.

"You look good in your dress, Kit." His eyes are bright.

"Thanks," I whisper. My nipples bead against the floral fabric; I'm not wearing a bra so it should be obvious his effect on me. A slow smile stretches his scarred lips. I wait for him to do more but he steps away.

"I'm going to leave you with these guys for the afternoon. Don't worry, they're nuts but you'll be safe."

"I want to come with you."

"No can do, Kit. It might be dangerous."

I start to protest and he places a finger on my lips, silencing me. "Tell you what. I'll pick you up before dark, and we'll have dinner in."

"All right. I'll cook for you," I offer softly.

"I'd like that."

He drops a kiss on my forehead, pats my ass, and after growling out orders to the three shifter Stooges to "watch and protect her with your life," he gets on his bike and roars away.

I swallow hard and hug my coloring book to my chest as the silly shifter trio turn curious eyes to me.

Grizz

My bear snarls as I motor away. But it can't be helped. Sooner or later, Augustine's gonna realize Jordy's gone, if he hasn't yet. And when he does, he'll be pissed. Vampires don't like other people playing with their toys. Even if they mistreat their toys. It's a power thing.

And while part of me relishes the chance to take on Augustine and teach him a lesson, I'm stupid to get myself involved. As soon as this job is done, I'm back on the hunt for the vampire who killed my mother. I eat, sleep, dream revenge and that's no life for Jordy. She deserves more.

At least she told me where the secret vampire club meeting place is. I can continue telling myself it's worth keeping her around.

The blue restaurant sign zooms by on my right. I slow and do another pass before parking in an alley. Jordy couldn't give me an exact address, but no worries. I can sniff out the rest on foot.

It takes me less than five blocks before I smell it. The cold, earthy smell of vampires underneath another meaty scent.

I break into the building with a crowbar and a heavy shove from my shoulder.

It's an old dance hall of some sort, complete with a stage. I head up there. Good for an auction.

And in the basement: bingo. This would be where they keep the cages.

Blood, sweat, tears. Smells like a shifter auction site to me.

I've got one more errand and then I'll get back to Jordy. Hope she's faring okay with the three Stooges, as she calls them. Fates, but she's cute.

I do one more lap of the building, checking out all the nooks and crannies. Creepy place, but nothing too sinister, not until I go in to the room behind the stage. The green room it's called by theater types. There's furniture back here, old fashioned velvety chairs and chaise lounges, perfect for a diva. It smells like vampires. But that's not what has the hair on the back of my neck prickling.

In the center of the room, there's a large brown stain on the floor. I crouch down but don't need to smell or touch to know what sank into the wooden floorboards so deeply.

Blood. Lots and lots of blood.

~

Jordy

THE THREE STOOGES stand around the Camaro, stuffing their faces with burgers. It's barely 11 a.m. The grey-haired guy, Parker, waited with me while the other two lined up at the door until an employee let them in. They returned with enough bags to feed an entire pack.

The dark-haired one, Declan, turns to me and says something with his mouth full.

"Pardon?" I ask.

"He asked if you wanted a burger," Parker says between bites of his own sandwich.

I decline, still hugging the coloring book to my chest. I can't help keeping an eye on the road, hoping Grizz will come motoring back on his bike.

Declan swallows a bite. "I know what ya are."

I turn back to him and blink at his pointed finger.

"Wee, sleekit, cowran, tim'rous beastie."

"Declan," Parker sighs.

"That's a poem," says the third shifter, a tall and skinny man who smells of feathers.

"I know it's a poem," Parker says. "It's by the Bard."

"Not the Bard, ya idjit," Declan scowls. "That's Shakespeare."

"Whatever," Parker waves a hand, balls up his wrapper and tosses it into the trash can. "All dead white poets sound alike to me."

"But it's in brogue," the feather-scented man protests quietly as Declan and Parker start arguing loudly. I blink at them. Whatever I was expecting from the guys Grizz left me with, it wasn't a discussion about poetry. By the end, Declan has stolen Laurie's hat, and he and Parker have almost come to blows. They wad up their burger wrappers and pelt each other with them.

Once they settle down, I step closer to them, hiding a smile behind my book.

"That's it, come sit a spell," Declan grins at me and scoots over to make room on the hood of the Camaro. I sit carefully, tugging down my dress.

"So, wee beastie, tell us what you're doin' w' a bear like Grizz."

"I'm helping him," I answer firmly.

"Are ya now?" The Irishman raises a brow. "'Cause ya know what he needs most of all—"

"Declan," Parker says in a warning tone, but it phases the Irish wolf not at all.

"—is to get laid."

Parker swats Declan hard enough for the black-haired man to rock in his boots, but he continues with a wink at me. "He needs it, bad."

"Oh, that's what I'm helping him with," I blurt, before I can stop myself.

"Ya sure? He's a great big grizzly bear, and you're a wee little thing. Aren't ya afraid of him?" Declan says it in his jaunty manner, but his dark eyes search my face carefully.

"No. I'm not afraid of Grizz. He's big and scary, but not to me. Never to me."

"Declan, shut up." Parker pulls Declan's hat over his eyes and turns to me. "I apologize for his rudeness." He's so formal I can't help but smile at him through my blushing.

"It's okay. I'm okay with it." I wave a hand in the air.

"See, she likes it," Declan tugs up the hat and swats Parker back. "Obviously has the right stuff, if she's taking Grizz on."

"Don't tell him, though," I bluster on. My face is probably cherry Kool-aid red. "It's a surprise."

"A surprise?" Declan's thick brows creep up into his cap, then he flashes a white-toothed smile and pats me on the back so hard I stagger forward. "I luv it. You've got more guts than I gave ya credit for, but I like your spunk and no mistake."

"Ok. Thank you."

"Glad this is all settled," Parker rolls his eyes. "Didn't realize you were so concerned with the sex lives of bears."

"Not just any bear. Our prize fighter."

"P-prize fighter?" the tall, thin man asks with a stammer. When I look at him he doesn't meet my eyes, so he's even more submissive than I am. A weak shifter—probably a bird. That would explain the feather smell.

"Yep," Declan declares cheerfully.

"Oh bother," Parker grunts, grabbing Declan's hat and setting it on his head at a rakish angle. "Not another big bet on a crazy fighter."

"That's right. We're all in. We just gotta keep the Tucson pack from killing our investment."

I stiffen. "They want to kill him?"

"Oh yes. Ever since he sided with the vampires."

"He's not siding with the vampires," I say and bite my lip. I don't know how much information I can give out.

"Whelp, then we just gotta convince the wolves that. Otherwise, they could try to take him out before the fight. They wouldn't win—you saw him against all those cats. But they could wound him, and the odds of the fight get worse."

"Tell me you didn't make this bet," Parker groans and tugs the hat over his eyes.

"Oh, I made it," Declan pronounces. "Friday night, we'll be rich."

"As long as Grizz doesn't lose," Parker says.

"You saw him fight," Declan picks up a burger and waves it. "What was that? Ten, fifteen to one?"

Parker raises the hat but doesn't look happy. "'Cause there's no other reason Grizz could lose. Like, perhaps, throwing the match for the vampires."

Declan unwraps the burger and scarfs it in three bites. "That would be bad. Do not pass go, do not collect three million dollars."

Parker groans again. "Don't tell me you borrowed money to make this bet."

"It's a sure thing," Declan licks ketchup from his fingers.

"Famous last words," Parker mutters and goes to sit inside the car, cranking down the driver's seat and laying out with the hat over his face.

"So," Declan turns to me. "Where d'you meet our Grizzly?"

"Um," my skin heats, toasting my freckles. "A club."

"Which club, luv? The Fight Club, or the club of kinky vampires?

"The...um," I stammer, "vampire one."

Declan leans forward to say to the third, quietest Stooge, "She's cute when she blushes. Sets off her red hair."

"L-l-leave her alone," the tall, thin one replies.

I smile at him gratefully. "It's all right."

"What was a nice girl doing in a place like that?"

"I was there with my vampire master."

Declan blinks rapidly and I meet his gaze head on.

"You're a s-s-s-sweetblood?" the tall shifter stammers.

"I am. Well, I was." I don't know what Grizz will do with me when he's done, but I doubt he'll let me go back to a vampire master.

"You're not anymore? Did the vampire give ya away?" Declan asks.

I bite my lip and shake my head.

"Then how are you with Grizz?"

"Grizz broke into his house and, um, took me."

Declan sags. "Jay-sus." He hops off the car hood and paces back and forth. Inside the car, Parker sits up.

"What's wrong? Laurie, tell me."

Laurie points to me. "Grizz s-s-s-stole her from a vampire."

"Aw, fates," Parker swears and scrambles out of the car.

Declan continues pacing back and forth in front of the car, head down, mumbling an occasional curse word.

"You bet on a fighter who's crossed a vampire. Who took from a vampire." Parker whirls on me. "Which vampire did you say you belonged to?"

"Augustine."

Declan stops to frown at me. "Tall guy? Looks like a male model? Wears suits all the time?"

Parker nudges the Irishman in the ribs. "You just described every vampire ever."

"I did not!"

"Oh really? What vampire doesn't look like a male model?"

Declan ponders this. "There was that small, skinny one. Remember? Ben something."

"Benedict?" I offer.

Declan snaps his fingers. "That's the one. Good ole Benny. Looks like he belongs in a boy band."

Beside me, Laurie laughs softly.

Declan grins at me. "Tell me I'm wrong."

"You're not wrong," I smile back. After the way he treated me in the club last time, Benny isn't my favorite vampire. Not that any vampires are my favorite.

"Congratulations," Parker says sourly. "You know who doesn't look like a model or a member of a boy band?

Frangelico." At the name of the vampire king, everyone's smiles drop away. "How will Frangelico feel about Grizz stealing from vampires?"

I shrug, my heart plummeting.

"I don't think he cares much either way." Declan rubs his chin. "He's pretty lax about his sireds, the vampires he's made. But Augustine…that's another story."

I wrap my arms around myself, suddenly chilled. Augustine is going to be pissed at Grizz if he finds out where I am. I totally forgot about that.

"W-what will A-augustine do?" Laurie asks.

"To a shifter who stole from him?" Parker shrugs. "Anyone's guess."

"What's your guess?" Declan asks.

"I don't know," Parker waves a hand. "Hunt Grizz down and rip his head off?"

All oxygen leaves the vicinity. I sway and slump against Laurie who puts an arm around me.

Declan runs to the driver's door, smashing into Parker who squawks and tries to push him off. They tangle together and start wrestling, arms flailing.

"In the car," Declan shouts. "We gotta find him!"

"Are you okay?" Laurie whispers and I nod. My head is still spinning. I need to get to Grizz. I need know he's okay.

"Calm down, dingbat," Parker growls, pushing Declan off him. The Irishman dashes to the car and climbs in the driver's seat.

"We gotta save him! Where are the keys?"

Parker holds them up. "It's daylight. No vampires are awake."

"Right," Declan says, pushing his hair back from his face. "Right."

"But you gave him intel on the shifter slavers, and sent him after them," Parker says, folding his arms across his chest.

"Jay-sus, why'd I do that?" Declan rubs a hand up and down his face.

"I don't know. So he wouldn't kill and eat you?" Parker stoops and picks up the crushed hat, dusting it off before handing it back to Laurie.

"Oh me heart." Declan lays a hand on his chest, panting. "I can't take this violence."

"Should've thought of that before you bet on a fight," Parker rolls his eyes.

CHAPTER 9

rizz

THE INTEL DECLAN gave me earlier leads me to an abandoned truck stop a few miles out of town. I buzz around on my motorcycle until I'm sure no one's around, then park to sniff things out. Again, there's nothing here but snatches of fur and the occasional feather. Someone's moving shifters in and out of here for sure. The question is: why? Did Frangelico's vampires all get a taste for shifter blood?

I kick around but don't find much more. Just a crumpled piece of paper advertising a midnight auction with 'fresh merchandise'. There's no address, but a picture—of the old theater building I just left.

Coincidence? I think not.

I pocket the flyer. The sun's still pretty high in the sky, but won't be for long. I need to call Jordy. I won't be back before dark—I have another errand to run. It's been a few days, and I've found enough to report to the vampire king. Not enough for him to pronounce a sentence, but he'll want to know about the secret vampire club, the auctions, the blood on the green room floor. He'll be pissed if he finds it out another way.

A coyote trots by, its yellow eyes flash at me, but it doesn't seem too nervous around me.

Overhead a hawk circles, shrieking.

Cold sweat breaks out on the back of my neck. Something tells me to get out of here.

I slow jog to my bike. Once I'm on the highway back into town, my bear relaxes.

Until I pass a familiar national park sign. I got so consumed by the hunt, I went deep into wolf territory. Not usually a problem, except I ain't exactly the wolves' favorite person right now.

Sure enough, when I motor by a gas station, two bikes come alive and turn onto the road after me.

As soon as I get back into a decent service area, my phone goes berserk, vibrating like it's trying to dig a hole and escape my jean pocket. It's annoying until I remember the only one who knows this burner number is Declan. My body goes cold. Jordy.

I pull over and yank it out. "Is Jordy all right?" I snarl.

"Grizz? Is that you?" Parker asks.

"No, it's the fucking pope," I bite out. My vision blurs and I have to loosen my hold on the phone before I crush it in my grip. "Where's Jordy?"

"She's right here," Parker says quickly. "She's all right."

"Put her on." I can't think straight until my bear knows she's safe.

"Grizz?" Her voice greets me, breathy and worried. "Is everything okay?"

My body unclenches. "Fine. What's going on? Why do you sound scared? Did they hurt you?" I shake, ending on a roar.

"No, Grizz." I relax as she sounds relieved. "I'm fine, really. The guys are great. I'm just worried about you."

"Me? I'm fine. Nothing's wrong." I lie. The two bikes have stopped behind me.

"Declan says Augustine will be mad at you for taking me. He'll hurt you."

"It's okay, Kit. No one's gonna hurt me." Damn those Stooges for scaring her.

Behind me, the two bikers haven't moved. Their orders must be to scout and report back. I wave at them.

"Come back soon," Jordy says.

"Soon, Kit. I got one more stop, but it'll be after dark, okay? Be good."

"I will. You want me to put Parker back on?"

"Yeah." I wait until Parker says my name and order, "Take Jordy to the movies. Watch two in a row and buy her anything she wants. I'll pay you back." I hang up on him before he can agree.

Behind me, a distant roaring is getting closer. I turn on my bike but it's too late. A bunch of motorcycles tear up the road behind me. In seconds my bike is surrounded. I'm hemmed in, three riders deep. They've all got their knuckles tattooed with the phases of the moon. Wolves.

I reach in my jacket for my flask before I remember it's empty.

On either side of me, the riders draw aside their leather vests, showing guns.

"Bring a gun to a claw fight?" I scoff. "Not fair."

"All's fair in war," the biker mutters back.

"This war?" I ask.

In front of me, Trey turns bright eyes on me. "It's whatever you want it to be, grizzly. Our alpha wants you to come in for a little chat. We can do this easy or do it the hard way. It's up to you."

I rebalance my bike. Shifters all around three deep. Twelve, at least. Better odds than the cat pack, but these guys aren't a bunch of pussies.

"Well?" Trey demands.

"What's it gonna be?"

I look left and right, calculating.

"Oh please," the biker to my right mutters. "Please choose the hard way."

Fucking wolves. Always spoiling for a fight, especially when they're in a pack. I could take them, I know I could, especially if I had the juice. But I'm all out.

"I guess I have time for a chat," I tell Trey. I wanted to talk to Garrett, anyway.

The big wolf nods. "All right then. Ride out."

I follow them to their pack's headquarters, a nightclub on Congress Street called Eclipse. It's not open to the public yet, which means the wolves can use it as their clubhouse. I park my bike with the rest of them and follow Trey inside. As my eyes adjust to the dimmer light, some wolf fuck takes a swing at me, knocking me in the ribs.

"What the hell?" I bark. I expected a meet with their pack leader, Garrett, not a fucking ambush.

Another wolf swings at me, and then another.

I punch back, defending myself, jogging in a loose circle.

They're not serious about hurting me. I can tell because the attacks are slow, measured. One by one. It feels more like sport fighting. Roughing me up.

Fine. They can rough me up if that's what they need to do. Piss all over me to measure the lengths of our dicks.

I catch the whiff of a scent that makes my hackles rise but I can't see where it's coming from because I'm too busy defending myself.

"He doesn't look that big to me." The stomp of heavy boots on the floor makes me turn toward the scent.

Bear.

A huge dark-haired man clomps toward me—bigger than me with a full on mountain man beard. My bear bristles because his eyes are animal-bright. Like he's having a hard time keeping his animal under control. Like he's half feral.

I catch a couple more fists to the ribs.

"Enough." Garrett's growl comes from the front door. He eyes the other bear warily and gives a single nod. "Caleb."

"Garrett." The bear appears equally wary.

"This is pack business."

Caleb shrugs. "I wasn't asking to be involved." He gives

me one more look and leaves through the same door he came in.

"They brought that crazy bear in special for you, Grizz."

I stare after the strange bear. "The fuck?" I don't have a clue what he's talking about.

Garrett tips his head. "That's who you're fighting Friday night."

Of course it is.

I shrug. "He got his rabies shots?"

Garrett folds his arms over his chest. "What's going on, Grizz?"

I match his pose. "I got no beef with wolves."

"You're working for the leeches. You infiltrated our pack as their spy. I definitely have a beef with you."

I stay calm, but keep my muscles loose, ready for an attack. The wolves are itching for a fight, but I know Garrett's a reasonable guy. And I haven't taken any steps against his pack, no matter what he thinks. "Not a spy. I never spied. I worked for both of you—that's it."

"What does Frangelico have on you, Grizz? What's the big secret you're keeping?"

I shake my head. "No secret." It's a lie, but my secret doesn't concern them.

"What dirty work are you doing for the vampire king right now?"

I keep my face impassive. "You already know. Looking into the shifter disappearances."

"And?"

I shrug. "I have a few leads."

Garrett crosses his arms. "Which are?"

Fuck. I don't want to share my intel with them. They will only get in my way. Still, I'm not gonna walk out of here without my body torn to pieces if I don't give him something.

"I found the site of a shifter slave auction. I don't know who's behind it, yet."

"What's your angle?"

"That's not relevant."

Garrett fists my shirt and shoves me back against the closest high top table. He's not my alpha, but I don't fight back. Not when he's got his entire pack here to back him up. If he needs to show a little force in front of his blood-thirsty guys, I get it. I know the wolf dynamic. "I don't like your secrets, Grizz," Garrett growls in a low voice. "I don't like you playing both sides. And I sure as hell don't like not knowing what you're up to."

"I'm finding the vampire responsible for the shifter slave market. And when I do, I'm gonna take care of him."

Garrett must see the gleam of true resolve in my eye, because he studies me for a moment, then lets me go. "I want to know when you find him."

"Not to be a dick, but I don't work for you any more. Your wolves fired me," I remind him. His boy Trey, the owner of Fight Club, flipped out on me a few months ago when he found out I was working for the leeches too.

Garrett punches me in the stomach. "If you want to fucking show your face around this town, you deliver when I ask you for something. Understand?"

I grunt, partly because he knocked the wind out of me and I don't want to show it.

"What's that?"

"Fine."

"Good." Garrett steps back, as if to let me pass. "I expect the same reports you're giving Frangelico, if not better."

His wolves press in on me from all sides, eager to get their punches in, too.

"Fine," I repeat, not because I'm scared of Garrett or his pack, but because I need to get back to Jordy, make sure she's all right. I don't have time for a pissing contest with these guys.

"Let him go," Garrett mutters and the wolves part to let me through. A couple more throw punches as I pass, but I let them fall and walk out, shaking my head.

From the back I hear the feral roar of the vicious bear.

I don't know what the hell his story is, but I'm not afraid to fight him. If he can't keep his animal in control, he'll be easy to best.

CHAPTER 10

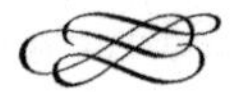

rizz

I ROLL up to Frangelico's house right at dusk. It's a brand new mansion set on a private lot down a long drive and up on a hill. The Italian-style marble columns look weird against the desert backdrop. The gate at the bottom of the hill opens for me slowly. There's no sign of security, but I'm not fooled. This place is crawling with guards, both human and drones.

I park behind a red Lamborghini and white Tesla Roadster and sit a spell, watching the sun sink behind the mountains. My fingers itch to call Jordy, but I hold off. She's safe with Declan and Parker. Their odd behavior allows people to write them off, and they fly under most people's radar.

I head into the house, striding between the white marble columns to the front door.

Two goons emerge from opposite sides of the house and stop me. I strip out of my leather jacket slowly, holding out my arms for them to wand. Inside, I walk through an archway I know holds a hidden metal detector. Vampires are paranoid fuckers, and their king is the most paranoid of them all. That's what's kept him alive.

Frangelico steps into the living room without fanfare. As much as he loves ceremony, he's pretty direct and good to work with when we're alone. Or maybe he just doesn't want me in his house for long.

"Broderick. Welcome."

I shake my head at the sound of my real name. I don't know how Frangelico found it. The last person to call me Broderick was my mother. The king just calls me that to mess with me, but I won't stoop to telling him to stop. That's a power game I won't win.

Frangelico crosses to the bar and pours himself a glass of wine. I refuse his offer of a drink and wait as the king holds the glass up to the light, swirls the red liquid, brings the glass back down to take a deep sniff and on and on. He does everything but marry it before taking a sip. "I take it you have something to report?"

I tell him everything I've found, with one exception. Jordy. I leave out any mention of her. Just because the king and I are allies doesn't mean he isn't dangerous. I'd rather keep Jordy off his radar.

"So your sources told you of the movements of the shifter slavers, and from there you discerned the location of the auction house?"

"I found this." I pull out the flyer of the theater and smooth it before handing it over the king. He studies it briefly before handing it back.

"I had a lead that led me to the theater first," I admit, in case Frangelico has me followed.

"A lead?"

"Confidential." I fold the flyer and put it back in my pocket. "But obviously correct. Your vampires are playing around behind your back."

Frangelico sighs and heads to the French doors looking out onto a stone patio. The doors open as he approaches and he exits. I follow, staying a few feet behind him as he leans against a column. His throat works as he tips back his drink.

He listens as I tell him all I know about the secret club. "There seems to be a contingent of your vampires who has a taste for submissive shifters. A new type of sweetbloods."

"Ah yes." He swirls the dregs of his glass. "Shifter submissives. One of my vampires has mentioned his sweetblood has gone missing. A pet fox, I believe."

I freeze, schooling my features carefully.

"You wouldn't know anything about that, would you?" He smiles when I don't answer. "I admit, I've been lax about my children. I indulge them. It's so hard to create a vampire, you see. So I tend to keep them alive, even when they turn against me." His smile, half hidden behind his wine glass, is chilling.

"You've had evidence of a coup for some time now."

"Ah yes. Little Nero and his bid for an empire." Frangelico taps a finger against his glass. The moon has risen, washing the mountains with ghostly light. The polished columns of his portico frame the desert vista perfectly. The mansion is on a hill, too, facing east as if waiting for the first touch of dawn's early light.

I wonder how long it's been since this vampire saw a sunrise. Frangelico is old, older than anyone knows. It'd wear on me, all those years in the dark.

As the silence stretches, I resist the urge to move or cough, to remind the vampire king that I'm here. Just because Frangelico is as still as a statue, his profile limned with silver-grey moonlight and frozen like a Roman emperor's face on a coin, doesn't mean that he's forgotten I'm here.

Finally Frangelico straightens. "It's an incredibly difficult process to sire a vampire," he murmurs, still not looking at me. I get the feeling he's talking to himself instead of me. "So much time and blood. So many defeats. And when it finally works..." He sighs and bows his head. "You still have to support them. Wean them. Such a delicate process to produce another of my species. Humans blink and pop out brats. That's why they'll win in the end. They'll breed us out."

He turns and I avert my eyes.

"I used to think it right that our food was so plentiful. So prolific." A mocking smile curves his lips and I resist the urge to back away. Nothing scarier than a smiling vampire. "I thought that if I created enough vampires, I'd bring balance to the world. Like introducing wolves to Yosemite, to bring down the overpopulated deer." He looks at me then. "You must be amused, hearing me compare our species to wolves."

Nope, not amused. Fucking terrified. I don't know why Frangelico's getting all nostalgic and ranty, but I don't want to know. Some monsters are better left in the dark.

"Anyway," Frangelico moves back into his living room, and the moment is broken. "It seems my sired are rising against me," he says coolly. "Not just Nero, but a large contingent. There may soon be some…unpleasantness."

Unpleasantness. Another way to say 'complete slaughter of my enemies'. Another sign I've been working with Frangelico too long, I know exactly how he understates things.

Frangelico continues, "I understand if you wish to decline the remainder of this job."

"Nah," I say. "I'll see this through."

Frangelico's features flicker. "I did not expect you to say that. I thought you would be relieved to return to your quest to avenge your fallen family."

"Oh, I'm not giving up on that," I say grimly. "As soon as I get to the bottom of this, I'm back on the hunt for that murdering bastard."

"As much as I wish for you to focus on the business I assign you, I admit I am impressed by your dedication. I wish I could help you more on your quest." Before I can tell him how he can help me, he continues, "You have spoken of this vampire before. Are you any closer to finding out his identity? Then I might be able to help."

"The only thing I know is he's male. Tall. Big."

"With one eye, you told me."

"Yeah, one eye. He lost it…in a fight." The fight that killed my mother.

"I have no acquaintance with such a vampire."

"You might have known him when he had both eyes."

"True." Frangelico sets down his glass. "I regret that I cannot help you identify him."

"Don't need your help with that. The only way you can help me is to give me more blood."

Frangelico sighs. "Ah yes. I wondered when you would ask."

"I need it."

"Has it ever occurred to you that the side effects of drinking my blood might be…life-changing?"

"You don't mean turning, do you?"

"Oh no," the king's voice turns cold. "Not turning. I would not give you my blood if there was any chance at turning you. A shifter turned vampire—would be an abomination."

The hair on my arms prickles at his tone.

"No," Frangelico continues, heading to the bar and going behind it to open the mini fridge. "I do not allow you this blood because I wish to sire you. If there was any chance of you rising as a vampire, I'd kill you right now and burn your body."

"Good," I can only mutter while my stomach roils. "I'd slit my own throat before becoming a vampire."

"And I'd remove your head," Frangelico agrees, his tone turning smooth and genial. "This is why I work with you. We are on the same page."

"Fan-fucking-tastic," I say. I hate how eager I am, watching the king stack several blood bags on the bar. The first time I had to make myself drink the blood, I only did it because I knew the edge it'd give me.

After the tenth time, I stopped gagging. After the twentieth, I savored the power coursing through my veins.

Now, after a hundred doses and several vampire kills, I live for the hit, the high it gives me.

He glances as me, and must see some of my need on my face. "Are you sure you want this?"

I turn away. "It's not about wanting. I need it." It's only a partial lie.

"I've never heard of a shifter taking so much and surviving. Most vampires would not allow it. I only do because we work so well together."

"And I'm willing to do your dirty work."

"That too. But the day may come where we find ourselves at the end of our bargain. You would be wise to weigh the toll the blood takes on you before then."

I stare at him—not his eyes, a spot on his face. If he thinks I'm going to break down and tell him how the blood affects me, how each hit leaves me weak and blacking out afterwards, he's got another think coming. I don't need his sympathy, or his advice.

I don't need him to tell me that one day when I take this blood, it will be my last. Either the dose will kill me, or it'll leave me so weak my enemy does it for me. I don't care. I just need to take out the one-eyed vampire before I go.

The king finishes stacking the blood bags on the bar. "Good luck on your hunt," he says softly, and leaves. I wait until he's well and truly gone before heading out. Finally, I can get back to Jordy.

But first, I go to the bar and take the blood. I have to.

Without it, I can't take a vampire and win. I need the blood to give me power to fight. I need the blood to hunt down the vampire that killed my mother and have my revenge.

~

Grizz

THE WHITE CAMARO sits in much the same place I left it, a few parking spots over. It's later than I'd like, well after dark. I had another errand to do after I left the vampire king.

I ride my bike right up to the parked car, squinting against its headlights. I can't see anyone. Then a figure darts in front of the car and my entire body tightens. Jordy.

She runs right up to me, her little white Keds flashing, her dress swirling around her knees. The Camaro's headlights outline her form, but the halo of light around her is not as bright as her smile.

"Hey," she says, breathless. Her sweet, unassuming beauty punches me in the gut. she's a flower blooming in a trash littered parking lot. A star blazing in the night.

Forget this shitty day. Forget the wolves, the vampires, and debriefing the Stooges. I gotta get her home, now.

Fuck if I can talk. I hand her the helmet. After she buckles it on, I check the strap and jerk my head for her to hop on. Her arms go around me, I pull them tighter, cause I'm a masochist. The feel of her pressed against my back, her hands locked around my abs makes my dick hard enough to punch through a steel door.

Gritting my teeth, I wave at the three stooges. I'll call them and give them the news and my gratitude later. I'm racking up favors all over town. Jordy leans into me, her head resting on my back and I think, *Worth it.*

The drive to my mountain takes for-fucking-ever.

She jumps off and goes ahead of me, leaning against the house as I open the door. Once inside, I dump the bags I'm carrying and flick on the lights, before catching Jordy. I haul Jordy into my arms and she lets me, not a squeak of protest as I lift her and give her a hard kiss.

"Missed you, Kit."

"I missed you." A smile plays on her lips. I haul her weight against me and she arches like a cat and rubs herself against my hardness. Fuck, I could get used to this. This is why Augustine kept her collared and caged.

The thought of the vampire is like a bucket of cold water on my dick. I loosen my hold and let her slide down to the ground.

"Grizz? What's wrong?"

"Nothing. You hungry?"

"A little," she says hesitantly.

"I'll whip something up." I go to the fridge and start pulling items out and slamming them onto the counter.

She hovers behind me. "Did I do something wrong?"

"No," I bark and repeat in a softened tone. "No. You're perfect. I just—it's been a long day."

"Of course." She dusts her hands on her dress. "Just… let me know what you need me to do." She scoots off, bustling around the kitchen. I try to go back to preparing food, but I still have the scent of her in my nose, the taste of her on my tongue. I pounced on her as soon as she walked through the door, but she didn't protest. I kissed her and she let me, as if I was just taking my due. I grit my teeth. Would she be so willing to offer her charms to the conquering victor?

I gotta get my head straight and let her know where she stands. Whatever we feel for each other, whatever we're heading towards, it can't last.

The thought makes me want to howl.

"Bags, Kit. Go unpack," I order her. Tuned into her as I am, I listen to the bags rustle and wait until her breath catches before turning.

She's holding a big sketch pad.

"Is this for me?"

"I'm not much of an artist. Anyway, I told you I'd get it."

"You didn't have to, but thank you."

"No problem." I dump everything into a crockpot and turn it on low. "We have some time before dinner. Make yourself at home."

I stomp to the bath to clean up. Strip off my shirt and examine myself in the dingy mirror. Fucking wolves got a few shots in, but the bruises are almost gone. The cats' scratches have all but disappeared. Only a few red tears where they got me with their claws. I'm not surprised they tipped their nails in something that would delay shifter healing.

The door creaks open and Jordy stands there, eyes round as she surveys my bare chest.

"You're all healed up," she says, coming and touching

my back. Her fingers dance over my skin, light and gentle. I still and she must take it as a sign of encouragement because she strokes both hands down the expanse of muscle then wraps her arms around my middle and presses her body into mine. Her breasts brush my back as she hugs me. Fates.

She has no idea how close I am to whirling around and pouncing, wrenching her legs open and pounding my cock into her sweet little cunt until she's screaming my name.

I take a deep, steadying breath. "Course I'm healed," I tell her gruffly. "Just took some punches."

"And scratches and bites," she says, a hint of chastising in her tone. I turn and cradle her face. "You don't like me fighting, Kit?"

Biting her lip she shakes her head.

I drop a kiss onto her forehead, right where the reddish hair meets freckled skin. "Better get used to it, 'cause I'm a fighter. It's who I am."

"I know," her voice is muffled against my bare chest. Her fingers slide over my pect, tracing a raised mark. "You have all these scars."

"You should see the other guy."

She doesn't crack a smile. "How did you get these? Not fighting shifters."

"No."

She frowns up at me. Her fingers still swirl over my scar, muddling my thoughts. A potent torture I can't resist. A few more minutes, and I'll spill my guts for a chance to get her in my bed. Gotta say something, get her off this dangerous subject.

"Did you ask Augustine so many questions?"

Her little body stiffens. Fates, why did I bring that leech up? Jordy starts to pull away and I haul her back against me.

"Hey, I didn't mean it."

"You know I didn't," she says shakily. "That was not the relationship we had. He was my master. I had to obey."

"Jordy, I'm sorry."

Angling her head, she eyes me with her hair half obscuring her face. "You're not my master."

"No, I'm not." I bite back anything else I might add. I don't want to be her master. Do I?

She's frowning thoughtfully, her narrowed eyes flicking up and down my body. Sizing me up, weighing me. I get the feeling she sees every part of me. For the first time in my life, I'm not proud of who I am.

Even if I wanted to own her, she shouldn't allow it. I don't measure up.

"Jordy…" her name is sweet on my tongue. "I'm not a good man."

Her frown deepens.

"I've… done things. It's not that I'm not proud of them, it's just that what I am, what I do, it doesn't fit in the normal world. The world you live in. The world you deserve." Fates, I'm not explaining this right. "I'm not like normal guys."

Understanding lights her eyes. "I don't want normal."

I sigh hard enough to blow her hair back. My hand finds her face. She closes her eyes. There's a picture, my tattooed and fight roughed hands on either side of her sweet freckled cheeks. She's so perfect and innocent. My skin looks dirty against hers. I don't want to touch her. I don't want to ruin what she is.

But I will. If she stays.

"I should send you away."

"Where would you send me?"

"Somewhere safe," I mutter against her hair. "Somewhere far away…from me."

"I don't want to go." Her hand seeks my cheek. "I don't want to be anywhere but here. With you."

"You can't know that. You don't know what I've done. What I plan to do…."

She turns and draws the dress over her head, turning a little. I stand stunned as she lets the clothing drop to the floor and smiles at me over her shoulder. Her hips sway, and all the blood rushes out of my head, going straight to my dick.

"Well?" She pauses in the doorway of my bedroom. "Are you coming or not?"

CHAPTER 11

rizz

"FATES," I mutter and stride to her so quickly, her eyes widen. I scoop her up in my arms and toss her on the bed so fast she gasps.

I draw back. "Did I hurt you?"

"No." She's laughing. "This is what I wanted." Her hands roam over me and when I find her mouth and claim it, she arches into the kiss.

Then she wriggles down my body.

"Kit—?" I go to grab her, haul her back up, but her hands are busy on my jeans and I freeze.

"Shh," she says. "Just relax and enjoy it."

I huff. "That's my line."

"You don't have to—"

"I know. I want to." She unbuttons and unzips and opens my jeans like unwrapping a present. It's dark, but I feel the reverence in her touch. Hot breath hits my skin.

"Hang on." I can't believe I'm stalling her, but the chance to watch her is too perfect to pass up. "I want to see you."

I reach over, flick on the light.

She blinks up at me. I lie back and let her settle over me, reaching to stroke her face.

"Don't let me stop you."

"Mmm," she purrs, and nuzzles my cock. She starts kissing it, her eyes closed as if she's reached nirvana. Fates, she's not gonna suck my cock, she's gonna worship it.

Her head drops and I groan as she licks my balls, swirling her tongue like she's licking an ice cream cone. Dizzy with pleasure, I let her take her sweet time. How did I get this lucky?

"Jordy…baby…you gotta stop."

She jerks her head up. "You don't like it?"

"You know I love it. But I'm gonna explode."

She smiles, and I see the vixen in her.

"Naughty," I growl. "Suck my cock."

"Yes, sir."

Fates, I'm gonna blow. "Now," I order and she sits up, dipping her head down immediately.

That's when I see it, a white mass of scars over her left breast.

"What the fuck?"

Her head snaps up, worry creasing her brow.

I touch the raised flesh, white weals where the skin

was marred and healed. How have I not noticed this before?

"It's nothing," she says, her expression dulling. A huge change from her usual sunny self. Like light shutting off.

"He fucking mauled you." I splay my hand over the raised flesh, so angry I can't see straight.

Jordy bows her head. "I don't want to talk about it."

"Who did this to you? Was it Augustine?" I can barely growl out his name.

Her eyes closed, she shakes her head. I catch her hair, holding her still. "Who?"

"I don't know. He was another vampire. I don't know who he was. Augustine gave me to him…as a reward. You know my relationship with him. I did as I was told."

"And he hurt you." It's not a question. Fangs tearing into her like that, it had to hurt.

She jerks away and sits on the edge of the bed, folding into herself. I get a lungful of her scent. Not fear, not anger.

Shame.

My anger washes away.

"Shh, it's okay. I know he marked you. It's okay."

"It's not," she says in a small voice that kills me.

I scoot to her, and when she shrinks away, I straddle her small body between my heavy thighs, enclosing her. My arm goes around her middle just in time for me to feel her give a dry sob.

Oh fuck.

"Hey," I say, desperate. "Hey, it's okay. I didn't mean to react like that. It's just…" I search for words to describe the rage brewing in my chest. "The thought of you getting hurt like that…makes me want to destroy worlds."

"It's my fault," she says.

"Jordy, no. No way it's your fault."

She keeps her head bowed.

"What happened? You want to talk about it?"

She shakes her head.

"Okay, you don't have to talk about it." Fates, what do I say? I thrust my forearm in front of her. "See this?"

She nods.

"What do you see?"

"Tattoos. Lots of them."

"A whole sleeve."

"Yes."

"Feel it, Jordy. Touch it."

She does and I grit my teeth. Her touch still has me hard. I wait until she reaches my favorite part of the tattoo, a giant redwood. She runs her finger up the trunk and pauses. There.

"You feel that?" I ask, burrowing my face into her hair. Even her scent is perfect. "You know what that is?"

"A scar."

"Yep. Big one. Got caught with a knife."

"But how—" she stops. She knows what scars a shifter.

"Vampire blood. I tried to stake the fucker. Got hit with blood, and it made the knife wound scar."

She turns in my lap, eyes wide at my declaration. "You fought a vampire."

More than one, but she doesn't need to know that. She looks absolutely shocked and I get it. Because I fought a vampire, and I'm still breathing.

"It's not possible," she whispers.

"Feel my arm."

She does, more hesitantly. The weal runs through the heart of the redwood tattoo and becomes a wave on an ocean, the Great Wave by Hokusai. Further around my arm, on more placid water, a ship sails into the horizon. "How did you get away?

"Luck." It's a partial truth. "I can't tell you much."

"You don't remember?"

I shrug. Something in her eyes makes me ask, "Do you remember?" I touch her scar again, gently, but she flinches.

"No." Her face shutters again. "Not completely."

"He'd have to spill vampire blood on you to make it scar. Lots of it."

"I know," she says softly.

I don't want to ask. What sick fuck vampire tears into his victim, and soaks her in his own blood just so she'll scar?

No wonder Jordy has nightmares.

"So how'd you scar, then?" she asks.

I don't want to go down this road, but if it draws her away from her dark path, I will. "Same way you did. Vampire blood. Lots of it."

"He bled on you?'

"Not by choice. It burned like a mother, but I got him, in the end."

She's silent, contemplating, her fingers still working down my arm. Her touch falls away, and she turns to the subject I absolutely do not want her thinking about. "You fight like a vampire. I know you do. I saw you."

"Jordy—"

"How do you do it? How is it possible?"

I shake my head. Pressing my lips together. We cannot go there.

"Declan and Parker were talking about it. Vampires are bigger, faster, strong. Shifters are all those things, but head to head, vampires beat shifters every time."

"He's right. As far as I know, I'm the only shifter to ever beat a vampire. There's a way to do it, but only I know how." Fates, why am I telling her this? If any vampire finds out what she knows, her life is forfeit. Not to mention mine.

"How?"

"It's a secret. I can't tell you."

Her hand drops to her own chest. "I dream about him, sometimes. The vampire who did this."

"I know, Kit." I've held her through those nightmares. "I'll kill him."

"No. I wish I was bigger, stronger, faster. So I could defend myself. But I'm not. I'll always be small." She sounds so sad. I want to comfort her and have no idea how. "And now I'm scarred. Ugly. Augustine was so mad after…he saw me. He never treated me the same after that."

"He should've protected you," I growl. "It wasn't your fault."

She closes her eyes, tears spilling, magnifying the freckles.

"Kit, sweetness," I shift her closer in my arms. "Don't cry. You're breaking my heart. If I had been there, I would've protected you."

"I know."

"I'm here now. No vampire will ever touch you again."

She shakes her head. "I've got to go back. You know that. You can't take from a vampire."

"He's not getting his hands on you again," I growl.

Her eyes slide to the door.

I grip her hair. "No. No running. We're in this now, together. If you think you're going back to him after this—"

"Grizz, please."

"No, Jordy." I tip her face up. "He doesn't get to have you."

Her eyes open and meet mine. "Then who does? Who gets to have me?"

"No one."

"I don't want to belong to no one."

"You belong to yourself."

"I know. But I want to give myself to someone."

I shouldn't ask, but I can't help it. "Who?"

She licks her lips. "You."

"Jordy. I can't…" This is killing me. The knife in my arm, the burn of vampire blood hurts less.

"I know." She lays her small fingers over my scared lips. "Shh, I know."

"I'm sorry. It's not fair to you, Kit. I should let you, but I can't. Not until—" Not until I find someone better to take her. I should say that, but I can't.

With a small nod, she pulls away. I let her go. But then she starts to slip down between my knees again.

"What are you doing?" Hope and alarm mixes in my voice.

"You saved me from him." She sets her hands on my knees, her face at my crotch. "Let me thank you."

"I want more than your gratitude," I growl, tugging her head back by her hair.

"Then what do you want?" Her whiskey-colored eyes spear me, open and guileless and absolutely devastating. Stripping me down, wrecking every wall I've raised between us.

"You, Kit. I want you. But I can't have you…" My voice grows ragged as she tugs against my hold, putting her lips right near my upright shaft.

"Just for tonight then. Just for tonight."

If I tug her hair any tighter, I'll hurt her, so I let her go. She wants to suck my cock? Fuck if I can stop her. I can barely think with her auburn hair spilling over my thigh, her lips skimming my cock.

"Fuck, yes. Kit, baby—"

"I love how you call me Kit," she says, her breath blowing over my turgid length. "Your baby fox." Her tongue darts out, and she licks me. Fuck, I'm gonna explode.

"Kit, please."

Her smile is smug. "I like being your baby. You make me feel small and cute."

"You are small."

She wrinkles her nose.

"You're cute, too, but not just that." Reach down and spear her hair with my blunt fingers. "You're beautiful."

With a quiet satisfied smile, she opens her mouth and engulfs my cock. Lights flash in my brain, my hips jerk up, fucking her mouth. She goes with it, bobbing her head, her mouth providing perfect suction. She takes me to the root—insane, given how big I am and how small she is.

She's humming—Fates—vibrations through me, my balls gonna explode.

"Jordy," I jerk her. "I want you." I want to come in her but there's not time. "I'm gonna come." I want her. She sucks harder, vacuums every bit of cum outta me.

With a roar I thrust hard into her mouth, she takes it, every inch.

Cum dribbles out of the side of her mouth. Obscene. Should be angry for defiling her, instead I want to lay her down, make her scream, wreck and ruin her and make a beautiful mess in my bed. Then hold her in my arms and croon how precious she is. She'll let me. She'll let me do every depraved thing I want to do, and lie there, tattered innocence, and smile.

Fisting my hand in her hair, I hold her still and kiss her, hard enough to bruise. My stubble scrapes her soft skin, but if it hurts her, she makes no sign. She wriggles under me, her legs wrapped around my hips, tugging me closer, begging for more.

I kiss down her body, browsing over her heart, breasts chafed, her hands begging.

"Please, Grizz, please, oh, yes—"

I prop her legs over my shoulders and bury my face in her snatch. Fates, she tastes so damn good. "Gonna eat you, baby. Gonna lick up every drop." My tongue rough and wide, lapping over as much of her tender skin as I can. She writhes under the onslaught, but her hands grip my hair, pulling me tighter.

That's it baby, let go. My hand finds her breast and

plumps it, squeezing it. She'll wear the marks from my rough stubble, my conquering hands. I pull her legs apart and attack her sweet pussy with my tongue again, drawing fresh moans. Fuck, I want more.

I flip her over and swat her ass, growling with pleasure at the red handprint on her pale flesh. I want to mark her. I want to own her. I want her to feel me in every way. I smack her again, without malice, but hard enough to leave a mark.

She arches her back and thrusts her bottom at me. "Harder," she orders. "more."

"You don't give the orders here." I thrust my fingers into her sopping pussy. It would be too rough if she wasn't so very wet.

"Fuck, Kit, you're so ready. You want me?"

"Yes," she moans, her head dropping to the bed. "Yes please."

"Gonna fuck this pussy. But not tonight. Tonight, I feast." I lie on my back, pulling her to straddle me. She blinks, dazed, her hair falling around her face as she looks down at me. Her nipples stand at attention. Her scent surrounds me.

My hands steady her hips. She tries to move off me and I grip her tighter. "Gonna eat you. Grind into my face, baby. Get your orgasm, take it all." I tug her lower and growl right into her pussy. "That's an order."

Her hips drop and she does as I command, rocking back and forth, rubbing against my face. I open wide and eat her, my tongue driving up into her tight hole, my fingers digging into her heated ass cheeks. She gasps and grinds harder, a huge moan rising from her lithe body.

Her thighs clench on either side of my head. Fuck, I want to reach my cock and jack off, but if I let go, she'll topple right over.

Her orgasm strikes like lightning and I fight to keep her upright, as her body is wracked with spasm after spasm. My arms prop her as I tongue her as deep as I can, loving the feel of her inner muscles clenching on me.

"Fuck, you're gonna feel so good on my cock."

With a final cry, she tips over, and I let her, rising up to arrange her on the bed. I kneel over her, a conquering warrior surveying his claim. Her pussy is soft and wet, raw and red from my beard. She'll take my cock there, but not tonight. Tonight I mark her as mine.

I jerk my cock over her prone body. With lazy eyes she reaches up to help and I wrap my hand over her little one, tugging on my cock until my seed spurts over her body. I grab her wrist. "Touch it. Spread it over yourself." I wait until she smears my cum all over her goosebumped flesh.

I don't know where this is going, but tonight, she's mine. When I kissed her by the door, I set her aside. She chose to follow me into the bathroom. To strip naked in the hall and beckon me into the bedroom. She had a chance to avoid this, and she chose me.

For better or worse her fate is sealed. But she doesn't seem to mind.

When she's done painting her flesh with my cum, she brings her fingers to her mouth. And licks them clean.

Fates. I'm done.

Jordy lies sweet and sated in my bed. I get a cloth and clean her, admiring every mark I've made on her body. Of course, that leads to me kissing every inch of her reddened flesh, from her flushed cheeks to her well spanked ass. I end up laying her over my lap again, holding her down by the scruff of her neck while my fingers work her to a final orgasm.

When the timer on the crock pot goes off, I have to fight to bring her back to reality. "Kit. Baby, time to eat."

She's so wrung out and droopy, I have to prop her up in my lap and hold little bites to her mouth, feeding her bit by bit. Which suits me just fine. Between bites, I kiss her, tasting the gravy. She sits up more once I get some food into her, her face still flushed from all her orgasms.

"Bad bear," she murmurs, tracing a finger around my mouth. I nip at it.

"Bad fox, coming into my house, eating all my meat and sleeping in my bed."

She pouts at the crock pot. "This meat's too hot." She looks at the piece I'm holding. "This meat is too cold." She wriggles in my lap and despite getting off twice my cock thickens. "This meat is just right."

"Bad fox," I growl, and hold my hand to her mouth. "Open."

She obeys, waiting for me to place the bite in her mouth.

"I'll feed you my meat as often as I can."

"Mmmm."

I put another bite up to her lips, and she shakes her head, diverting it to my mouth. I eat the portion meant for her, and when she reaches into the stew pot, I let her continue to feed me as I fed her. I indulge her, licking the gravy off her fingers.

"Enough," I say between sucking on her fingers. I lift her and carry her back to the bed.

"You need to eat more."

"I'd rather eat you."

"You already did."

"I want more."

She laughs.

"Later. Maybe." I set her down and arrange the pillows behind her. "Right now I gotta clean up. You stay," I order her when she starts to follow me. "I want you to relax."

"Okay, Grizz," she says happily. I hand her the sketch pad and she thanks me again.

"I'll draw something for you."

"I'd rather you draw something for yourself."

She cocks her head. "Like what?"

I hold out my arm and flex my biceps under my tattooed sleeve. "You like my ink?"

Her eyes are hooded, drowsy with desire. Fates, it's such a turn on.

"You can get a tattoo of your own, you know. If you want, you can cover up the scars."

"Do you think I should?" She bites her lip.

"I think you're beautiful as you are. But if they bother you, yeah, Kit. Draw something to ink over them. They're part of you now. Might as well make them something beautiful."

"All right," she says softly. "I'll see what I can draw."

"Good girl."

I leave her to it, knees drawn up, sketch pad in front of

her, tongue peeking out as she concentrates. Cute little Kit.

I clean up the kitchen, puttering, marveling that this could be my life. Doing domestic things while a sweet little vixen waits in my bed.

My machine is blinking with a message I got just after 7 pm. I hit the play button and go back to the dishes. A rasping voice comes on, one I vaguely recognize. I freeze.

"Grizzly." A pause and the speaker breathes hard and angry. Teeth click—a vampire grinding his fangs. My hackles rise at the sound. "You got something of mine. I want it back." The message ends.

So Augustine figured out who took his pet fox. He wants her back.

"Too fucking bad," I tell the message machine. If that leech was here I'd—

A soft noise makes me whirl. Jordy stands in the kitchen entryway, wide-eyed. She meets my stare with her horrified one.

"Go back to bed," I say, without a push to make it an order. I want to go back in time and erase the message. Or better yet, to the time before her family sold her, so I could find her, seduce her and steal her away.

Too bad time doesn't work like that.

"Was that—" Her lip trembles. More than anything I want to hold her.

"Yes." I go to hit the delete button and she stays my hand. She hits replay and we both listen to the message again. This time, when I go to delete it she doesn't stop me.

"Did he have your number?"

"No. Must have got it out of the books at Toxic." I try to sound bored. My information is in the king's files, same as everyone. "It's okay. My address isn't listed."

"He'll come for me."

"He doesn't know where you are. It's okay, Kit, I got this."

I go to the door and check the locks, just in case. Making this place my den will keep a vampire from coming over the threshold, but won't keep out other thieves. Fortunately, they'll probably all be human. I'm the only shifter I know who will work with a vampire.

Humans, I can take.

When I turn back, Jordy's still by the answering machine, frozen.

"It's all right," I tell her again.

"You gotta let me go," she whispers.

"Fuck no." I cross to her and tug her to me. She squirms and I clamp down tighter. "It's not happening."

"Grizz, please." Normally I like the sound of her begging, but not now. "He knows you got me. He's not gonna stop."

"He's not getting you back—"

"He'll kill you," she blurts. Her pupils are blown. Full panic.

"He can try." I pick her up, shaking her a little. "Calm down, Kit."

"He's a vampire!"

"And I kill vampires," I snarl in her face. She stills in shock. Fuck, my secret's out. "I kill vampires," I repeat, quieter. I'm not mad at her. My hand itches a little, wanting to reach for the juice. I got enough blood and rage right now, I could fight the world, and win.

"You just said you killed one. That it was luck."

"The first one I fought I didn't kill. I got away, and that was luck," I admit. "He killed someone I loved." I swallow. I haven't told anyone but Frangelico this. And I only told him so he'd know how serious I was about our alliance.

Jordy is silent and still, waiting. Or maybe she's just trying to process what I've told her.

I carry her to the bed and sit, keeping her in my lap.

"It happened when I was a teen. Soon after I'd turned. A vampire was…hunting. He got a taste for shifters or maybe my mom just surprised him."

"And you were there?"

"Not until too late. He killed her." For a moment reality dips away. I see a galley kitchen, a wooden table, blood spilling down the wall and dripping down to the body crumpled behind the chair. "I tracked him down and barely escaped with my life. That was before I learned how to fight vampires." I hadn't killed the vampire murderer, but I had spilled his blood. Licking my wounds later, I felt the buzz, the burst of energy, and I figured out how I could have my revenge.

"I'm sorry," Jordy says softly. Her face swims into view.

"It was a long time ago. I haven't seen the bastard since."

"But you're still looking."

"Yeah. As soon as I'm done with this job, I'll go back to my hunt."

"Does…" she hesitates.

"Ask."

"Does Frangelico know you're hunting a vampire?"

"He does. That's why I partner with him. He knows my past. He supports my quest. That's why I can't own you, Kit. I gotta let you go. I'm not…I can't be in a relationship."

"So you are going to release me."

"Not yet," I growl more loudly than I mean to. "Not until I've dealt with Augustine. Punished him for what he's done to you."

"Grizz." Her small hands cup my face. "You can't keep me here."

"I'm going to keep you safe."

"He'll come after you. I don't want you to be hurt because of me. I'm not worth it," she says, sadness flaring in her scent.

"You are to me. Don't you ever say that again. You're worth everything. I wanna give you the whole world."

"Grizz." She closes her eyes.

"I'm not giving you back to that leech," I swear savagely. "He used you and abused you. He doesn't get you back. Ever."

"You can't keep me from running to him."

"The hell I can't." My bear snarling for vampire blood, I rise up and throw her over my shoulder.

Jordy

I PUSH up to see where Grizz is taking me. He goes to his

drawers and rummages around. His big hand claps down on my ass when I struggle.

"Be still."

"Grizz, c'mon. Be reasonable." I'd submit if I wasn't so terrified for him. At any moment Augustine could drive up and attack.

"He can't get in, Kit. I have a threshold. This place is my home."

"He can send people in."

"Humans," he snorts as if that says it all.

"They might have guns."

"I can heal before a bullet kills me."

"Not a bullet to the head." I argue. Stubborn bear. He tromps back to the bed and tosses me down. What can I say to make him care about his safety? "And what about me? I might get caught in the crossfire."

"Yep. Already thought of that." He's got a rope in his hand.

"What are you doing?"

"Tying you to the bed." He grabs my wrist and starts to secure one arm to the headboard.

Normally, the thought of big, beautiful Grizz tying me up would make me ecstatic. Tonight, I just want to howl. "That won't work," I snap. I've never been this feisty in my life. Grizz is rubbing off on me. He gets close to my face and I bare my teeth. I'll gnaw out of anything he puts me in.

"Fine." He grits out. Face like stone, he straightens and winds the rope around his wrist.

"What are you doing?" He's not holding me down, but I'm too curious to run.

"Tying you to me." He reaches for me and I scramble away. I get as far as the door before he snatches me. He's fast as a vampire. Of course he can catch me. With one arm around my middle, he carries me back and drapes me face down over his lap.

"What are you doing?" I squawk.

"Punishment, Kit."

"No," I cry, but he's already spanking me. Not too hard—not even close. If we were playing, I'd tell him I can take it a lot harder. All his palm is doing is turning me on.

Bad bear!

He slaps my butt and I kick my legs, howling.

"I thought you were submissive," he chuckles. His fingers graze my pussy and I shriek louder. "Nevermind. You're dripping wet."

He tips me back up. Before I can protest, he's looped our wrists together. I don't know how he ties a knot one handed, but when it's done, I tug and tug and nothing. He pulls his arm back, grinning right in my face.

"You're stuck now."

"How are you gonna fight a vampire tied to me?"

"Don't need to fight a vampire. Augustine isn't gonna find us tonight. Way I see it, I just gotta keep you tied to me so I can get a little rest. If you keep struggling, Kit, I can fuck you into compliance."

I suck in a breath. *Like that will deter me.* I want to say. But I have to be strong. "You think that will work?"

"Yeah." He cups my pussy with his other hand. "I do."

It's so annoying, but he's not wrong. His fingers stroke me and I still, not wanting him to stop.

He does and I sigh, trying to remember what we were arguing about.

He holds up our bound wrists.

"You can gnaw through this. But you might hurt me. And if you leave tonight, Jordy, and run from me, you will hurt me."

My breath catches as pain stabs my heart. There's no way I can run from him now.

I stay awake a long time after he turns the light off, my mind spinning even as he holds me tight, safe, and warm. Wondering if he knows the truth I've realized: the rope around my wrist is the least of the ties that bind me to him.

CHAPTER 12

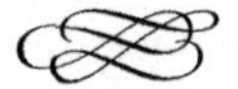

rizz

THE SCENT of sizzling bacon hits my nose, and I jerk awake. Instantly I'm reaching for something, groping the bed beside me. Jordy. The place next to me is still warm, but my hand comes up empty. Something hits my face and I flail until I realize what it is. Rope. The one I wound around our wrists. Fuck.

I'm on my feet and halfway down the hall before I link the smell of bacon to Jordy's absence. I hit the kitchen and brake. She's standing in front of the stove, dressed in nothing but one of my t-shirts, frying bacon. She got free, but she stayed with me.

"Hey." Her cheek curves in my direction and every bit of blood in me rushes to my dick. I lean against a cupboard, gritting my teeth against the demands of my morning wood.

"Did you sleep all right?" She covers the pan and turns fully to me. Her eyes snag on my erection. "Is that for me?" She colors sweetly, and padding over, drops to her knees in front of me. Her head tips back and her smile almost brings me to my knees. "Let me take care of you."

Oh hell, yes.

She grips the base of my cock to make it jut out even further and swirls her tongue around the head.

A shudder of pleasure runs through me, striking at the base of my spine. "Fuck, Kit." I tangle my fingers into her hair, tighten them into a fist. She lifts her eyes to mine as she takes me deep into her mouth, then down the back of her throat. I have to force myself not to think about the fucker who trained her to do this. I should be grateful because it's the best damn blowjob of my life. Nothing compares to the feel of her swallowing me back.

I use my fist in her hair to direct her movements, pulling her on and off my cock. My thighs start to shake, balls tighten. Between her hands, lips, and clever darting tongue, I spurt into her mouth before the bacon burns.

Breakfast is good too.

"Damn, Kit, you can cook."

She smiles down at her plate. "I'm glad you like it."

"Fuck, yes," I swear vehemently and she laughs. "No one's cooked for me since..." I hesitate and her eyes fly to mine. "Since my mom," I tell her honestly. "I haven't even shared a meal with anyone."

"I'm sorry." She reaches over and squeezes my hand. I catch it and turn it over, cradling it in my rough fight-worn paws. It's like catching a little bird. Small, soft, fragile. Unmarred.

"Me too."

After a moment, she slips into my lap. My dick's already responding, but I wait to see what she'll do. Cupping my face in her hands she sets her forehead against mine. She rubs her face against mine and fuck if it doesn't feel like absolution. The tightness in my chest eases a little.

Fates, she makes me soft.

"You eat enough?" I ask brusquely, and when she nods, I order her off my lap. "Get dressed. We're going out."

She doesn't ask questions, just obeys, and I shepherd her out of my den and onto my bike.

She still doesn't ask questions, even when I pull up to the battered black storefront with a sign in red script proclaiming "Custom Tattoos." She hops off the bike and lets me guide her forward with my hand at her back.

"Guy here works on shifters. He did this." I hold up my scarred arm, the one with the full sleeve. "He does all the wolf pack's ink." I pull her sketch book out of my jacket. "We got a few hours. Figured you could draw something and get it, if you like."

Inside, I introduce her to Dick, the artist. Once she's comfortable, I excuse myself. I made it clear that she doesn't have to get anything if she doesn't want to, but if she does, I'll pay. I head outside to give her space. A tattoo's a personal thing, and I'm just a guy she's known a few days. She'll have this ink forever.

Standing on the sidewalk, I make a few calls. One to the company that leases the theater to see if I can get any leads there. The line rings and rings. Nothing. I'll see if Frangelico can make inquiries.

My phone buzzes with an incoming call. Declan doesn't even say hello, just launches in. "There's a fight tonight. Don't forget."

"I haven't forgotten. Will you be there?"

"Wouldn't miss it."

"Great. I need you to watch Kit again."

"No worries. She's no trouble."

I grit my teeth. "Actually, there might be trouble. Augustine knows I took her."

A stream of curses meets that news. "Taking from vampires. That'll get ya killed."

"I know. I'm working on it."

"You're working on getting killed?"

"No," I snarl. "I'm working on getting her free. I wanna know who leaked news that she's with me."

"Damned if I know. Probably one of the shifters ya fought, wanting to get back at ya. Ya have enemies, Grizz. And vampires know how to get information. Their spies are everywhere."

Ugh. Dead end. Declan knows nothing. "Fine. But you're gonna help me watch Kit. She's not going back to Augustine, and that's final."

Declan sighs. "Anything else?"

I tell him what I found around the truck stop and at the theater. "I need eyes on both. I'll pay. You think you can make that happen?"

"Yeah. It'll cost ya."

"That's fine. I'm good for it." I'll pass the bill on to Frangelico.

As if he can hear my thoughts, Declan says, "It's dangerous, working for the vampire king."

"I know. I wouldn't do it unless I had to." I must be crazy, offering up that bit of information. Hanging around Jordy has made me soft. More willing to reach out and make a connection. If I don't get a hold of myself, I'll be handing out friendship bracelets and getting the Stooges to braid my hair.

"I don't know what drives a shifter to partner with a vampire," Declan says carefully, "but I do know this. Vampires are dangerous, and the king—he's the most dangerous of them all. You're swimmin' in shark-infested waters, Grizz."

I sigh. "Don't I know it."

"Make sure ya don't bleed."

I kill a few more minutes making phone calls. I'm about to re-enter the shop and see what Jordy wants for lunch when the door opens and she comes out.

"You ready to go?"

"Yeah."

"Didn't want to get anything?"

With hesitant hands, she tugs down her shirt and shows me the bandage made of white gauze and tape above her left breast. She got something to cover up the mass of scars on her heart.

"Very good, Kit." I hide my disappointment that I didn't get to see it. If she wants to share, she'll share. Not my place to know, or ask. "Vamos."

Jordy

Grizz and I spend the day together, doing whatever we want. After a quick stop to get tacos, I tell Grizz I love his bike and he takes me on a long, meandering drive around town. His Harley circles lazily up 'A' Mountain—the mountain with the giant white A for University of Arizona—and we eat at the overlook. Afterward, he takes me to a small park and we walk a trail through the cacti, holding hands like a couple. Dinner is at a diner, where Grizz shocks the waitress with the amount of food he plows through.

"Gotta fight tonight," he tells me. "Need to fuel up."

"Is that why you took it easy today? To get ready for the fight?"

"No." He sets down his fork and cups my cheek. "I wanted to spend time with you."

I can't stop beaming at him. It's stupid and inelegant. I should play hard to get. But whenever I'm with him, it's like a light switches on. I grin and glow and feel all warm and toasty, like I've swallowed a sun.

"I like seeing you happy, Kit," he tells me.

I am happy, I want to say. *But only around you.*

The closer we get to nightfall, the more serious he gets. His smile slips away, fading with the light. The last rays die behind the mountains, and he stands, throwing a hundred dollar bill down on the table between the empty plates.

"Time to go."

I hold on tight as we ride to the industrial part of

town. Behind us, two more motorcycles rip onto the road and flank us, catching up to us when we stop at a red light. Grizz stiffens in my arms, but he keeps his head straight. The light turns green, and he roars away, but the two bikes follow, growling angrily. By the time we're at the turnoff to the Fight Club, more bikes have joined us.

"Who are they?" I ask when we're stopped again at a light.

"Wolves. Tucson pack."

I look back and one of the bikers salutes me. A big dude, as big as Grizz. He has the phases of the moon tattooed on his knuckles. They all do.

My own tattoo itches under its bandage. It didn't hurt too bad. I called on my submissive training, breathing deep and surrendering to the needle. The worst part was the burn of vampire blood to set the ink. I wonder if the wolves know about the vampire blood, how it's the quickest way to make a shifter scar. Stop shifter healing in its tracks.

We park and Grizz waits until I hop off to dismount. His hand covers my back as we walk to the Fight Club door. There are groups of shifters waiting, lots of bikers and gangbanger types. I almost trip when I recognize some of the cats who attacked Grizz.

"It's all right," he whispers and throws his arm around my shoulders. "We're safe tonight. The wolves won't let anyone touch me. Not until I'm in the ring."

Sure enough, the biker wolves are following us. By the time we get to the door, they've completely surrounded us. I breathe deep and will my fox not to panic. She doesn't like being surrounded by all these predators. I'd be more scared if I wasn't with Grizz.

Inside, the wolves fall away and Grizz leads me straight to the bar. The club is a lot nicer than I thought it'd be. The raw, reclaimed wood tables and bar, the exposed Edison bulbs, the concrete floor, even the rough pockets of shifters fit together with a sort of rugged charm.

Grizz orders and the bartender plunks down two glasses. Clinking his with mine, he tips back the shot. I sip mine and sputter.

"Sorry, Kit. Should've warned you." Grizz rubs my back even as amusement glints his eye.

"That's okay," I cough. "I don't drink much. You take it."

He shoots mine back almost absently, his eyes roving around the club. "Fight's about to start. You're gonna sit here," he leads me to the corner. "And keep quiet. Keep out of trouble."

"What about you?"

"I'll be in the ring." He definitely is amused.

I crane my neck to see beyond the clusters of shifters to the spotlit cage in the center of the warehouse. "I can't be closer?" I can't hide my disappointment that I'm so far away.

"No," Grizz says gently, stroking my back. "I gotta focus. I can't do that if I'm not sure you're safe."

"I'm gonna root for you," I tell him and he dips his face close to mine.

"You sure, Kit? You'll be the only one."

"Yes," I say decisively, and tug him closer for a kiss. He

breaks it off first, scanning the warehouse. With so many potential threats around, he's not able to relax. The club is full of predators. I should be all worked up, but I'm not. I bask in his protection until three familiar faces pop up behind Grizz.

"Heya, Kit. Miss us?"

"A little." I lean in and hug Declan, then Laurie. A rumbled growl makes us jerk apart. Grizz looms over us, his eyes bright with his bear. Jealous grizzly. I almost giggle.

"It's okay," I say. "We're just friends." But Parker and I fist bump instead of hug.

"Ya ready for this?" Declan asks.

Grizz shrugs. "Ready as I'll ever be. You got details on this fight?"

"Parker does." Declan jerks his head to the grey-haired shifter, who nods and starts walking farther into the warehouse, towards the cage.

"I got bad news," Grizz says to me, humor lightening his tone. "You gotta stick close to these guys for the night."

"Bad news bear." I mock frown.

"Yeah." He starts to lean in for another kiss when a shadow falls over us. Grizz straightens, his face going blank.

One of the big wolves who followed us stands close by, two of his own pack behind him as backup. "Grizz."

Grizz jerks a nod, but doesn't look at them.

"Fifteen minutes."

"You here to escort me to the cage?" Grizz grins, but it's a cold, hard thing, with none of the warmth he gives to me.

The wolf shrugs. "Don't want you to trip and fall on your way there."

My hackles go up as the cheetahs stroll in, joining the rowdy crowd. They turn bright yellow eyes on Grizz.

"I'm touched by your concern." Grizz straightens. "Be good," he says to me and chucks me under the chin.

A few of the wolves look at me curiously.

"No one touches my crew," Grizz says to the big wolf, who nods. Two of the wolves stay behind, standing a little apart from us like guards. I'd be grateful if they weren't blocking our view.

Whoops and shouts echo around the big space. More shifters pour in through the door, crowding the bar, surrounding the cage.

"Just a few more minutes," Laurie murmurs.

I wipe my palms on my jeans.

"He'll be okay," Declan says. "Grizz is the best. In fact —" A roar goes up by the cage and we all strain to see.

"Did ya catch that?" Declan asks Laurie, but the bird shifter shakes his head.

Declan hops up on his stool and swears. "Aw, shite."

"What is it?" I push up as far as I can, but the room's too packed with huge shifters. Their heads block my view of the cage.

"A pre-fight," he mutters. "They want him to fight someone else first."

"Who?" I crane my neck, then give up and stand on my stool too. Chills run up and down my body as the new fighter enters the cage. It's the gorilla.

"Guess he's fighting two tonight."

"Is that allowed?"

"First rule of the Shifter Fight Club," Declan grimaces and shakes his head.

"What is it?" I lean down and whisper to Laurie. "What's the rule?"

"There are n-n-no rules."

~

Grizz

I FACE the silverback who instigated the fight that led to my black out.

"You gonna fight for yourself tonight? Not get a bunch of pussies to do your dirty work?"

The gorilla's lips peel back, showing flat, yellowed teeth. "You're gonna bleed, Grizzly."

"All right. No monkey business."

The gorilla roars at me, but the crowd laughs. They don't like me, but they like my attitude.

"Go Grizz." Amid the jeers, a single voice cheers me on. "You can do it."

Jordy. I'd pick her out of any crowd. There may as well be no one else here but us.

I tug off my leather jacket and wrap it to hide the flask. I hand it carefully to Parker. "Guard that."

He nods. He knows I carry a flask, but has no idea what it contains. No one does.

I face the gorilla, shaking out my shoulders. I don't need the juice to fight this banana brain. I can take him.

"Ready?" A wolf calls from the sidelines. I nod at him and he blows a whistle.

A foot comes out of nowhere. I barely have time to duck. The gorilla lands and whirls. I block another kick with raised forearms, staggering back under the heavy-weight. The crowd whoops, loving that I got caught off guard.

I lower my arms, meeting the gorilla's crazy eyes. The fucker is barefoot, wearing loose black gee pants. I should've picked it out immediately.

I shrug and roll the kinks outta my shoulders. MMA? Why the fuck not? I'm down for some karate.

Making a fist, I press it into my palm, bowing without lowering my head or dropping my gaze. The gorilla rolls his lips back again in a snarl-smile. He launches into another leap, coming at me feet first. I dodge, grab his ankle and swing him into the cage wall.

The crowd's cheering cuts off as if someone hit a switch.

The monkey picks himself up, shakes his limbs out, and comes at me again. On all fours, like an animal. He hits my middle and we fall to the floor together. I punch his head repeatedly until he rolls away. I sit up without using my arms and rise. When he comes at me again, I duck and grab his arm at the same time, rolling him off my back into the cage wall. He bounces and rebounds—right as I kick out. Foot, meet face.

The crowd's on its feet, hooting and howling. They sound more animal than human. Fine by me. I'm the biggest predator here. My bear surges forward. I drop to all fours, fighting the instinct to change. My mouth opens and I roar. A few shifters cover their ears. Others drop their gaze. *That's right, fuckers. Grizz is in the house.*

The monkey sits up, dazed. Beyond him, outside the cage, Parker is shouting something. What is it?

"Behind you—"

The gorilla smiles. I whirl around as a big, bad bear enters the cage, shrugging out of his leather jacket, smirking at me with the biggest canines I've ever seen.

All around the cage, the wolves begin to howl.

CHAPTER 13

Jordy

"WHAT IS IT? WHAT'S HAPPENING?" I tug on Declan's leg. When the fighting started, it was so fast, so glorious and brutal, I couldn't watch without my eyes watering. I got down from my stool to give Laurie a turn. But now, hearing the crowd screaming for blood, and the grim expressions on the two Stooges' faces, I know something's wrong.

"Grizz." I turn back to the cage. My bear is there, prowling around the perimeter, turning his head back and forth from one opponent to another.

Two on one?

"Feck," Declan mutters.

"Grizz," I breathe in horror. I've seen him fight more

than one opponent before, but everything about this is worse. The stakes are higher. The shifters around the cage laugh and shout.

I gotta get closer.

Cupping my hands around my mouth, I shout this to Declan and his eyes widen. "Kit, no—"

I'm already racing towards the cage, weaving in and out of the groups waiting at the bar. The shifters don't part for me and for once I'm glad I'm small. I fight through the crowd, squeezing between bodies and slipping away before anyone can grab me.

I end up near one of the bleachers. If I'm lucky, no one will notice me.

Grizz waves to the second fighter, and he orders a timeout.

Calmly, my big bear walks to the side of the cage and hooks his fingers in the links.

"Parker," he growls. "Juice."

Parker fumbles the leather jacket and holds up a flask. He lifts it to the cage, pushing the neck through the links. Grizz takes a pull, pressing his face to the cage wall. His throat works for a long second before he pulls back and nods to Parker to put the flask away. A red drop clings to Grizz's lips before he dashes a hand over his mouth and turns back to meet his two opponents.

"Let's do this," he says to everyone and no one.

"Round two," the big wolf shouts and blows on a whistle. "Fight!"

~

Grizz

I PACE the perimeter of the fight cage, keeping both my opponents in my peripheral vision. I gotta work to keep from giving either of them my back.

Two against one? Not great odds, but I've had worse.

The vampire blood sizzles in my veins. Frangelico didn't skimp on this dose. This is heart blood—the most potent. The hangover's gonna be a bitch, but it'll give me enough energy to last a few hours.

Time to get this fight started.

I move first, tackling the gorilla. He leaps onto the cage wall, practically levitating. I tear him down and give him a taste of my fist.

Behind me, the crazy bear paces. Good, he's not feral enough to be comfortable fighting these uneven odds. He'll wait his turn, which gives me time to teach this monkey a lesson.

The gorilla fights with kicks and punches, which I block easily. I catch his thigh with a kick of my own. Close to his crotch. Yeah, it's a cheap shot, but I'm not fighting fair.

"Still hiding behind better shifters, I see," I taunt him. A scream of rage and the gorilla hurtles through the air towards me. I dodge and let him crash to the ground, following it with a kick to the head.

"K/O," Parker shouts. The crowd forgets its animosity towards me, and chants my name as I straighten with satisfaction.

One down. One to go.

"Feel free to forfeit," I tell the bear.

"You don't fucking scare me," Caleb growls back. He licks the gorilla's blood off his arm, tongue running over his lips as if he likes the taste. Fuck, he really smells broken.

We wait as the wolves enter the cage and pull the gorilla out by his feet. The first fighter leaves a long smear of blood on the floor.

~

Jordy

THE TWO REMAINING FIGHTERS CIRCLE, staring at each other. Grizz stands tall while his opponent remains hunched, prowling almost, on all fours. The hulking fighter looks more animal than human. Grizz jogs in place, rotating his shoulders and stretching his neck. At last he stops pretending to warm up. He hits his chest and holds out his hands. "We gonna do this? Or just dance all night?"

The opposing fighter backs up into the cage, leaning against the chain links. Pushing back further and further until the links strain. The metal creaks as the posts start to bend. The crowd quiets.

"You break the cage you buy it," Grizz warns. A few hecklers start shouting.

The fighter raises his head and roars. Chills run up and down my spine and every shifter in the place stills.

A laugh rings out. Grizz stretches his arms open and bares his teeth in a savage grin. "Bring it."

The bear snaps forward and lumbers toward Grizz, practically on all fours. At the last second, Grizz ducks out of the way, pivots, and leaps onto the creature's back. His tattooed arms tighten around the bear's neck.

"Yeah, yeah, yeah," someone shouts. Declan. He's closer to my hiding spot, probably looking for me. Right now he's paused, mesmerized by the fight.

The fighter staggers under Grizz's weight. His head goes back and for a moment it looks like the fight is over.

Then the fighter's skin ripples.

"That's right," someone chuckles. One of the wolf pack, watching with an evil look on his face. "Fight that, traitor."

"What's happening?" I whisper.

"No," Declan shouts in horror.

"Yes," the wolves correct. "He's changing."

"That's against the rules!" Parker is banging on the cage.

"This isn't San Diego. No rules here."

I remember Grizz telling me some fights shifters have to keep human forms, or be disqualified. Looks like that isn't the case here.

"Rule one of Shifter Fight Club?" a wolf shouts, and the pack roars back, "There are no rules!"

"Oh no," I breathe. In the cage, Grizz struggles to hold on to the bear's neck.

"You can do it," I shout, my voice thin in the heavy silence. I cup my hands around my mouth. "Grizz, you got this!"

One second I'm inching closer to the cage. The next my arm is almost yanked from my socket. I spin around and stare into the eyes of a vampire.

"Got ya," he hisses through his fangs. *Benedict.*

"No," I gasp, the noise of the crowd swallowing up the small sound.

"Augustine can't wait to get his hands on you," Benedict snickers.

I remember too late I shouldn't look into his eyes, and everything goes black.

~

Grizz

Fucking insane black bear fucker. I loosen my grip as fur sprouts under my arms. The bear's on hind legs now, swaying even as his bones pop and resize. Sinking my teeth into the matted fur, I tighten my hold. He might be tripling his size, but I'm not gonna make it easy for him. After a second, I stop biting him and spit out black fur. Fates, when was the last time this idiot bathed?

The shift complete, the giant black bear lands on all fours, shaking the floor. I must look like an ant clinging to his back. I wait for my opening and kick away from him, leaping back to a far corner. I have to get out of here. Get to Jordy. That's when the juice kicks in, and I blur. I know I've moved faster than anyone thinks possible when the crowd gasps. The wolves howl, and the sound falters as I whiz around the cage.

"Traitor! Vampire pet!" The wolves start booing, and the rest of the crowd takes up the chant.

I rush my opponent, dance out of the way of giant fangs, and get two body blows in, knocking the bear back. Soon as I finish this fight, I'm challenging some wolves. I'll teach them to call me a vampire pet.

Something niggles at the back of my mind. I take a moment to scan the crowd. Where the fuck is Jordy? There, by the bleachers. Or at least, she was there.

A flash of red and my blood turns to lead. She's there, slumped over someone's shoulder. I catch the vampire's pale face before he blurs out the door.

Fuck, Jordy, no!

My bear's right there, ready to break free. I fight it back. If I shift now, I won't have the wits to hunt.

I race to the cage door but it's locked. I grab the poles and yank. Teeth sink into the back of my neck and I snarl, but don't turn. I rip away, letting blood spray, and blur to the other side of the cage where I climb the links and drop to the other side.

Gotta get Jordy. Gotta move!

Shifters scramble out of my way. Those who don't get tossed aside.

"Grizz," someone calls desperately. Declan.

"Follow me," I order him and he, Laurie, and Parker race into my wake. I'm almost outside. Almost free.

A wolf steps in front of me before I can reach the door.

"You leave and you forfeit," Trey yells. I keep coming and he steps out of the way. With a warehouse shaking roar, I hit the door and send it flying. The door frame groans as I smash through it, leaving the crowd staring at a Grizz shaped hole.

Fuck everything. I gotta get Jordy.

Gravel flies out from under my feet as I race in the direction the vampire took her.

Fucker hasn't gotten far, even with blurring. I can track him. I pick up speed and catch up just as Benny reaches the arroyo.

The skinny vampire turns, his eyes widening. He looses that oily smoothness and stumbles as he watches me blur towards him.

I see it all in slow motion: the pale face, Jordy's limp form, Benny's lips moving. "Impossible—" he says. I'm almost on him when he slings Jordy down.

I roar and he blurs away. Fuck, gotta catch him.

Frantic footsteps make me whirl. Parker and Declan, racing my way. They slow, gasping for air, clutching their chest.

"Juice," I order before they can speak.

Parker digs in his jacket and offers me the flask. I drain it. I'll feel it later, but now I need all I can get to get Benny. He took my girl. He's working for Augustine. I don't care who's behind the shifter slavers, they tried to kidnap Jordy, so they're all going down. This ends now.

Jordy lies in a huddle at my feet. I tip her back and check her pulse. It's strong and steady, but her eyes flutter and she doesn't wake. Totally under the dark. Fucking vampires. I grab her and thrust her at Declan and Parker. "Get her outta here."

"Where?" Declan asks, even as Parker and Laurie start walking her back to the club.

"Somewhere safe." I give them my address.

"Wait," Parker shouts as I straighten. "Where are you goin'?"

I snarl my answer to the moon before taking off after Benny. "Hunting vampire."

~

I CATCH up to Benny in Marana, a dead zone near the tattoo parlor I took Jordy to. Fucker's probably headed back to the theater. I pause long enough to rip up a palo verde tree, snapping and peeling a section of the trunk into a nice stake.

I've got enough juice in me to run down a flock of vampires, but not fight them all. Darkness lurks in the edges of my sight, threatening to bring me down. Can't succumb yet. Gotta get Benny, make sure Jordy's safe. Then I can go back to her.

Benny pauses in an alleyway. We're somewhere near the theater, I'm not sure how close. He leans against the wall. At his feet are steps leading down somewhere, probably to a basement door. Makes sense, that's where the vampires congregate. Benny just led me right to their secret lair.

He's stopped there, just waiting. I prowl in the shadows as he lights a cigarette. He doesn't smoke it, just holds it between shaking fingers. Vampires love fire. Something about playing with what could cause their ultimate doom.

Benny won't get such a quick death. Not when I half-stake him, tie him up, and drag him to Frangelico. We'll question him, and the king will squeeze answers outta him. We can get to the bottom of all this. Jordy will be safe and I can get back to my ultimate mission.

The thought of returning to my search for revenge doesn't feel as good as it should, though. Wish there was a way I could keep Jordy while I continue the hunt. At first she was just a distraction, but having her at my side trumps anything else. I need her in my life. Such a small person, to weight the balance like she does.

Shadows flicker around Benny's hands. He's holding the cigarette steady. Any moment he'll decide he's calm enough to keep on. Time to make my move.

Again, I blur so fast Benny has no time to react. I slam him against the building. It's so satisfying, I do it again.

"Caught ya," I say.

The cigarette falls to the ground. "That's—"

"Impossible? Nope." I set the sharper end of my makeshift stake at his heart. "Say goodnight, Benny."

Unconscious, vampires weigh more than you'd think. Even skinny guys like Benny are like fuckin' concrete slabs. By the time I get back to Fight Club, dawn's about to break. If Augustine thought he'd get his fangs into Jordy tonight, he's fresh outta luck. I just have to store this body before light clears the mountains.

A contingent of wolves hang around the dumpster out back. A few snarl when they see me, but they back away when I drag Benny right up to the side of the building.

Trey steps out of the door, eyes flashing. "What the—"

"Need a favor," I say. "Gotta store this one somewhere for questioning." I give Benny a kick. He may as well be a bag of blood for all the fight he gave me.

The wolves back away and eye me nervously. I grin at them. *Never seen a shifter take down a vampire before?*

Trey doesn't even blink. We may have our differences, but he's a solid guy.

"Here," Trey says and flips open the lid of the dumpster. If closed properly, no light will get in and fry the sucker before questioning.

"Perfect."

After barking to his pack to clear the club out, Trey helps me load the vampire into his smelly coffin.

"Thanks." I dust off my hands. "I owe you," I say to him.

He shrugs. "We won a bunch of money betting against you on the fight. You taking that vampire to Frangelico?"

"Yep. Caught him snooping around a shifter slaver site. Gonna bust that ring wide open."

"Good." Trey's eyes flare. "Then we're even."

I turn, take two steps, and stumble. My hands hit the gravel.

"Whoa, easy." Trey's at my side. He helps me up. "What the fuck, man? You drunk?"

"Nope," I slur.

Trey's eyes narrow. "You're on something."

My tongue fills my mouth. "Gotta go," I mumble.

"Sorry, buddy. You're not going anywhere in this condition." He slings my arm around his shoulder and kicks open the Fight Club door. The back of the place is empty, so no one sees my walk of shame. My bear cringes at showing such weakness. Next thing I know I'm in a cool, dark cube of a room—the back office—and Trey is leaning over me. "Here," he offers me a drink of water. "Just take it easy."

"Gotta go. Gotta get to Jordy—" At least that's what I try to say. My voice is too garbled to come out in real words. I clutch his shoulder and he puts his tattooed hand over my scarred one.

"No one's coming in here," he assures me, misunderstanding. "No one has to know. I don't kick a bear when he's down."

"Jordy—" I try again, but Trey still doesn't understand. My grip on his shoulder loosens as I fall backwards, sliding into the dark.

~

Grizz

Jordy! I have to get to Jordy. My female's gotta be terrified. I suck in a breath and try to orient myself. The memory of Trey bringing me into Fight Club seeps back as I get up.

True to his word, Trey locked the place up. I sneak out, only pausing on the doorstep when light hits me in the face.

What the—

It's daytime. Judging by the sun, well past noon. *Fuck.* That means I was unconscious for over twelve hours. And I still feel like I've been hit by a Mack truck.

I have to get to Jordy and make sure she's okay. I pray the three stooges got her safely to my place.

Fuck, I pray she was able to come out of that vamp-induced sleep Benny put her in.

I rally my clumsy limbs and trudge to my bike. It takes me a few tries, but once I'm on and balanced, my body remembers itself and I break every speed limit zooming home.

CHAPTER 14

rizz

THE SECOND I walk into my home, my bear calms.

Jordy's waiting at the table, dressed for the day in a skirt and button-down shirt that hugs the curve of her breasts. She rises, her face composed.

"Kit."

"Grizz." She's still standing by the chair, looking me over. "You're all right?"

"I am now." I open my arms. Emotions scroll over her face—worry, relief, delight—and then she stops thinking and rushes to me. And as soon as her weight hits my body, her scent rushes over me, and I'm home.

I lift her in my arms, squeezing her tight.

I wasn't rushing home because Jordy might be upset. I

was rushing because I needed to see her. I needed to know she was all right.

I need her.

The realization doesn't rock my world. It spins it right round and settles it firmly on its axis where it belonged.

"I was so worried," she whispers.

"It's okay, baby. I'm here. I'm here now."

We hug a long time, and while I'm rock hard and aching against her, I can't put her down to kiss her. I need her to know how much I need her, and until she does, I can't let her go.

Finally, she raises her head. Her sweet smile is more potent than a punch. "I cooked for you."

I let her wriggle out of my arms, gritting my teeth against the new surge of arousal. She takes my hand and tugs me to the chair. The kitchen smells lemony fresh and the counters almost sparkle. She waited for me. She cooked. She cleaned.

"Jordy." I tug her back and claim her mouth. I feast, all that sweetness dissolving on my tongue like sugar, but when I grab her hips and set her against my erection, she laughs and tuts. "Not now."

"Yes, now," I growl.

"No." She slips away. Damn wriggly fox. I go after her and she races around the table. If it weren't full of food she made, I'd flip the furniture out of the way, drag her to the ground and claim her. She's mine. There's no need to wait any longer.

"You need to eat."

"I will eat. You."

Smiling and blushing, she shakes her finger. "No. You

need real food. You were gone a long time. I know how much it took out of you."

I start to growl and she puts her hands on her hips. "One plate. At least."

"I want you now."

"You'll get me," she soothes. "But first, I need to know you're okay." She pulls out my chair. "Sit."

I hide a grin. "You giving orders now?"

"Yes." She blushes as she says it and ducks her head. Well, hell, now I can't refuse her.

"All right, Kit. One plate."

"And then we talk," she announces and starts uncovering dishes.

"That sounds ominous," I mutter, but don't push it. Now that she's pulled the cover off the crock pot, I want food.

"Looks good, baby."

"It's *cochinita pibil*," she says. "Slow cooked pork. My recipe."

I grab her ass as she serves it up. She laughs and dances away when my hand strays between her legs. She didn't say anything about me not feeling her up. I wait until she's out of reach, sitting across the table from me, to pick up my fork. One bite and I'm plowing through the meal.

"Damn, Kit, this is good."

She says nothing, but beams.

"You gonna eat?"

"I already did." She puts her elbows on the table, resting her face against her folded hands. Almost like she's praying, but her eyes are on me. She doesn't speak. Her hands hide her expression.

As soon as my plate is clean, I reach for her. I could eat more, but first I need a bite of her. "Come here."

She obeys, and doesn't protest when I guide her to sit on my lap.

"Grizz—" she starts and I kiss her, drinking more of her sweetness. My fingers fist in her hair, angling her face the way I want it. For a long time she allows it, but then jerks back.

"Grizz, we need to talk."

I nibble a little more at her lips. "Later," I murmur.

A few more kisses and she shakes her head, rubbing her face against my stubble. "Now."

I sit back with a sigh. Her face is so serious it turns the food in my stomach to concrete.

She strokes my hair as if soothing me. Cute little fox. "You were gone a long time."

I almost close my eyes at the worry in her voice. "Is that why you cooked for me, Kit? Get me softened up so you could give me the third degree?"

She just looks at me.

I sigh. "Look, I—"

"You didn't come back because you couldn't. You passed out again, like after the last fight. Right?"

Fuck. I don't want to lie to her. I nod.

She blinks and says to herself, "It has something to do with how you can blur."

Alarms go off in my head. "Kit, I can't tell you. It's not safe."

"It's the flask, isn't it? It contains something that helps you fight faster."

I weigh the truth against the cost. "Yeah."

"What is it?"

"I can't tell you that." Frangelico won't want any word of this spreading. If I tell her the final secret, her life will be in danger.

Silence stretches like a chasm between us.

Her head bows and she mutters something.

"What's that?" I raise her chin.

She meets my eyes unflinchingly. "I said, 'it's killing you.'"

I open my mouth but my protest dies under her direct stare. I can't look at her, the woman I love, and lie.

And I love Jordy. I don't know when I started but I know I'll never stop.

So when she takes my hand and leads me to the bathroom, I follow. Big bad bear meek and mild around her. She tugs off my shirt and I stifle a snarl. Fates, that hurts.

"You're not healing," she says, grabbing down the mirror and angling it to show me the nasty bite on my shoulder, where the bear fighter bit me. "It's slowing you down. And these blackouts? They're getting worse. I timed them. Last one was — hours. This one was almost fifteen."

"Look I'm sorry I left you—"

She slaps the counter. "I don't want your apologies. You don't owe me. But whatever you're doing, you're hurting yourself. You need to stop."

"I can't."

"Why not?" she whispers.

I spear my fingers into her hair. How did I come to this moment? Where a lovely young woman looks me in the eyes like I hang the moon?

"I can't, Jordy. I don't do it because I want to. I do it for revenge."

"Revenge for your mother?"

I nod, unable to speak.

"Revenge is a death trap. It's hurting you. It could kill you."

I lick my lips and tell her the truth. "As long as I take out my mother's murderer, I don't care."

"Grizz." She looks so sad. "I care."

I jolt as if electrified. But she's not done.

"I don't want you to die," she whispers, and I jolt again like she shouted it. How long has it been since someone cared whether I'm alive?

"Kit," is the only thing I can say. I rub the red strands of her hair between my finger and thumb. The fine strands catch on my callouses.

She tugs me closer and lays her forehead on mine. "I wish I could give you what you want. I wish I could give you your revenge." She slides her face against mine until we're cheek to cheek. "How long until you get it?"

"I don't know."

"Soon?"

"I don't know," I repeat. "It never mattered before. I'm gonna get it if it takes the rest of my life."

"What happens after?" she asks softly. "After you get your revenge?"

I try to answer, try to think, and there's nothing. "I

guess I never thought beyond it. I guess I assumed I'd..." I stop before I say "die", knowing the word will hurt her.

She raises her head and studies me. "Isn't there anything else you want? Something that will give you a reason to live?"

"There wasn't." My chest is tight, I can barely get the words out. "Until a few days ago, there wasn't." I cup her cheek, my thumb playing over her soft freckled skin. "And then I met you."

She searches my face, nodding to herself. Then she pulls away, taking my hand and drawing me from the bathroom. "I have something to show you."

Jordy

THE COOL DEPTHS of the bedroom swallow us and I force my breathing to calm. All night and morning I waited for Grizz and pretended I belonged in his home.

I decided: I don't belong to Augustine any more. I belong to Grizz. I can only hope he wants me.

It's time to show him my true feelings. Now or never.

I lead him to the bed. Another time it'd be amusing how our roles are reversed. I'm leading; he's following. After today, I might never be so bold again. I'm shaking now, facing Grizz, smoothing the button-down shirt I'm wearing. After this he might decide he doesn't want me. He might kiss my forehead, call Declan and Parker, and send me away forever. I don't know what he wants. Either way, he'll know my choice.

"I want to show you something," I repeat.

He reaches for me and I step back.

"Kit, you're scaring me."

"Don't be afraid," I tell myself as much as him. My fingers fumble with the buttons on my shirt. "I don't know if it's too soon, but I want you to see."

"Jordy, what—" I part my shirt and his eyes drop to my revealed flesh. Wincing at the bite of the tape, I peel the bandage away from my tattoo.

Grizz's eyes widen and I let my hands drop. I straighten, letting him see what I drew for the artist, what I chose to put on my body. Over my heart, covering the ugly scar tissue.

"Kit," Grizz swallows, not taking his eyes off my tattoo. The flesh around the ink is red. It's still healing, but there's no mistaking the design. A bear print.

"Is that—?"

I nod slowly.

"Kit." Such warm depths in his voice, I can sink happily. I can drown. He touches the ink stain, gently. I jolt as if electrified. "Did you get this for me?"

"Yes. I want your mark."

He lets out a shaky breath.

"I want to belong to you. That is, if you'll have me." I bow my head, partly in submission, partly because I can't bear to look into his eyes.

Slowly, as if a sudden movement will frighten me, he extends his hand. I hold my breath as he spreads his hand over the mark. His touch is light but burns, a heat spreading through my body.

"Look at me," he orders. My eyes snap to his. I force myself to keep breathing as his bright gaze swallows me. "You wear my mark."

"Yes."

"You belong to me."

I nod. Everything I want to say clogs my throat, choking me up.

"Yes." He seizes me. Fisting my hair, he draws my head back, lips sucking on my pulse until they release me with a pop. "Yes."

My body instantly goes soft, my natural instinct for submission flaring to life with his commanding touch. I feel my pulse beating everywhere—at my throat, behind my knees. Between my legs.

"Grizz."

He palms my backside, squeezing it roughly. In a flash, I'm up in the air, legs straddling his waist as he nips at my breast through my shirt. I arch into him, offer myself to his plunder.

"Little fox," he murmurs, shoving my bra down to get at my nipple. "My Kit." He uses his teeth on my nipple as he settles me on my back on the bed. I reach up to tangle my hands in his hair, but he grasps them, pinioning them above my head with one hand. I smile and wriggle, loving his domination.

His grin is feral. "You like that, little fox? You need me to hold you down while I make you scream?" He's back to work on my nipple, worrying it with his teeth, flicking it with his tongue, sucking so hard I feel the answering tug right between my legs.

He unhooks my bra and pulls it and my open shirt off. Then he returns to my breasts. He kisses a circle around the tattoo, his facial hair brushing against the tender skin and making me shiver.

"Does that hurt, baby?"

"I like the hurt," I tell him, voice thick with lust. My skin tingles everywhere with delicious sensation. My senses are on overload: the weight of Grizz pressing down on me, his intoxicating smell in my nostrils, his slow thrusts in the notch between my legs. All the while, his tongue circles my neglected nipple, flicking, teasing.

He sucks this one, too, and I choke on a cry, arching into his mouth.

Grizz thrusts against me, hard, almost like he couldn't help it.

"Fuck, Kit. You don't know what you do to me," he growls, shifting to palm my mons. I moan and rock my pelvis into his hand to get pressure on my clit. He slides his hand inside my panties and fingers my wet folds.

"Is all this wetness for me?"

"Yes," I breathe, wrapping my legs around his back to encourage him into the position I crave.

He screws one finger into me, then another as I squirm and gasp. Submission falls away as I grow more desperate. I twist my head and nip at his arm, trying to drive him into giving me what I need.

He chuckles. "Are you getting nippy little fox? I might have expected that more from a cat shifter. Or were you begging for a spanking?"

I smile up at him. It feels like a naughty smile—one I didn't even know I was capable of. He grins back, rolling me over to my belly and slapping my ass. He drags my skirt and panties off and delivers five more slaps before he strokes my wet slit again.

I shiver with pleasure and roll my hips.

"You like it from behind, Kit?"

I never really considered my own likes before. I enjoyed submitting, so I liked whatever pleased my master. That's still true. Anything Grizz wants from me I would offer in a heartbeat. It would bring me genuine joy to please him. But what do I like? Do I want it from behind?

"Yes," I answer honestly. Because it sounds delicious. But also, "I like it any way with you, Grizz. I want it every way." There I go making demands. Again, so not like me.

And yet I know Grizz wants to hear.

He shucks his clothes quickly and climbs over me, palming my butt with both hands and squeezing. There's no need for a condom. Shifters don't have sexual diseases and my bear is claiming me. So he wouldn't be afraid of putting a cub in me.

Or a kit.

"Spread your legs, Jordy." Grizz's voice is thick with desire. The sound of a deep rumble makes my pussy clench.

I part my thighs to make room for his massive length and he lines up with my entrance.

"Who do you belong to?" he demands, right before he plows into me.

My muscles squeeze around his thick member and I

lose my breath—not because it hurts. It's more the sensation of being filled so fully startles me.

But it also feels so right.

"You, Grizz. I belong to you." Tears sting my eyes at the honor of being claimed by this male. This brave, strong, loyal male.

He arcs in and out of me, filling and emptying me and every stroke brings new bliss. I turn my face into the pillows and moan softly. Grizz wraps his hand in my hair and lifts my head, leaning over to mate our mouths. His tongue twines with mine in a hectic, sideways kiss and then he's ramming into me, slapping my butt with his loins, getting deeper with every thrust.

My moans take on a higher pitch—a keen—and desire starts to coil into restless need. "Please, Grizz. Claim me. Oh please."

"Fates yes, I'll claim you," he growls, slamming even harder—harder than I would've thought possible.

I sob in ecstasy as he splits me in two, shatters me. He releases my hair and wraps a large hand around my nape to hold me in place for his brutal thrusts.

His movements grow jerky, breath short. "Fuck, Kit. Fuck! You better come now, little fox." He slams in doubly hard for four more thrusts and then stays deep. I swear I feel the hot stream of his cum fill me as I shake and squeeze and scream out my own release.

Stars explode behind my eyes. Pleasure engulfs me. I sink into the total ecstasy of release.

I barely register Grizz pulling out and carrying me into the shower.

~

Grizz

TAKING care of Jordy satisfies me as much as claiming her. I love the way she trusts me completely. There's no resistance, no walls up. She stands under the spray of the water and lets me suds her from head to toe.

She's still blissed out from her orgasm. Almost as drugged as the subs look leaving Toxic. Which is a relief, because I'm not sure I'm into giving her much more pain than a few spanks to color her ass.

I turn off the water and climb out. "Wait here, Kit. I'll get you a towel."

She nods, eyes still glazed, cheeks flushed pink from the steam and heat. I grab a towel, cursing inwardly that I don't have any newer, softer towels. My little fox deserves something more luxurious against her delicate skin. I dry her off, then pull her back into the bedroom to get under the covers.

Yeah, I want to cuddle.

Me.

It's fucking strange, but beautifully true.

"I want you to draw me something," I tell her. "Anything. I want your mark on my body."

"I thought you said bears don't mark their mates."

I smile under her fingers. "This one does."

She smiles back, a little quirk of her mouth. "I'll draw you something."

"Or lots of things. I can cover all my scars."

"But I love your scars." With an impish wrinkle of her nose, she kisses down my chest, settling between my legs and browsing with her mouth at the slash across my abs until my body is tight and drawn up to the point of her mouth. Then and only then do her lips brush my cock. Her backside sways as she gets to work.

"Kit," I grate out. No, she's not a kit. She's a beautiful, full-grown female fox.

A vixen.

CHAPTER 15

rizz

A CRY WAKES ME. Jordy thrashes in my arms, fighting demons in her sleep.

I shake her gently. "Shh, baby, wake up."

She gasps and her eyes fly open, round and wide. "Grizz?"

"It's okay, shh." I rock her in my arms, feeling helpless. I wish I could fight the ones who prey on her in her nightmares. *Never again,* I vow. *No vampire will touch you again.*

She cries in my arms and I grope for the light, desperate. My hand falls on the sketch book.

"Here." I turn so she's in my lap and place the book in hers, along with the pencils. "Draw it."

"What?" She sniffles.

"You keep having nightmares," I explain. "You don't have to tell me what they are."

"I can't." She wipes her face. "I would if I could, but I don't fully remember. Just bits and pieces."

"It's okay. Draw it. Get it out."

A pause, then a shuddering sigh blows through her. Her pencil scratches over paper. I avert my gaze to give her privacy. No need to see what she draws until she's willing to show me.

I hold her like that until she murmurs she's done and sets the notebook aside. Then I curl up around her and hold her until her breathing evens and I know she's asleep.

MY BEAR WAKES me close to dusk. I know the hour even though no light reaches us in the bedroom. A lifetime of hunting vampires has trained me to come alert before nightfall. Time to be up and on the hunt.

For the first time, I don't want to move. I've got a beautiful vixen in my arms.

She's a restless sleeper, twitching and frowning, worry lines moving across her face like clouds. She slept still enough after I fucked her, though.

I wait until she whimpers to wake her. "Jordy? Wake up, baby. You're having a bad dream."

She comes awake with a strangled gasp. "Grizz?"

"I'm here." I snuggle her closer. "You're safe with me."

Her whole body instantly relaxes. I tip her back and brush her hair from her brow. "Another nightmare, Kit?"

With a sigh, she nods.

"You wanna draw it?"

"I'm okay." She burrows deeper into my hold. "I feel safe with you."

"I'm glad."

"I never thought I'd feel that way. Not in a hundred million years," she continues in a small voice.

My forehead creases. What the fuck did Augustine do to her, that she's tormented every time she sleeps?

"What time is it?" She stretches and yawns.

"Close to dusk. Maybe a little after. I gotta go."

"Do you have to?" She wriggles against me, waking delicious memories. And a monster—the one in my pants.

"Careful, Kit," I growl. She giggles and I kiss her, swallowing her laughter.

"All right, enough." I roll out of bed. "Rise and shine. Up and at 'em." I swat her as she dances from the bed into the direction of the bathroom. I want to pull her back to bed.

No! Bad bear. I need to head to the Fight Club to grab Benny, and take him to Frangelico for questioning. This hunt is close to being over. I can feel it.

I shake out the bed sheet and something flops to the floor. Jordy's sketch pad. I go to grab it when an image on the page hits my eye. I recoil like it's a rattlesnake.

"What is it?" Jordy asks from the doorway. She's wearing nothing but her button-down shirt, and it's not buttoned down. A second ago I would've been tempted.

I snatch up the sketch pad, holding it in the lamplight. I wasn't mistaken. The image is clear—the one-eyed vampire.

"Grizz? What is it? What's wrong?"

I keep my back to her. It's too much to reconcile: the woman I love and the object of my hate. I never told her what he looked like. Did she know all along? Did Augustine know?

I can't stop my thoughts from taking a dark turn. It's too much of a coincidence that the monster haunting Jordy's nightmares is my mother's murderer.

Is it possible Jordy's playing me? No. Not consciously —the vampires are pulling the strings. Is she a plant?

It makes sense. She's the perfect bait. Augustine saw me slavering over her at Toxic, and conspired with my enemy to lure me out. At any moment, she could make a call and bring the vampires here. She just has to wait until this place is home to her, then she can invite them over the threshold.

No. Stop. This is Jordy we're talking about. She couldn't betray me. Could she?

I turn and the look on my face makes her back away.

"Grizz?" She glances from me to the sketch pad, hesitant and uncertain.

"What is this?" I hold the sketch in front of her face, my voice intentionally cold. "Why did you draw this?"

She shakes her head, her fingers trace the drawing lightly. "You said I should draw my nightmares."

I drop the book and grasp her shoulders. "Who is he? Is Augustine in league with him?"

"Grizz, please—"

"Answer me!" I roar, even as my bear protests my rough treatment of her.

"I don't know," she cries. "I don't know who he is. He's

in my dreams. I don't remember. Augustine brought me to him, and I think they…I don't remember."

"Are you lying to me?" I tip her head back.

Tears hit her eyes. "I've never lied to you."

She's telling the truth. I sniff her over and can't sense a lie. She might still be a pawn in this, but that's not her fault.

"I'm sorry." I back away. She tips her face up, pleading, but I can't touch her, reassure her. I run my hand through my hair instead. "I was wrong. I didn't mean to hurt you. I just saw—" I gesture to the image. Fuck, my heart's racing.

She picks the sketch pad up. "What is it? You're scaring me."

"That's the vampire that killed my mother." I stare at the face that haunts me. I haven't seen his image in over fifteen years.

The blood drains out of Jordy's face. She looks as tortured as I feel. "I didn't know." She sinks on the bed, the sketch pad in her lap, damning image on display.

Of course she didn't. I've got to think clearly. Rationally. If I'm not the hunter, then I'm the prey.

I rub a hand over my face and clear my throat. "When did you meet him? Do you know?" There, that's rational. Ask questions, figure things out. I'm Sherlock fucking Holmes.

Jordy hesitates. Her face twists in painful memory. When she speaks, she looks at the image. "It was recently. The past few months. I was blindfolded at first, but then they…got into things."

"Sexual?" I ask, my voice cold, clinical.

She winces. "And other things. They fed. Just my pulse

points at first but then—" she gestures to her heart. "I don't remember that part."

Makes sense. Heart blood is the most potent, but the most dangerous to take. Easy to kill your victim.

"Do you remember anything else?" She hesitates and I growl. "Jordy. Tell me now."

"I felt like I was dying," she whispers and my heart seizes. I'm an asshole, forcing her to remember. But I need to know. Everything I've worked for is at stake. "The vampires drank and drank, and I thought I would die. I passed out a few times. When I came to, they were giving me blood. Their blood."

What. The. Fuck. Vampires sharing blood? With a shifter? Sounds like my arrangement with Frangelico. But why would they do that for Jordy?

When I ask, she shakes her head. "I don't know. But it healed me. The blood made me feel strong again. But later, Augustine told me I'd failed. That I was too weak. He hated me after that."

"So you tried to forget that night." Until I made her remember. Yeah, I'm an asshole, but it's time she knew. I've been playing house with a cute little fox for too long. Playtime's over.

I tug the sketch pad from her hands and rip out the image of my enemy. A quick page through doesn't reveal anymore telling images. I pause a moment on a sketch of my face, drawn lovingly, scars softened. "Kit—" the word sticks in my mouth. I swallow the endearment down. Gotta stay cool. No heart. No emotion. Nothing but the hunt.

I toss the pad on the bed next to her. "I'm going out.

Stay." I put enough dominance into the order to root her to the spot.

"Grizz—"

"I mean it." If she leaves and Augustine finds her, he'll get her to lead him straight to me. The hunter becomes the hunted. Not if I can help it. Once Frangelico and I question Benny, the truth will come out. Frangelico will give me enough blood to take out the one-eyed vampire and company. I just have to focus. That means getting a seductive fox out of my head.

With that thought, I head out of the bedroom without a second glance.

"Grizz," she cries.

I stop in the doorway but don't turn. "What?"

"I'm sorry."

I make an impatient gesture. A sob hits my ears as I walk out, but I harden my heart. Stone cold hunter, hell bent on trapping his prey. I forgot for a moment, but it's time for us both to learn: there's no room in my heart for anything but revenge.

CHAPTER 16

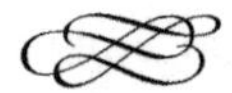

rizz

My cell rings just as I climb onto my bike. I answer with a grunt.

"Where have you been?" Parker snaps. "I've been fielding calls all day from the wolf pack. They want to know when you're returning to the Fight Club to collect the package you left."

"On my way right now. Meet me there. I need your car to transport the package."

Trey is waiting for me by the back door when I roll up.

"You here to collect the leech?"

"Yep." I resist the urge to lift the dumpster lid and check on Benny. Don't want him burning to death too soon. "Just waiting on transport."

Trey offers me a beer while I wait. At my startled expression he shrugs. "You threw a match. Won the pack a ton of money. I think everyone's pretty much forgiven you. Everyone but Caleb. He wanted to beat your ass."

"That bear has too much crazy in him. It would've been bloody."

"Who was that redhead, anyway?"

I shake my head. The fewer people know who Jordy is, the better. I know there's another fox shifter in town—or at least half fox. She's mated to one of the wolves, but things are too hot to introduce them. Keeping Jordy safe is way more important than building her social life.

"Wouldn't have guessed there's anyone in the world you cared about," Trey muses.

So much for hiding my feelings. Fates, I gotta figure out what to do with Jordy.

"If I needed safe passage for someone out of town, could the wolves provide it?"

His eyes light. "A favor?"

I swallow my pride. "Yeah."

He stares a moment, then shakes his head. "No favor required. Not if you're helping someone out of the goodness of your heart."

A day ago I'd say I was helping Jordy for the benefit of my dick. Now, I'm not so sure.

We wait in silence. The white Camaro appears as the last fingers of daylight loosen their grip on the mountains.

Trey and I load Benny's still body into the trunk of the Camaro to the soundtrack of Parker's griping.

"This is a new car! Well, new-ish. We just got it cleaned!"

I slam down the hood, silencing the complaints. "See ya around," I say to Trey.

"Yeah," the werewolf rubs the back of his neck, slaps the trunk, and disappears into the Fight Club. If everything goes right, I might not be back here again.

If everything goes wrong, I'll be dead.

"Grizz? Ya ready or what?" Declan calls.

"Yeah." I pivot on my boot and point to Laurie. "You take my bike. The rest of you, into the car." I tromp to the driver's side and glare at Parker until he scrambles out of the seat.

The club looms in the rearview mirror until I turn out of the parking lot and gun it, ignoring the further protests of the shifter Stooges.

No more nostalgia.

I've got vampires to catch, and a murderer to kill.

"WHERE ARE WE GOING?" Declan asks.

"Frangelico."

There's a flurry of frantic activity in the back seat. "We can't go there! He'll kill us!"

"Pull over," Declan shouts, grabbing the wheel.

I do. "What the fuck?"

Laurie and Parker are already out on the sidewalk.

"We made a bet that you'd win the fight."

"So?"

"So we might have borrowed a wee bit of money to do it."

I sigh. "And you borrowed from Frangelico. You don't need me to tell you that was fucking stupid."

"You were supposed to win the match!"

My hands tighten on the steering wheel. I gotta get Benny to Frangelico now. Every second that passes is another chance for the one-eyed vampire to get away.

"Get in the car," I order. "I'll put a word in with Frangelico for you."

"Really?" Parker perks up. "You'd do that?"

"He won't kill you on my watch. Won't even bleed you." They'll just be in his debt, which is arguably worse.

We pull up to the mansion and I park in front of the gate.

"Tell Laurie to park my bike out here," I order before exiting and grabbing Benny out of the trunk. The sucker gurgles as I arrange him over my shoulder. He better not drool blood on me.

"And you'll talk to Frangelico about our debt?"

"Yep." I wave without looking back. I flag the attention of a lookout camera and tip Benny into view.

The gates creak open and I jog up the hill. Benny feels lighter. Loss of blood? Vampire anatomy is so weird.

This time, no guards greet me at the front door. The king trusts me. Or he's impatient to get his claws into Benny. Or fangs.

"Don't envy you, sucker," I mutter to the unconscious vampire as the front door swings open.

Frangelico appears in the foyer, dressed in jeans and a white button-down shirt. It's the most casual I've seen him. "Is this for me?" He rolls up his shirt sleeves. I'm about to point out that white is a bad color for what we're about to do when Benny gurgles and jerks. The stake falls out and my burden starts to thrash.

"Shit, he's waking up."

Frangelico is by my side in a flash. Literally. I didn't see him move. He didn't even blur. *Shit, fast vampire!* My defenses stutter while Frangelico grabs his sired.

"Shh, I got you," the king croons as if he's holding his child. Which, in a way, he is. Benny's eyes flutter and land on the king's face, where they widen in terror. A moan breaks from the smaller vampire when he realizes who's holding him.

"Good evening, Benedict," Frangelico says in the fucking creepy crooning voice of his. "Have you been a bad boy?"

I turn away before I barf, just in time to miss Frangelico breaking Benny's arm. The lesser vampire screams, but the king just lifts him. "Get the door, will you?" Frangelico asks me and I scramble. "We'll finish this in the dungeon."

It takes less than an hour for Benny to break. Usually I'd get involved, but the way Frangelico tortures his own is too much for me. I've given plenty of beatings—taken them too—but Frangelico uses both emotional torment and physical pain that's beyond what I can stand. Plus his dungeon is full of medieval torture devices—actually from the Middle Ages. Fucking creepy. Benny thinks so, too, because he spills everything about the coup against Frangelico and all the players involved. Pretty much all of Frangelico's sired were planning to overthrow him. When he finds that out, Frangelico drops all pretense about caring for Benny, and gets really cruel.

I almost pity the vampire victim. But then Benny screams something out about "Augustine's fox."

"What was that?" I lean closer to Benny's face. No need to look down his body at what Frangelico's doing.

"Augustine has a pet. He said you took her. He said he needed her back."

"Did he say why?"

Benny shakes his head frantically.

"What about the one-eyed vampire," I ask. "How is he involved?"

"He wanted the fox back too. The experiment is over, they said, but they still wanted the fox back. Something about hiding evidence."

"Experiment? What experiment?"

Frangelico does something and Benny screams. "I don't know! They don't tell me everything."

I nod to Frangelico and he makes Benny scream some more, but we don't get anything else about the one-eyed vampire. Just the location of their secret club—behind the basement door where I cornered Benny.

Finally, Frangelico announces that we've gotten enough for tonight.

"Join me for a drink?" he invites. As he leaves, he caresses Benny's limp hand. "I'll be back for you later." At Benny's whimper, we leave.

"I gotta go," I tell Frangelico after we've washed up.

The king's shirt is covered in Benny's blood, but he doesn't seem to mind. He washes his hands and inspects his nails as if he spent the last hour getting a fucking manicure.

"In a minute," Frangelico says.

"Now," I growl. Every second here gives the vampires a chance to clear out of their club.

"I promise to make it worth your while."

Okay then. I follow the king into his living room.

"What are you going to do with your sired?" I ask. The king ignores me, going to the bar and pouring two glasses of whiskey. I accept mine but don't drink.

Frangelico drinks his in one gulp and pours another. Is he trying to get drunk? Do vampires even get drunk? Shit, I don't have time to play drinking games.

Before I can bow out, Frangelico murmurs, almost to himself.

"Do you have any idea how hard it is to sire a vampire? What's involved?"

I shrug. "Blood exchange."

"Yes. A careful, constant feeding. The number of exchanges varies. Too many and you weaken the victim. Too few and the virus doesn't take hold. Oh yes," he takes my shock for interest. "Vampirism is a virus. After all the exchanges are done to ensure the victim is primed enough to accept the virus, it's time for the final step. The sire kills them. The heart must stop and the victim must die. Only then can the virus take over. It takes heart's blood. The deepest, richest, and most deadly blood of all. The victim spills their heart's blood, the sire replaces it.

"It's excruciating," he whispers, studying the color of

his drink. "Waiting by your youngling's side, not knowing if they will rise again. If you snuffed their life out before its time.

"Of all the sins on my head, the deaths of my children are why I am damned. But damnation is a small price to pay to avoid the long penance: eternal life." He sets down the glass with a clink. Again, he's murmuring so softly I wonder if it's meant for my ears. "I will live forever, alone."

Lucius Frangelico, all-powerful king of the vampires, is lonely.

Enough of this. I'm not his therapist. I drain my glass and set it down on the bar with a clink.

"I'm going after the one-eyed vampire," I say. "I need blood. Lots of it."

Without another word Lucius goes to his bar and draws out a small cooler.

"Here," he says. I take the cooler's handle but he doesn't let go. "This is more than I've ever given you. Use it wisely. Drinking all of this could—"

"Kill me, yeah, yeah. I know."

He raises a brow and I realize I just mocked a vampire king. After a second he smiles and I relax.

"I was going to say 'bring a person back from the dead'. That's another use of vampire blood—did you know? Vampire blood—the most healing substance on earth." He picks up his glass and murmurs to the liquid, "The humans would hunt and breed us, if they knew."

I wait until he's finished swallowing before saying, "One more thing…"

"Yes?"

"The shifters who borrowed money from you. To place on me during the fight."

"Yes? What about them?"

Fuck. How do I say this? "They're...they're my friends."

The vampire king grins broader. It is not a pretty sight. "And you're telling me this because..."

"Because I like my friends." It better not get back to the Stooges that I said any of this. "I'd be very upset," I enunciate carefully, "if any of them got hurt."

"Ah. I see." The vampire laughs. "You've been hanging out with vampires too long. Learning the art of the subtle threat." He bends to the mini fridge and fills his drink with ice while I grit my teeth. I'm this close to saying a stake isn't so subtle when he shrugs.

"I have no interest in killing any of my debtors. You can't squeeze blood from a stone. Or a dead shifter." He gives me one of his chilling smiles. "If they cannot repay me, they will simply owe me a favor."

I suppress a shudder. The Stooges might be better off dead. "Got it."

"I wish you well on your hunt."

I'm halfway to the door before I remember my original question. "And your sired? What are your plans?"

The king has moved to a spot in front of his French doors, looking out on the portico. Without turning he waves his hand. "Finish your quest. Have your revenge."

"Don't worry, I'm planning on it. But if I run across Augustine and the rest of your sired, do I have permission to deal with them?"

"If they have turned against me, they are no longer under my protection. You may kill them. Kill them all."

I leave him looking out at the night sky. I have a feeling he won't move for a long time.

CHAPTER 17

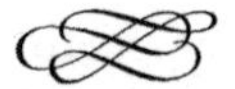

ordy

"BUCK UP, lass, it's not so bad," Declan says. He and the other two have been trying to cheer me up since picking me up from Grizz's house. "You get to spend the day with us."

I stare out the car window but see nothing except Grizz's angry face.

"Here we are," Declan sings as Parker pulls into a trailer park. Each lot holds a single wide, a patch of gravel for a yard and, towering over everything, a palm tree. "Home sweet home."

The guys pour out of the car, carrying bags of takeout. I follow more slowly, rubbing my aching tattoo.

I thought Grizz and I shared something. I thought maybe, he'd give us a chance. We could be together if he'd just choose me.

But he didn't, and I shouldn't be surprised. My family threw me away. I give my all, and it means nothing.

As I enter the trailer, Parker's on the phone. When the grey-haired shifter sees me, he ducks out of the room.

"Kit, come on." Laurie waves at me to sit by him on a threadbare couch.

I try to follow Parker and Declan pops up in front of me. "Want some beer? Or some of this?" He holds up a flask and pries off the top. "My own brew." He takes a swig and coughs until his eyes redden and water. "Delicious," he gasps. Laurie jumps up and pounds him on the back.

I take the offered flask. Looks a lot like Grizz's. I sniff the top and the fumes scald my nose. Parker returns and I hand the flask back to Declan.

"Was that Grizz?" I ask Parker eagerly.

The grey-haired shifter won't meet my eyes. "It was. Says he's left Frangelico, and he's on the hunt."

The hunt. Of course. "Did he ask about me?"

"He said we should get you out of town, and quickly."

I suck in a breath. I was expecting this, but not so soon. But why not? Grizz doesn't want me. He just wants revenge.

"It doesn't have to be tonight," Parker continues gently. "But soon."

"It's all right," I say. "I can go."

"No, no, lass." Declan throws his arm around my shoulders. "Kick back. Stay awhile."

For the next few hours, I sit on the couch and watch reruns on the television with a digital antenna taped to the window. Every so often the channel cuts out. Declan and Laurie take turns kicking the console until it flickers back to life.

"You didn't eat your burger." Parker nudges me.

"Can I eat it?" Declan asks, and Laurie smacks him.

"S-stop it. She's s-s-sad."

The three of them look at me.

"It's okay." I force a tiny grin. "Here, you can have my food."

As I pass the wrapped sandwich over, headlights flare in the window, and then cut out.

"We expecting anyone?" Declan asks. Laurie shrugs. Parker heads to the door while I hop up and rush to the window. Could it be Grizz?

Hope withers when I see the sleek black sedan with tinted windows. A chill pours into my blood.

The vampires are here.

~

Grizz

Fuck, where are these vampires? The basement is empty. So is the theater, even though someone's been here since I last searched. A spotlight is on, directed at a single wooden chair set in the center of the stage.

On the chair is a tattered teddy bear with one button eye missing. The torso is stained with old blood, and when I pick it up one of the legs falls off. Lovely. A nice little threat left by the one-eyed vampire, just for me.

I take a sniff to get the fucker's scent, and my blood runs cold. The stuffed toy smells like vampire… and Jordy.

I leave the bear and theater and mount my bike. I'm deep in the hunt now, and nothing's gonna stop me. Good thing Frangelico gave me a cooler to keep his blood in. When I find the nest, I'll be ready.

~

Jordy

"WHO IN THE HELL—" Parker starts to open the door and I tackle him.

"Get down," I hiss at the others.

"Jordy? What—"

"Shh." I cover Parker's mouth. "You can't let them hear."

"Who?"

"Vampires," I mouth to him and his eyes go round.

"Little fox, little fox, let me come in." It's Augustine. He's come for me.

A blow to the trailer makes us jump. A long tearing sound rips down the trailer, from one end to the other. A pause, and it begins again.

"What's that?" Declan whispers. "What's he doing?"

I hold my breath as the ripping and wrenching continues. It sounds like he's tearing the siding off the trailer. I feel like a sardine in a tin can.

"I'll tear this trailer apart, bit by bit," Augustine explains calmly. "Your friends won't like my remodeling much. Pity. So much work on my part, unappreciated. No matter. If I get hungry, I can always grab a little human snack."

I close my eyes. He's here, unchecked, in the trailer park. He won't hesitate to kill a human. He thinks they're lower than bugs.

"What do ya want?" Declan shouts before Laurie grabs a pillow and shoves it in his face.

"I only want what's mine. The bear stole her, but she belongs to me."

No. Not anymore. I belong to Grizz. Or I did, until he left. I clutch the tender skin over my heart. The scars the vampires gave me, and the paw print I chose for myself.

I can be a victim. Or I can choose.

"It's up to you, slave," Augustine snaps. "Give me what I want, or—" The door shudders. Once, twice, and then it's still.

"It's like three little piggies," Declan mutters.

"Shhhhhh," Parker and Laurie hiss.

I wait with my hand over my heart. One, two, three heartbeats. My heart beats for Grizz, and now he's gone. I gave him my all, but I have one thing I can give.

I stand up, ignoring Parker's desperate cry, "No!", and open the door.

"I'm here."

I step outside.

~

Grizz

I'M SITTING at a light when I realize my pocket's vibrating. I pull out my phone and answer with an annoyed grunt.

"They took her!"

Chills run up my arms. "Who? Jordy?"

"The vampires! They came and—" a muffled sound like the phone was dropped.

"Declan? Parker?" I grit my teeth and my phone cracks. Fuck, I almost broke it. I force my grip to loosen.

"Grizz?"

"Talk to me." The light turns green and some fucker in a Honda Civic honks at me. I turn and glare until the Civic creeps around me and screeches away. "What happened?"

"The vampires came. We were in the trailer, but they started to take it apart and—" he gasps, gulping air.

"And what?" I growl. I'm gonna shift into a bear in the middle of traffic if I'm not careful.

"And Jordy went out to them. She sacrificed herself. She saved us."

Jordy. No.

"The vampires have her?"

"They threw her into the trunk and drove off. We tried to follow but lost them."

"Where?" I bark, already turning my bike. "Tell me where, dammit—"

"Oro Valley."

"Fuck," I explode, and hang up. I know where they're taking her.

I turn my bike and book it. All this time hunting vampires, and they were hunting her. I left her in danger. I promised I'd keep her from the vampires, and I failed. I left her. Should've gotten her out of town when I had the chance.

Might as well gift wrapped her and given her to Augustine. And the one-eyed vampire.

The stoplight ahead turns yellow and I zoom through it as it turns red. *Hang on, little Kit.*

Gotta get to Jordy before it's too late.

I weave through traffic but get stuck behind an eighteen wheeler and have to put my foot down to steady the bike. I slam the right handle and it dents.

Does the one-eyed vampire know what she means to me? He'll kill her for sure. Shit, the teddy bear. Drenched in blood and Jordy's scent. Maybe Jordy's blood. She said she remembered him feeding on her. And then reviving her with his blood. What sick fuck feeds a shifter blood unless…unless….

Fuck. I know what the vampires are trying to do.

Shifters. That's why they're using shifters. They're—fuck, they're using slavers to supply them. The shifter slavers—they're not snatching dominants. They're snatching weak ones.

All to make a vampire army. *Do you know hard it is to make a vampire?* So hard, too hard. Too long a process—unless your victim is stronger.

They want to create more vampires. Faster. Stronger. Better. With an army they can overthrow Frangelico.

It all falls into place. And Jordy, Jordy is the key.

I've got to save her.

CHAPTER 18

ordy

I STAND NAKED on the carpet of the large bedroom. Augustine paces around me. I haven't said anything since he grabbed me in front of the trailer and shoved me into the trunk of a car. I expected him to take me to the club or back into the green room, but not here.

"Welcome home," he said as he dragged me up the walk to the house where he kept me. I bite my tongue to keep from correcting him. This was never my true home.

"Jordy," he croons now, running a finger along the back of my neck. His nail cuts me but I don't flinch. "You've been a bad slave."

I'm not your slave. I don't belong to you anymore.

"What a merry little chase you and your teddy bear led me on. I must say, I'm almost impressed."

I say nothing. My fists clench against my legs. I will not bow. I will not shiver, or break. I will not give this vampire the satisfaction.

Because he was never my master. He was a poser, a user, and he took from me what wasn't his. I never truly belonged to him.

Just a few minutes longer. Hold out until—

"Did you think you could hide forever? Did you think he'd protect you?"

"He did protect me—" I say and my head snaps to the side with Augustine's slap, a blow I expected but never saw coming. My cheek goes numb.

"He left you," the vampire sneers. "And now you're back here. Alone. Unarmed. Pitiful. Nothing more pathetic than an unowned slave."

I'm not unowned. My love may not want me, but I chose him. I wear his mark on my heart.

Oh Grizz, I wish I could see you. One last time.

My former vampire master circles me. "Kneel."

"No. I don't kneel for you."

"You belong to me."

"I don't. Not any more." And I smile. His hold over me is broken. I don't submit to anyone. Submission is a choice, and I don't choose anyone but Grizz.

"Who did she tell?"

I come face to face with my nightmare. The one eyed vampire.

For the first time in my life, I look the vampires in the

eye. I'm going to die, anyway. Might as well stand up for myself.

"She won't tell me," Augustine grits out.

"So we make her," the one-eyed vampire says, and for a moment things fade away.

I come to with Augustine slapping my face.

"It's no use. She knows nothing, and we're running out of time."

The one-eyed vampire's voice fills my head, a nightmare come to life. "Then we make sure she doesn't talk again."

And then: pain. So much pain.

Grizz

I PULL up just as a black car with dark tinted windows pulls away. Tires squeal around the corner and hideous laughter rings in my ears. Before I can give chase, a flash of red catches my eye. Down the walkway, leading from the house are red footprints, soaked with the scent of blood.

Not a good sign.

I'm off the bike and in the house in seconds. The flask burns a hole in my pocket, but instead of reaching for it, I clench my fist. I'll need every drop for the confrontation with the vampires, and something tells me that they're already gone.

Augustine's house is silent, but the scent of vampire is everywhere. My bear is out and wild. This place is silent as a fucking tomb, and something tells me this hunt won't end well.

I follow the bloody footprints backwards from the front door to the hall. They end in front of a half-open door leading to a bedroom. I push open the door. It sticks on the wet carpet, pushing through a tide of red. Blood and more blood, and just in view, a spill of red hair.

Oh no.

I stop pushing the door and enter the dark bedroom.

Jordy lies on the carpet, limbs askew. A broken, blood-stained doll for me to find. The vampires had their fun and left her.

This is my fault.

I fall to my knees and grab her hand and she whimpers. Her wrist is broken. Her eyes scan my face, wide with pain and frightened. "Grizz."

"It's okay, Kit. I'm here."

I don't bother checking her wounds. She's covered in blood. The worst tearing is over her heart, her blood leaking out with every pump. The vampires ripped her open. I want to roar and tear this place apart.

Instead I crouch beside her.

"You're here," she rasps, her fingers fumbling over my face.

"Of course I'm here." Did she think I'd stay away? Leave her to die? I shake my head. "I fucked up."

"You gotta go." She tries to raise her head and I soothe her back.

"I'm not leaving you, Jordy."

"You have to. The one eyed vampire was here. You can find him. You can track him. You can go. Have your revenge." She squeezes my fingers and lets them drop. *"Go."*

"Jordy."

"Go kill him, Grizz. Then you can be free." Her head lolls on her neck. Fuck, she's lost too much blood. Her fox is trying, but the shifter healing isn't happening fast enough.

"Don't leave me, Kit."

Her breath rattles in her lungs. "Wanted to give my life to someone," she rasps. "I'm glad it was you."

Fuck, no. It can't end this way. It can't.

I pull the flask from my pocket and fumble with the cap. Gotta be quick, there's not much time.

"Here." I put the flask to her lips. "You need to drink this." *Vampire blood—the most healing substance on earth.*

Her lips move as if to protest. I shove the bottle into her mouth and tip it. Blood pours into her mouth. Dark, rich red.

She sputters, shaking her head.

"You will," I order. "Drink it all."

I wait until she drains it and race out, return with the cooler. The blood of the vampire king—the most potent there is. If anything can heal her, this can.

"Drink," I command with all the dominance in me. I force bag after bag into her, and pour the rest over her broken body. All of the blood meant to give me revenge. Every drop.

Finally, it's done. She lies in a red pool, her eyes closed.

I wait for a long time, listening to her breath. Slow, but steady. Not much, but it's something.

I rush to find all the blankets I can and put them around her. Fates, is her chest still moving? The wounds still look bad, but there's no fresh blood leaking out of her. With any luck, the healing's begun.

"Fight through it, Kit. You can do it, little fox." I lay beside her and smooth her hair from her face. Her skin is chilled. Fuck. "You can't leave me, Jordy. You just can't. Not now. Not when I'm finally coming to my senses." Fuck, my eyes hurt. I blink a few times. Must be the strain. I haven't cried since my mother died.

But there's wet on my face when I put an arm around Jordy and press my face into her blood soaked hair. "Live, Kit. Live for me. Because, from now on, I live for you."

A slight noise and her mouth parts, her chest rising and falling. "That's it. That's right," I murmur, pressing closer. The healing has begun. "When you wake up, I'll be here. Because I choose you."

A WHIMPER WAKES ME. I open my eyes and the sun hits me in the face. It's high in the sky. Shit, I fell asleep? Jordy lies still beside me. For a horrible second I think that—but no, her chest is still moving. Her face and body are matted with dried blood, but underneath her wounds have healed.

I head to the bathroom, grab a fancy towel, and spend a few minutes washing the blood off her face and chest. About halfway through, her eyes slowly open.

"Hey." I stroke back her hair.

"Grizz? What—" her eyes flash around frantically. "What happened? Augustine—"

"He's gone. The vampires are all gone." For now. But I gotta move her soon, in case they come back.

"But, I thought—"

"I couldn't leave you, Kit. I made a mistake, but I'm not going to leave you again."

Her forehead wrinkles and I smooth the lines away. She relaxes into my touch. It's scary, how much she trusts me.

"How you feeling?"

She tries to shrug and gives a little groan.

"Easy. You're okay."

"I don't know what happened. The vampires..."

"Beat you and left you for dead."

Her hand falls, her eyes round with pain. "I remember."

"Kit, I'm so sorry."

"It's all right." She starts to struggle upright, then sits up quickly, casting a wondering glance around her. "I feel…fine." She tests the word, raising a hand in front of her face and staring at it. "Better than fine actually."

"It's the blood."

She closes her mouth. Swallows. "Blood?"

"All the blood I had. A whole cooler. Frangelico gave it to me to fight vampires."

"You gave it to me?"

"I gave it to you. I didn't know if it would heal or kill you, but you were dying anyway. I could only hope." I touch her face tenderly. "And it worked. It healed you.

Took all the blood I had, but it was worth it. It saved you."

"You used the blood," she murmurs to herself. "But, what about the vampires? The one-eyed vampire? I saw him, he was there. You can still get him—"

"No, Kit. No more. We can't stay here. I can't go back to the king. And I can't hunt the one-eyed vampire anymore. I can't risk anyone finding out about you. The vampires were trying to turn you."

"Trying to—" her brow wrinkles.

"I figured out what they were doing. All those blood exchanges. They want an army to fight Frangelico. They tried to turn you." For a horrible moment, I wondered if the blood could have turned her into a vampire. But no. Jordy's alive and her fox is strong. The blood did its healing work.

"Grizz." She touches my face. "What about your revenge?"

"I don't need it. All I need is you."

She closes her eyes and lets her forehead meet mine. "I'm sorry."

"For what?"

"For ruining things. For using up all the blood. Now you can't get revenge."

"Jordy." I pull away and catch her chin. "You didn't ruin anything. You saved me. I was gonna drink that blood, fight the vampires, and die. I didn't think I had anything to live for but revenge. I was wrong." I tuck my face close to hers and whisper against her lips. "I have you." Fuck, I have to kiss her.

Her arm slides around my neck and I lift her, carrying

her swiftly out of the room. Away from the blood and gore. Away from the scene of her death and rebirth.

I get as far as the front door before I haul her against me and claim her mouth. I kiss her in the vampire's house, my hands running up and down her body, squeezing, claiming. She's soft and warm and whole. I was so fucking stupid. I could've missed this. I could've lost her forever.

A dog barks outside, a random warning. I break the kiss and Jordy puts a hand to her face, rubbed red by my stubble. She laughs at the beard burn, and I have to kiss her again.

This time she breaks away, still smiling. "We need to go."

Right. "We gotta get outta town before sundown. Out of the valley."

Her face falls and I cup her chin. "It's not like that. I'm coming with you this time. I promise this, Jordy. I will never leave you again."

"Okay," she says, looking up at me with such trust. I don't deserve her. I'll spend the rest of my life treasuring this woman, caring for her and protecting her and replacing every bad memory of vampires with a hundred good ones. She's gonna know how special she is. She's gonna know she's loved. I'll dedicate my life to it. To her.

"We'll have to be on the run for a little while. Make sure the vampires think you're dead, and I'm too devastated by your death to hunt. We'll run for a bit, but then I'm gonna take you to my place up north."

"Really?" she asks, her eyes shining.

"It's not much," I caution. "Just a cabin the woods, in

the Sierra Nevadas. No one around. Just you, me, and a bunch of trees."

"Sounds wonderful."

I shake my head. This fox. So cute. "You excited about that? Living in the woods with a grumpy bear?"

"Yes," she repeats, and laughs breathily as I tug her hair. "Yes. I'll go anywhere, Grizz, as long as it's with you."

EPILOGUE

rizz

I SIT in the old dentist chair, a half smile on my face. Jordy's got her sketch pad out and she and the tattoo artist are poring over her designs.

"I was thinking the mountain right here." She uses her hand to map out the placement on my body, "and the giant saguaro with the paw prints at the bottom."

"What sort animal is that?" The artist asks. "Wolf?"

"Fox," Jordy corrects. She glances at me and I wink at her. Her hand is still resting on my bare chest, and I capture it and place it more firmly over my heart. She wrinkles her nose at me.

"Let me see what I can do." The artist takes the sketch and studies it, rubbing his goatee. He's not as good as the one in Tucson, but he'll do. We've been running for over a month now, with no sign of trouble. Tomorrow I'll take her to my cabin in the woods, but first I want to imprint my memories on my skin.

The artist turns away, and I take the opportunity to haul my mate into my lap.

"Grizz," she protests, until I kiss her breathless. I squeeze her ass through her jeans and she rubs against me, the public place forgotten.

"Love you, Kit," I tell her, because I promised myself I'd say it out loud and often.

"I know," she whispers back, and wriggles off me before the tattoo artist returns.

"Ready?" he asks.

"Yep." I keep Jordy's hand in mine as the artist starts to prep the area. "You gonna cover up all my scars?" I ask her.

She shakes her head. "Scars make us who we are." She lifts my hand and covers the spot above her left breast where she bears the scars that made her who she is.

I stroke the spot through her shirt. "What about tattoos then?"

"The marks we choose tell us where our heart is. Who we belong to."

Satisfied, I relax back into the seat. With each breath I inhale her scent. By the time the needle starts to buzz, I'm in a trance, surrounded by Jordy.

In a few hours, I'll walk out of here wearing her mark on my skin, but I don't need a tattoo to know who I belong to. The moment we met, she owned me. The ink on my skin is nothing compared to the marks she left on my heart.

The End

From the authors: Thank you dear readers for continuing to love on our bad boy alphas! We know Jordy was never reunited with Foxfire—you'll have to read on in future books for that happy family reunion. Stay tuned for Alpha's Prey, the next book in the series, featuring Caleb, the wild bear from New Mexico!

If you loved **Alpha's Secret**, please consider reviewing it or recommending to a friend—your reviews help indie authors so much.

WANT MORE? ALPHA'S PREY - CHAPTER ONE

Please enjoy this short excerpt from the next stand-alone book in the *Bad Boy Alphas* Series

Caleb

Snow crunches under my boots. I shake my head to clear the metallic scent of blood from my nose.

I'm going fucking nuts.

No. Something evil lurks in these woods. It drew me out of my cabin this afternoon, sent me hiking through the brush.

It's a prickle at the back of my neck.

The imagined scent of evil in my nostrils. I know the scent isn't real because no matter how hard I look, I find nothing.

No mauled bodies left torn at the river's edge. No screams of my mate and cub.

It could just be a figment of my memory...the nightmare. From the trauma of their still unexplained death three years ago. From spending too much time in bear form since then. I'm more beast than man these days, and I know it shows.

I heard the wolves in Tucson mutter about me when I was there for a fight last month.

That bear should've been put down after he lost his mate. He's going to hurt somebody one of these days.

It's true.

Leaving my winter hibernation to go to Arizona and fight that grizzly was stupid. I should never have let the idiot wolf Trey talk me into it. I should be holed up in my cabin for the winter. But he knew just how to poke the bear. He insinuated something dark about the grizzly I was going to fight, and damn if it didn't make me have to go sniff the asshole myself.

Just in case he's the bear who killed my family.

He wasn't. He was an ordinary grizzly shifter. Rough, like most bears, but not wrong. Not evil.

But at least I came home with the money from the fight. I was flat broke before it. I gave most of my earnings from summer construction to one of my co-workers whose little boy needed surgery, and the rest of it had dwindled. That's the shit-can of taking winters off.

So I roused myself. Drove to the desert. Made enough money to keep me in blueberries and salmon for eight months.

But now I can't settle back in. I'm out here letting my dick swing in the wind as I hike restlessly through the forest.

Another woman's gone missing.

That's part of why I can't rest.

There's a serial killer, or kidnapper, loose up here.

I reach the main road sooner than expected. I walked three miles across my land without noticing. A blue Subaru pulls around the bend. I don't recognize it, which is strange. I know most all the cars that come and go over this road, at least during winter. I stare into the SUV as it passes me, and when I see who's driving, give a low curse.

A single female. A curvy redhead with a don't-fuck-with-me look on her face. Alone, with suitcases in her car.

Shit.

The prickles on the back of my neck grow stronger.

I know where she's going. She's headed to the University of New Mexico research station. It's a small cabin ten miles out on U.S. Forest road.

I wouldn't give a shit except three single females have disappeared from this forest in the last eight months.

Three.

And I consider this to be my fucking forest. I'm the apex predator. No other creature—beast or human—should be bringing down humans.

Especially females.

I'm not charming or chivalrous, and I sure as hell have never been known as a gentleman, but protecting females is hard-wired into me.

I skirt along the ridge, watching her car. She pulls in and parks at the only convenience store in our tiny town.

Goddammit.

Looks like I'll be spending the next week playing bodyguard to the determined researcher. The one too stupid to know not to come here in March. Alone.

Especially when there's a serial killer on the loose.

Miranda

I pull in at the roadside market in Pecos to get supplies for the week.

I didn't plan on coming up here again until late spring, but my tree ring research couldn't wait. I have a paper to publish by June and to meet that deadline, I need the numbers now.

Dr. Alogore's voice still rings in my head. *"Another delay, and you lose funding. Get the numbers, now."*

When I argued that it was March, still winter in our Sangre de Cristo mountains, the southernmost tip of the Rockies, and—

"I don't see your fellow researchers asking for the same type of special treatment for their projects."

My cheeks heat as he smirks at me. Around the table my fellow researchers, all male, smirk with him. I don't need to look around to know they're all laughing internally at me. They mirror everything Dr. Alogore says or does. They even wear what he wears—right down to the fashion offensive plaid tie and brown Dockers.

"Fine," I mutter, dropping my eyes to my yellow folder. It's a bright spot of color in a drab room, and I chose it to give me a spark of joy in my otherwise weary day. But today it's just yellow, the color of cowards.

"That's it, sweetheart," Dr. Alogore says to my blouse. I want to put my hand to my neckline, but stop myself in time. I feel the gaze of all my male colleagues resting on my modest sweater set. My grandma dresses less conservatively than I do, but I still

get leers like I'm in lingerie. The way these guys look at me, I feel like they're imagining me naked. Maybe they are. Yeah, I have big breasts. The rest of me is pretty curvy too. That doesn't mean I should be treated any differently.

"If that's all, let's head out to lunch. My treat," the professor says. Everyone murmurs gratefully except me. Dr. Alogore prefers lunch joints where the women dance on tables.

I grab my folder and scurry into the hall.

"Hey, Miranda," one of my tall colleagues separates himself from the Dockers-wearing pack and comes to breathe down my neck. I turn and get a faceful of onion breath. He smiles like a shark, his eyes on my chest. "I'll come up and help you collect that data."

Ew.

"No, thank you," I mutter and pull my cardigan closed. I'm not even baring cleavage. These guys are just creepers.

"Come on. I can help. It's scary up there in the mountains this time of year," he says with false concern. "We go up there together, and I can help you grab everything in record time. You can buy me dinner afterwards, to thank me." His grin gets bigger. "I can help you with the findings, and we'll split the credit, half and half."

And there it is. A blatant grab for my research.

"Ugh, no thank you." I hunch my shoulders and hug the folder to my front. "What, you think you can swoop in at the last minute and I'll let you put your name above mine on the paper?"

He shrugs. "Makes sense, alphabetically—"

"No. I got this." I duck my head and walk as fast as my legs can carry me. No one is cheating me out of my research. Not this time.

This paper could make the difference between another shitty year as a postdoc in Dr. Alogore's lab and getting an actual professorial position somewhere. Anywhere. Of course, a professor position still won't guarantee me respect in my field. I've seen enough women in science have their careers belittled on a daily basis to know I'll be fighting for my equal rights every step of the way. Probably until the day I retire.

Never give up, never give in. That's my motto.

I get out in Pecos and grab my empty canvas shopping bags to fill. Inside, I blink as my eyes adjust to the dimly lit, somewhat depressing market. I've been here before, so I know what to expect, but it still makes my skin crawl. Unswept concrete floors, ancient canned goods with old-fashioned price tags. Like any convenience market near an entry to a U.S. Forest, it carries extremely overpriced gas station fare. Loaves of Wonder Bread for almost five bucks, eight dollar jars of peanut butter.

I packed my own non-perishables in Albuquerque, so I head to the refrigerator case to grab a jug of milk, some eggs, bacon, and butter. That should be enough to get me by for the five days I plan to be up here.

I bring them up to the counter where an ancient man is talking to a local. He ignores me for a solid two minutes before he slowly drags the eggs toward the register while still gabbing away.

I clear my throat.

His companion, equally old, says goodbye and shuffles out. The owner turns and eyes me speculatively. Yes, his eyes drop to my cleavage. "What brings you up here, young lady? Isn't the right time of year for fishing or hiking."

"I'm headed to the research lab for a few days," I say politely. It's the exact same conversation we had last time I was here. Granted, that was six months ago, but still. I doubt they get a ton of women camping or hiking alone.

"Oh right, right. University of New Mexico, aren't you?"

"Yes."

He stops punching numbers into the cash register and squints at me. "You be careful up there alone. You've heard about the missing women?"

I push away the dread that ripples through me. The only thing to fear is fear itself. Right?

"I've heard, yes. But I've got my dog with me. And he's very protective."

That may or may not be true. I have a furry German / Australian Shepherd mix who loves to play fetch. But he does have a ferocious-sounding bark.

"Well, you might have to protect your dog. You do know we have a bear problem in this forest, don't you?"

Right, the bear problem. He told me about it the last time I was up here. As an ecologist, I rather dislike when humans presume the animals are the problem. Wouldn't our overpopulation and the shrinkage of wildlife corridors be the actual problem?

When I was here this past summer, he leaned on the counter and squinted at me. "You be careful up here. There's a rabid bear roaming this wilderness. Tore a woman and her child to pieces a few years back."

"If he was rabid a few years ago, he'd be dead by now,

don't you think?" I hated to use science and logic as a weapon, but...please.

"Well, he may not be rabid, but he's definitely feral," the old man had claimed.

I couldn't help the scorn that must've crept over my face. "Bears can't be feral. We don't keep them as pets."

The man thumped my change down on the counter and glared at me. "Crazy, then! There's a crazy bear out there. Uncanny-like. Enormous animal with eyes that glow yellow and a real desire to destroy things. Same time that woman and her child got killed, the bear scored every tree in a three mile radius with his claws."

"Yes, yes, I've heard about your bear," I tell him now. "But you haven't had any bear problems recently, right?"

"No, it's been a few years. But something was wrong with the animal, I'm telling you. You mind your dog, or that bear might kill him just for sport—mark my words."

Right. And Bigfoot might invite me to a tea party. I wanted to argue that bear attacks are incredibly rare, and just because an animal is an apex predator doesn't mean it's out to get humans. Most animals just want to be left alone in their natural habitat. And don't get me started on the villainizing of sharks and bears and wolves in animated children's movies.

The guy points at the number on the register. "Twenty-eight twenty-two."

Yeah, like I said—overpriced.

I hand over my money and try to quell the stirring in my stomach. "Okay, I'll keep him close at all times. Thanks for the warning."

Despite the fact that I'd put my reusable bags on the

counter with the food, the guy slid all my food into plastic ones.

I take them and dump the food into my canvas sacks and hand the bags back to him. "I don't need these, thanks."

As I head out the door, I hear him call after me, "You be careful, you hear?"

"Yep, I will. Thank you!"

Inside my Subaru, Bear gives a happy bark to see me return.

I open the door and put the bags of groceries on the passenger seat while Bear lunges forward and tries to kiss my face from the back seat. "You ready to go to the cabin, boy?"

He chuffs and tries to lick some more.

I angle my face away and give him a quick head rub. "Go lie down," I tell him.

He promptly hops over the back seat into the trunk area, where I put his bed, and curls into it.

I smile into the rear view mirror. "Good boy."

Snowflakes hit my windshield, and I say a prayer to the weather gods. The weather app I checked said there'd be a light wintry mix but would clear up tomorrow. It will be chilly, but I should be able to complete my research and get home by the end of the week.

ALPHA'S TEMPTATION (BAD BOY ALPHAS, BOOK 1)

Read now

MINE TO PROTECT. MINE TO PUNISH. *MINE.*

I'm a lone wolf, and I like it that way. Banished from my birth pack after a bloodbath, I never wanted a mate.

Then I meet Kylie. *My temptation.* We're trapped in an elevator together, and her panic almost makes her pass out in my arms. She's strong, but broken. And she's hiding something.

My wolf wants to claim her. But she's human, and her delicate flesh won't survive a wolf's mark.

I'm too dangerous. I should stay away. But when I discover she's the hacker who nearly took down my company, I demand she submit to my punishment. And she will.

Kylie belongs to me.

ALPHA'S DANGER (BAD BOY ALPHAS, BOOK 2)

"YOU BROKE THE RULES, LITTLE HUMAN. I OWN YOU NOW."

I am an alpha wolf, one of the youngest in the States. I can pick any she-wolf in the pack for a mate. So why am I sniffing around the sexy human attorney next door? The minute I catch Amber's sweet scent, my wolf wants to claim her.

Hanging around is a bad idea, but I don't play by the rules. Amber acts all prim and proper, but she has a secret, too. She may not want her psychic abilities, but they're a gift.

I should let her go, but the way she fights me only makes me want her more. When she learns what I am, there's no escape for her. She's in my world, whether she likes it or not. I need her to use her gifts to help recover my missing sister—and I won't take no for an answer.

She's mine now.

ALPHA'S PRIZE (BAD BOY ALPHAS, BOOK 3)

MY CAPTIVE. MY MATE. MY PRIZE.

I didn't order the capture of the beautiful American she-wolf. I didn't buy her from the traffickers. I didn't even plan to claim her. But no male shifter could have withstood the test of a full moon and a locked room with Sedona, naked and shackled to the bed.

I lost control, not only claiming her but also marking her and leaving her pregnant with my wolf pup. I won't keep her prisoner, as much as I'd like to. I allow her to escape to the safety of her brother's pack.

But once marked, no she-wolf is ever really free. I will follow her to the ends of the Earth, if I must.

Sedona belongs to me.

ALPHA'S CHALLENGE (BAD BOY ALPHAS, BOOK 4)

How to Date a Werewolf:

#1 Never call him 'Good Doggie.'

I've got a problem. A big, hairy problem. An enforcer from the Werewolves Motorcycle Club broke into my house. He thinks I know the Werewolves' secret, and the pack sent him to guard me.

#2 During a full moon, be ready to get freaky

By the time he decides I'm no threat, it's too late. His wolf has claimed me for his mate.

Too bad we can't stand each other...

 # 3 Bad girls get eaten in the bedroom

...until instincts take over. Things get wild. Naked under the full moon, this wolfman has me howling for more.

 # 4 Break ups are hairy

Not even a visit from the mob, my abusive ex, my crazy mother and a road trip across the state in a hippie VW bus can shake him.

#5 Beware the mating bite

Because there's no running from a wolf when he decides you're his mate.

Read Now

ALPHA'S OBSESSION (BAD BOY ALPHA'S BOOK 5)

A werewolf, an owl shifter, and a scientist walk into a bar...

Sam

I was born in a lab, fostered out to humans, then tortured in a cage. Fate allowed me to escape, and I know why.

To balance the scales of justice. Right the misdeeds of the harvesters.

Nothing matters but taking down the man who made me what I am: A monster driven by revenge, whatever the cost.

Then I meet Layne. She thinks I'm a hero.

But she doesn't understand—If I don't follow this darkness to its end, it will consume me.

Layne

I've spent my life in the lab, researching the cure for the disease that killed my mom. No late nights out, no dates, definitely no boyfriend.

Then Sam breaks into my lab, steals my research, and

kidnaps me. He's damaged. Crazy. And definitely not human.

He and his friends are on a mission to stop the company that's been torturing shifters, and now I'm a part of it.

Sam promises to protect me. And when he touches me, I feel reborn. But he's hellbent on revenge. He won't give it up.

Not even for me.

Read Now

ALPHA'S DESIRE (BAD BOY ALPHA'S BOOK 6)

She's the one girl this player can't have. A human.

I'm dying to claim the redhead who lights up the club every Saturday night.

I want to pull her into the storeroom and make her scream, but it wouldn't be right.

She's too pure. Too fresh. Too passionate.

Too *human.*

When she learns my secret, my alpha orders me to wipe her memories.

But I won't do it.

Still, I'm not mate material—I can't mark her and bring her into the pack.

What in the hell am I going to do with her?

Read Now

ALPHA'S WAR (BAD BOY ALPHA'S BOOK 7)

I marked you. You belong to me.

Nash

I've survived suicide missions in war zones. Shifter prison labs. The worst torture imaginable. Nothing knocked me off my feet... until the beautiful lioness they threw in my cage. We shared one night before our captors ripped us apart.

Now I'm free, and my lion is going insane. He'll destroy me from the inside out if I don't find my mate.

I don't know who she is. I don't know where she lives. All I have is a video of her. But I'll die if I don't find her, and make her mine.

I'm coming for you, Denali.

Denali

They took me from my home, they killed my pride, they locked me up and forced me to breed. They took everything from me and still I survived.

But one night with a lion shifter destroyed me. Nash took the one thing my captors couldn't touch—my heart.

Somehow I escaped, and live in fear that they will come for me. It's killing my lioness, but I've got to hide—even from Nash. I've got to protect the one thing I have left to lose.

Our cub.

Read Now

ALPHA'S MISSION (BAD BOY ALPHAS 8)

THE MONSTER WANTS HER. HE WON'T BE DENIED.

I've become a monster.

I hear blood moving in people's veins. Scent their emotions.

I want to feed. To hunt. To mate...

I'm no longer a human--my life is over.

I've left everyone I love. I've gone rogue from the CIA.

My only hope is my handler.

Annabel gray is tough enough to face my monster. If I lose control, she won't hesitate to take me out. But I'm not the only predator out there. Someone's hunting Annabel.

She needs my protection.

But if I don't get my animal under control,

I may be her biggest threat yet.

Read Now

ALPHA'S BANE (BAD BOY ALPHAS BOOK 9)

She ruined my life, got me thrown out of the pack.
The only revenge I crave is *her*.

Trey

I never thought I'd have a girl like Sheridan. A pack princess—beautiful, smart, one of the elite. She picked me. She gave me her heart, her innocence.

Hurting her was my biggest regret. But then she betrayed us all.

Now she's back—sent to spy on our pack.

She wants revenge.

But my wolf...he just wants her.

Sheridan

He crushed my heart and broke my trust. I ruined his life.

Now we have to work together, and it's killing me.

I want to hate him. But more than that...I want his mark.

Alpha's Bane is a stand-alone second-chance shifter romance. No cheating or cliff-hangers.

Read now: *Alpha's Bane*

ALPHA'S SECRET (BAD BOY ALPHAS BOOK 10)

SHE BELONGS TO MY ENEMY. I WON'T STOP UNTIL SHE'S MINE.

Grizz:

I'm the ultimate predator. I live by a code. Hunt or be hunted. Kill or be killed.

Then I meet her. The second I catch her scent, I know she was meant for me. She was born to wear my mark and I was born to protect her.

She belonged to my enemy until I took her. He wants her back. He'll wage war to get her, but no one's taking her from me.

She's mine, and I'm not letting her go.

*This steamy stand-alone bad boy romance contains a

grumpy grizzly shifter, a beautiful fox and a whole lot of paranormal intrigue. No cheating, happily ever after guaranteed.

Read now: *Alpha's Secret*

ABOUT RENEE ROSE

USA TODAY BESTSELLING AUTHOR RENEE ROSE loves a dominant, dirty-talking alpha hero! She's sold over a half million copies of steamy romance with varying levels of kink. Her books have been featured in USA Today's *Happily Ever After* and *Popsugar*. Named Eroticon USA's Next Top Erotic Author in 2013, she has also won *Spunky and Sassy's* Favorite Sci-Fi and Anthology author, *The Romance Reviews* Best Historical Romance, and *Spanking Romance Reviews'* Best Sci-fi, Paranormal, Historical, Erotic, Ageplay and favorite couple and author. She's hit the *USA Today* list five times with various anthologies.

Please follow her on:

Bookbub | Goodreads | Instagram

Renee loves to connect with readers!

www.reneeroseromance.com
reneeroseauthor@gmail.com

WANT FREE RENEE ROSE BOOKS?

Click here to sign up for Renee Rose's newsletter and receive a free copy of *Theirs to Protect, Owned by the Marine, Theirs to Punish, The Alpha's Punishment, Disobedience at the Dressmaker's* and *Her Billionaire Boss*. In addition to the free stories, you will also get special pricing, exclusive previews and news of new releases.

OTHER TITLES BY RENEE ROSE

Vegas Underground Mafia Romance

King of Diamonds

Mafia Daddy

Jack of Spades

Ace of Hearts

Joker's Wild

His Queen of Clubs (coming May 6)

More Mafia Romance

The Russian

The Don's Daughter

Mob Mistress

The Bossman

Contemporary

Black Light: Celebrity Roulette

Blaze: A Firefighter Daddy Romance

Black Light: Roulette Redux

Her Royal Master

The Russian

Black Light: Valentine Roulette

Theirs to Protect

Scoring with Santa

Owned by the Marine

Theirs to Punish

Punishing Portia

The Professor's Girl

Safe in his Arms

Saved

The Elusive "O"

Paranormal

Bad Boy Alphas Series

Alpha's Secret

Alpha's Bane

Alpha's Mission

Alpha's War

Alpha's Desire

Alpha's Obsession

Alpha's Challenge

Alpha's Prize

Alpha's Danger

Alpha's Temptation

Alpha Doms Series

The Alpha's Hunger

The Alpha's Promise

The Alpha's Punishment

Other Paranormals

His Captive Mortal

Deathless Love

Deathless Discipline

The Winter Storm: An Ever After Chronicle

Sci-Fi

Zandian Masters Series

His Human Slave

His Human Prisoner

Training His Human

His Human Rebel

His Human Vessel

His Mate and Master

Zandian Pet

Their Zandian Mate

His Human Possession

Zandian Brides (Reverse Harem)

Night of the Zandians

Bought by the Zandians

Mastered by the Zandians

Zandian Lights

The Hand of Vengeance

Her Alien Masters

Regency

The Darlington Incident

Humbled

The Reddington Scandal

The Westerfield Affair

Pleasing the Colonel

Western

His Little Lapis

The Devil of Whiskey Row

The Outlaw's Bride

Medieval

Mercenary

Medieval Discipline

Lords and Ladies

The Knight's Prisoner

Betrothed

Held for Ransom

The Knight's Seduction

The Conquered Brides (5 book box set)

Renaissance

Renaissance Discipline

Ageplay

Stepbrother's Rules

Her Hollywood Daddy

His Little Lapis

Black Light: Valentine's Roulette (Broken)

BDSM under the name Darling Adams

Medical Play

Yes, Doctor

Master/Slave

Punishing Portia

EXCERPT: KING OF DIAMONDS BY RENEE ROSE

Want to sample a new series? Check out Renee Rose's Vegas Underground mafia books including this book, King of Diamonds.

Sondra

I TUG down the hem of my one-piece, zippered housekeeping uniform dress. The Pepto Bismol pink number comes to my upper thighs and fits like a glove, hugging my curves, showing off my cleavage. Clearly, the owners of the Bellissimo Hotel and Casino want their maids to look as hot as their cocktail girls.

I went with it. I'm wearing a pair of platform-heeled wrap-arounds comfortable enough to clean rooms in, but sexy enough to show off the muscles in my legs, and I pulled my shoulder-length blonde hair into two fluffy pigtails.

When in Vegas, right?

My feminist friends from grad school would have a fit with this.

I push the not-so-little housekeeping cart down the hallway of the grand hotel portion of the casino. I spent all morning cleaning people's messes. And let me tell you, the messes in Vegas are big. Drug paraphernalia. Semen. Condoms. Blood. And this is an expensive, high-class place. I've only worked here two weeks and I've already seen all that and more.

I work fast. Some of the maids recommend taking your time so you don't get overloaded, but I still hope to impress someone at the Bellissimo into giving me a better job. Hence dressing like the casino version of the French maid fantasy.

Dolling myself up was probably prompted by what my cousin Corey dubs, *The Voice of Wrong.* I have the opposite of a sixth sense or voice of reason, especially when it comes to the male half of the population.

Why else would I be broke and on the rebound from the two-timing party boy I left in Reno? I'm a smart woman. I have a master's degree. I had a decent adjunct faculty position and a bright future.

But when I realized all my suspicions about Tanner cheating on me were true, I packed the Subaru I shared with him and left for Vegas to stay with Corey, who promised to get me a job dealing cards with her here.

But there aren't any dealer jobs available at the moment—only housekeeping. So now I'm at the bottom of the totem pole, broke, single, and without a set of wheels because my car got totaled in a hit and run the day I arrived.

Not that I plan to stay here long-term. I'm just testing the waters in Vegas. If I like it, I'll apply for adjunct college teaching jobs. I've even considered substitute teaching high school once I have the wheels to get around.

If I'm able to land a dealer job, though, I'll take it because the money would be three times what I'd make in the public school system. Which is a tragedy to be discussed on another day.

I head back into the main supply area which doubles as my boss' office and load up my cart in the housekeeping cave, stacking towels and soap boxes in neat rows.

"Oh for God's sake." Marissa, my supervisor, shoves her phone in the pocket of her housekeeping dress. A hot forty-two-year-old, she fills hers out in all the right places, making it look like a dress she chose to wear, rather than a uniform. "I have four people out sick today. Now I have to go do the bosses' suites myself," she groans.

I perk up. I know—that's *The Voice of Wrong*. I have a morbid fascination with everything mafioso. Like, I've watched every episode of *The Sopranos* and have memorized the script from *The Godfather*.

"You mean the Tacones' rooms? I'll do them." It's stupid, but I want a glimpse of them. What do real mafia men look like? Al Pacino? James Gandolfini? Or are they just ordinary guys? Maybe I've already passed them while pushing my cart around.

"I wish, but you can't. It's a special security clearance

thing. And believe me—you don't want to. They are super paranoid and picky as hell. You can't look at the wrong thing without getting ripped a new one. They definitely wouldn't want to see anyone new up there. I'd probably lose my job over it, as a matter of fact."

I should be daunted, but this news only adds to the mystique I created in my mind around these men. "Well, I'm willing and available, if you want me to. I already finished my hallway. Or I could go with you and help? Make it go faster?"

I see my suggestion worming through her objections. Interest flits over her face, followed by more consternation.

I adopt a hopeful-helpful expression.

"Well, maybe that would be all right...I'd be supervising you, after all."

Yes! I'm dying of curiosity to see the mafia bosses up close. Foolish, I know, but I can't help it. I want to text Corey to tell her the news, but there isn't time. Corey knows all about my fascination, since I already pumped her for information.

Marissa loads a few other things on my cart and we head off together for the special bank of elevators—the only ones that go all the way to the top of the building and require a keycard to access.

"So, these guys are really touchy. Most times they're not in their rooms, and then all you have to worry about is staying away from their office desks," Marissa explains once we left the last public floor and it was just the two of us in the elevator. "Don't open any drawers—don't do anything that appears nosy. I'm serious—these guys are scary."

The doors swish open and I push the cart out, following her around the bend to the first door. The sound of loud, male voices comes from the room.

Marissa winces. "*Always knock,*" she whispers before lifting her knuckles to rap on the door.

They clearly don't hear her, because the loud talking continues.

She knocks again and the talking stops.

"Yeah?" a deep masculine voice calls out.

"Housekeeping."

We wait as silence greets her call. After a moment the door swings open to reveal a middle-aged guy with slightly graying hair. "Yeah, we were just leaving." He pulls on what must be a thousand dollar suit jacket. A slight gut thickens his middle, but otherwise he's extremely good-looking. Behind him stand three other men, all dressed in equally nice suits, none wearing their jackets.

They ignore us as they push past, resuming their conversation in the hallway. "So I tell him..." The door closes behind them.

"Whew," Marissa breathes. "It's way easier if they're not here." She glances up at the corners of the rooms. "Of course there are cameras everywhere, so it's not like we aren't being watched." She points to a tiny red light shining from a little device mounted at the juncture of the wall and ceiling. I've already noticed them all over the casino. "But it's less nerve-wracking if we're not tiptoeing around them."

She jerks her head down the hall. "You take the bathroom and bedrooms, I'll do the kitchen, office and living area."

"Got it." I grab the supplies I need off the cart and head in the direction she indicated.

The bedroom's well-appointed in a nondescript way. I pull the sheets and bedspread up to make the bed. The sheets were probably 3,000 thread count, if there is such a thing. That may be an exaggeration but, really, they are amazing.

Just for kicks, I rub one against my cheek.

It's so smooth and soft. I can't imagine what it would be like to lie in that bed. I wonder which of the guys slept in here. I make the bed with hospital corners, the way Marissa trained me to, dust and vacuum, then move on to the second bedroom and then the bathroom. When I finish, I find Marissa vacuuming in the living room.

She switches it off and winds up the cord. "All done? Me too. Let's go to the next one."

I push out the cart and she taps on the door of the suite down the hall. No answer.

She keys us in. "It is way faster having you help," she says gratefully.

I flash her a smile. "I think it's more fun to work as a team, too."

She smiles back. "Yeah, somehow I don't think they would go for it as a regular thing, but it's nice for a change."

"Same routine?"

"Unless you want to switch? This one only has one bedroom."

"Nah," I say, "I like bed/bath." Of course that's because

of my all-consuming curiosity. There are more personal effects in a bedroom and a bathroom, not that I saw anything of interest in the last place. I didn't go poking around, of course. The cameras in every corner have me nervous.

This place is the same as the last, as if they'd paid a decorator to furnish them and they were all identical. High luxury, but not much personality. Well, from what I understand, the Tacone family—at least the ones who run the Bellissimo—are all single men. What can I expect?

I make the bed and move on to dusting.

From the living room, I hear Marissa's voice.

"What?" I call out, but then I realize she's talking on the phone.

She comes in a moment later, breathless. "I have to go." Her face has gone pale. "My kid's been taken to the ER for a concussion."

"Oh shit. Go—I've got this. Do you want to give me the keycard for the last suite?" There are three suites on this top floor.

She looks around distractedly. "No, I'd better not. Could you just finish this place up and head back downstairs? I'll call Samuel to let him know what happened." Samuel's our boss, the head of housekeeping. "Don't forget to stay away from the desk in the office."

"Sure thing. Get out of here." I make a shooing motion. "Go be with your kid."

"Okay." She digs her purse out from the cart and slings it over her shoulder. "I'll see you tomorrow."

"I hope he's all right," I say to her back as she leaves.

She flings a weak smile over her shoulder. "Thanks. Bye."

I grab the vacuum and head back into the bedroom. When I finish, I hear male voices in the living room.

"Hope you can get some sleep, Nico. How long's it been?" one of the voices asked.

"Forty-eight hours. Fucking insomnia."

"G'luck, see you later." A door clicks shut.

My heart immediately beats a little faster with excitement or nerves. Yes—I'm a fool. Later, I would realize my mistake in not marching right out and introducing myself, but Marissa has me nervous about the Tacones and I freeze up. The cart stands out in the living room, though. I decide to go into the bathroom and clean everything I can without getting fresh supplies. Finally, I give up, square my shoulders and head out.

I arrive in the living room and pull out three folded towels, four hand towels and four washcloths. Out of my peripheral vision, I watch the broad shoulders and back of another finely dressed man.

He glances over then does a double-take. His dark eyes rake over me, lingering on my legs and traveling up to my breasts, then face. "*Who the fuck are you?*"

I should've expected that response, but it startles me anyway. He sounds scary. Seriously scary, and he walks toward me like he means business. He's beautiful, with dark wavy hair, a stubbled square jaw and thick-lashed eyes that bore a hole right through me.

"Huh? Who. The fuck. Are you?"

I panic. Instead of answering him, I turn and walk

swiftly to the bathroom, as if putting fresh towels in his bathroom will fix everything.

He stalks after me and follows me in. "What are you doing in here?" He knocks the towels out of my hands.

Stunned, I stare down at them scattered on the floor. "I'm...housekeeping," I offer lamely. Damn my idiotic fascination with the mafia. This is not the freaking *Sopranos*. This is a real-life, dangerous man wearing a gun in a holster under his armpit. I know, because I see it when he reaches for me.

He grips my upper arms. "Bullshit. No one who looks like"—his eyes travel up and down the length of my body again—"*you*—works in housekeeping."

I blink, not sure what that means. I'm pretty, I know that, but there's nothing special about me. I'm your girl-next-door blue-eyed blonde type, on the short and curvy side. Not like my cousin Corey, who is tall, slender, red-haired and drop-dead gorgeous, with the confidence to match.

There's something lewd in the way he looks at me that makes it sound like I'm standing there in nipple tassels and a G-string instead of my short, fitted maid's dress. I play dumb. "I'm new. I've only been here a couple weeks."

He sports dark circles under his eyes, and I remember what he told the other man. He suffers from insomnia. Hasn't slept in forty-eight hours.

"Are you bugging the place?" he demands.

"Wha—" I can't even answer. I just stare like an idiot.

He starts frisking me for a weapon. "Is this a con? What do they think—I'm going to fuck you? Who sent you?"

I attempt to answer, but his warm hands sliding all over me make me forget what I was going to say. *Why is he talking about fucking me?*

He stands up and gives me a tiny shake. "Who. Sent. You?" His dark eyes mesmerize. He smells of the casino—of whiskey and cash, and beneath it, his own simmering essence.

"No one...I mean, Marissa!" I exclaim her name like a secret password, but it only seems to irritate him further.

He reaches out and runs his fingers swiftly along the collar of my housekeeping dress, as if checking for some hidden wiretap. I'm pretty sure the guy's half out of his mind, maybe delirious with sleep deprivation. Maybe just nuts. I freeze, not wanting to set him off.

To my shock, he yanks down the zipper on the front of my dress, all the way to my waist.

If I were my cousin Corey, daughter of a mean FBI agent, I'd knee him in the balls, gun or not. But I was raised not to make waves. To be a nice girl and do what authority tells me to do.

So, like a freaking idiot, I just stand there. A tiny mewl leaves my lips, but I don't dare move, don't protest. He yanks the form-fitting dress to my waist and jerks it down over my hips.

I wrest my arms free from the fabric to wrap them around myself.

Nico Tacone shoves me aside to get the dress out from under my feet. He picks it up and runs his hands all over it, still searching for the mythical wiretap while I shiver in my bra and panties.

I fold my arms across my breasts. "Look, I'm not

wearing a wire or bugging the place," I breathe. "I was helping Marissa and then she got a call—"

"Save it," he barks. "You're too fucking perfect. What's the con? What the fuck are you doing in here?"

I'm confounded. Should I keep arguing the truth when it only pisses him off? I swallow. None of the words in my head seem like the right ones to say.

He reaches for my bra.

I bat at his hands, heart pumping like I just did two back-to-back spin classes. He ignores my feeble resistance. The bra is a front hook and he obviously excels at removing women's lingerie because it's off faster than the dress. My breasts spring out with a bounce, and he glares at them, as if I bared them just to tempt him. He examines the bra, then tosses it on the floor and stares at me. His eyes dip once more to my breasts and his expression grows even more furious. "Real tits," he mutters as if that's a punishable offense.

I try to step back but I bump into the toilet. "I'm not hiding anything. I'm just a maid. I got hired two weeks ago. You can call Samuel."

He steps closer. Tragically, the hardened menace on his handsome face only increases his attractiveness to me. I really am wired wrong. My body thrills at the nearness of him, pussy dampening. Or maybe it's the fact that he just stripped me practically naked while he stands there fully clothed. I think this is a fetish to some people. Apparently, I'm one of them. If I wasn't so scared, it would be uber hot.

He palms my backside, warm fingers sliding over the satiny fabric of my panties, but he's not groping me, he's still working efficiently, checking for bugs. He slides a thumb under the gusset, running the fabric through his fingers. My belly flutters.

Oh God. The back of his thumb brushes my dewy slit. I cringe in embarrassment. His head jerks up and he stares at me in surprise, nostrils flaring.

Then his brows slammed down as if it pisses him off I'm turned on, as if it's a trick.

That's when things really go to shit.

He pulls out his gun and points it at my head—actually pushes the cold hard muzzle against my brow. "*What. The fuck. Are you doing here?*"

I pee myself.

Literally.

God help me.

I freeze and pee trickles down my inner thighs before I can stop it. My face burns with humiliation.

Now, the anger and indignation I should've had from the start rushes out. It's the exact wrong moment to get lippy, but I glare at him. "What's *wrong* with you?"

He stares at the dribble on the floor. I think he's going to... Well, I don't know what I think he'll do—pistol whip me or sneer or something—but his expression relaxes and he shoves the gun in its holster. Apparently, I finally gave the right reaction.

He grips my arm and drags me toward the shower. My brain is doing flip flops trying to get back online. To figure out what in the hell is happening and how I can get myself out of this very crazy, very fucked up situation.

Tacone reaches in and turns on the water, holding his hand under the spray as if to check its temperature.

My brain hasn't turned back on, but I wrestle with his grip on my arm.

He releases it and holds his palm face out. "Okay," he says. "Get in." He draws his hand out of the shower and jerks his head toward the spray. "Clean up."

Is he coming in there with me? Or is this really just about washing off?

Fuck it. I *am* a mess. I kick off my shoes and step in, panties and all.

I don't know how long I stand there, drowning in shock. After a while, I blink and awareness seeps back in. Then I freak out. What in the hell is happening? What will he do with me? Did I really just pee on his floor? I want to die of embarrassment.

Keep it together, Sondra.

Jesus Christ. The mafia boss who stands on the other side of the shower curtain thinks I'm a narc. Or a spy or rat—whatever they call it. And he just stripped me down to my panties and pointed a gun at my head. Things could only get worse from here. A sob rises up in my throat.

Don't cry. Not a good time to cry.

I stumble back against the tile wall, my legs too rubbery to stand. Hot tears spill down my cheeks and I sniff.

The shower curtain peeps open right by my face and I jerk back. I didn't know he was standing right outside it.

~

Nico

. . .

Minchia. Shit.

My remaining doubts about the girl evaporate when I hear her crying. If I made a mistake, it's a really fucking big one. Because I seriously don't want to have to explain to my head of HR why I stripped one of our employees and held a gun to her head. *In my bathroom.*

I've seriously gone off the deep end this time. The insomnia is fucking with me—making me paranoid and itchy. I need to get my little brother Stefano out here to help me run the place so I can sleep at least an hour a night. He's the only one I trust.

"Hey." I make my voice softer. The girl's standing under the spray of water, soaking her Harley Quinn pigtails and the pair of light blue satin panties she's still wearing.

Fuck if I don't want to yank them right off her and see what's underneath.

I'm pretty sure she's in shock, and who could blame her? I terrify my employees on my best days and that's without tearing off their clothes and flashing a weapon.

Her chest shudders as she lets out a silent sob and it gets under my skin, same way her sniffle did. Somehow, I don't think undercover feds or any kind of professional would pee on my floor and cry in my shower. So yeah. I seriously fucked up here.

I reach past her and shut off the water, soaking the entire arm of my suit jacket in the process. "Hey, don't cry."

A better man might apologize, but until I'm one hundred percent sure there's not something off here, I keep it in. I yank the shower curtain open, and pull her out to stand on the bath mat while I wrap one of the towels from the floor around her. Because she seems to still be in shock, I hook my thumbs in the waistband of her wet panties and tug them down her trembling legs. I must not be as depraved as I think, because I somehow manage not to look at what she keeps under them when I lower to a squat and grip her ankle to help her step out of the dripping fabric.

I toss them in the garbage can. Earlier, I threw a towel over the place where she peed, and her eyes dart there now.

I know she's gotta be completely humiliated by it, but the truth is, she's not the first person I've made piss themselves. I guess she's the first female. The only one I'm sorry for scaring.

She's trying to stifle her sobs, which, of course, only turns them into snorts and choked gasps. Now I really feel like a first-class asshole.

"Aw, *bambina*." I grab the two corners of the towel, and pull her against me. Her wet skin dampens my suit, but all I can think about is how soft her lush, naked form is against my body. The exhaustion in my limbs ebbs, cleared by the flames of white-hot desire. "Shh. You're okay."

She trembles against me, but her sobs quiet.

"Did I hurt you?"

She shakes her head, her wet pigtails splattering a drop of water onto my cheek. Her gaze tracks to it. A loose section in the front flops over her eyes.

I shift my grip on the towel to one hand and use the

other to brush the hair back from her face. "You're okay," I repeat.

She blinks up at me with long-lashed blue eyes. I love having her up close and captive where I can study her better. She's as beautiful as I originally thought, with porcelain skin and high cheekbones. It's not just beauty that makes her special. There's some other quality that makes her seem so out of place here. A fresh-faced innocence. Yet she's not overly naive or young. She's not dumb, either. I can't put my finger on it.

I don't release her. I don't want to. The heat of her body radiates through my damp clothes and crowds my mind with the dirtiest of thoughts. If I were a gentleman, I'd leave the room and let her get dressed, but I'm not. I'm an asshole with a hotel casino to run.

And I still don't know who the hell this girl is or how she ended up in my suite. And seriously, heads are going to roll for this. Even more because the girl suffered for it.

Right. If my brain were working better, I might acknowledge I'm the only one who can take blame for that part, especially since I'm still holding her naked and captive.

"It's just a girl who looks like you doesn't normally clean rooms in Vegas," I offer as the lamest excuse ever. It's true, though. I'm sure there are more girls like her out there. But I don't see them around here. All I see are the fake-boobed hustlers trying to work some angle. The professionals. Women who use their bodies like weapons. And I have no problem with them. I'm happy to use their bodies, too.

But this one—she's different.

Her full berry lips part, but she doesn't say anything.

I can't keep my hands to myself. I run my thumb across her lower lip, trace it back and forth over the plump flesh.

Her pupils dilate, giving me encouragement to keep touching.

"A girl like you is usually on the stage—some kind of stage—even if it's just a gentleman's club."

Her eyes narrow but I don't shut up.

"Girl like you could make a shit ton selling herself." Mary, Queen of Peace, I want to kiss the girl. I lower my lips but manage to stop above hers. A kiss would definitely not be welcome. I may be a scary prick, but I don't force myself on women. "You know how much a guy like me would pay for a night with you?"

This time I really went too far. She tries to yank back from me. I don't release her, but I do lift my head. She presses her lips together a moment before saying, "May I go?"

I ease back, but shake my head. "No." It's a decisive syllable, short and curt.

She flinches. The dilated pupils narrow back to fear. I don't like her afraid nearly as well as I like her trembling and soft, open to me, the way she was a moment ago. It's a subtle distinction, though, because I do love the power position of having her here, at my mercy.

"I still need some answers." I back her toward the sink counter, then pick her up by the waist and plop her bare ass down on the cool marble top. The towel flaps open when I release her, and I get another eyeful of her perfect, full breasts as she scrambles to find the corners and pull it closed.

I shake my head to clear the fresh flood of lust rocketing through me. My cock's gone rock hard. I'm a man used to getting everything he wants, which usually includes women. The fact that this one isn't available makes me want her even more. "Seriously," I mutter. "I'd pay five large for a night with a girl like you." Even as I say it, I know I'd never want her that way. I'd want to coax the willingness out of this one.

And that's my strangest thought yet. Because I never, ever spend time dating.

"I'm not a prostitute," she snaps, blue eyes flashing.

Her anger pulls me out of my sleep-deprived fantasy. I blink several times. "I know. Just saying you could make a lot of money in this town."

I shake my head. What the fuck am I saying? I don't want this girl to become one of those women.

And she just wants to get the hell out of here. So I need to get back to my interrogation.

"Who are you and why are you here?"

She draws in a shaky breath. "My name is Sondra Simonson. My cousin, Corey Simonson, works here as a dealer. She got me this job in housekeeping while I wait for something better to open up." She speaks rapidly, but it doesn't sound rehearsed. And it has enough details to ring true. "Marissa is my boss, and I offered to help her clean the rooms up here because the regulars are out sick. Her kid got a concussion and she had to leave me up here by myself. All I did was clean." She lifts her chin, even though her pulse flutters at a frantic pace in her neck.

I wait for her to go on, not because I'm still that suspicious, but because I like hearing her talk.

She babbles on, "I just moved here from Reno…I taught art history at Truckee Meadow Community College."

I tilt my head, trying to assimilate this new information. It only adds to the wrongness of this girl being in my room. "Why is an art history professor working as a goddamn maid in my hotel?"

"Because I have terrible taste in men," she blurts.

"That right?" I have to work to keep from smiling. I lean my hip up against the counter between her spread thighs. When she blushes, I know she must be thinking about how close her pretty little bare pussy is to the part of me most eager to touch her.

I'm even more fascinated by this lovely creature now. What kind of guy does an art history professor fall for?

She swallows and nods. "Yeah."

"You follow a guy here?"

"No." She lets out her breath with a sigh. "I bailed on one. Turns out we had an unshared interest in polyamory."

I lift an eyebrow. She's studying me right back, her blue eyes intelligent now that the fear is wearing off.

"Let's just say finding him banging three girls in our bed will be forever burned into my mind. So"—she shrugs — "I took our car and headed to Vegas. But karma got me because it got totaled when I arrived."

"How is that your karma?"

"Because half that car belonged to Tanner and I stole it."

I shrug. "Whose name was on the title?"

"Mine."

"Then it's your car," I say, like I'm the guy who makes the final ruling on all things to do with her ex. "So that still doesn't explain why you're in my bathroom."

Or maybe it did. My brain is still short-circuiting from lack of sleep. The real truth is probably that I don't want to let her go. I'd like to string her up in my room and interrogate her with my leather flogger all night long. I wonder how that pale skin would look with my hand prints on it.

Too much, Tacone. I try to pull back. The room swims and dips as my vision trails. Fuck, I need sleep.

She blinks rapidly. "Because you won't let me leave?"

I was right. She's smart.

The corners of my mouth twitch.

"Housekeeping is the only place I could get a job on short notice. I'd rather work as a dealer. Think you can hook me up?" Now she's getting sassy.

Funny, I don't have the urge to take her down a peg the way I usually do with employees. Unless, of course, it involves her naked and at my mercy.

Oh yeah. I already set that up.

But the suggestion of her working as a dealer irritates the fuck out of me. I don't know if it's because she'd be ruined by Las Vegas in a month, or because I really want to keep her in my room. Cleaning my floors. Naked.

"No."

She flinches because I say the word too hard. I'm definitely having a difficult time modulating my behavior. But she just shrugs. "Well, this is temporary, anyway. Just until I earn enough to get a new car and find a teaching job."

Okay, even not trusting my instincts, I think she's who she says she is. Which means I have no good reason to keep her prisoner here. I step back and take another long perusal of her now that I know more about her. Seriously. I want to keep her.

But considering the things I just did to her, she'll probably quit the second she leaves my suite. I point to her crumpled dress and bra on the floor. "Get dressed."

Before I do or say anything else to traumatize the girl, I leave the bathroom, shutting the door behind myself.

ABOUT LEE SAVINO

Lee Savino is a USA today bestselling author, mom and choco-holic.

Warning: Do not read her Berserker series, or you will be addicted to the huge, dominant warriors who will stop at nothing to claim their mates.

I repeat: Do. Not. Read. The Berserker Saga. Particularly not the thrilling excerpt below.

Download a free book from www.leesavino.com (don't read that either. Too much hot, sexy lovin').

EXCERPT: SOLD TO THE BERSERKERS

A MÉNAGE SHIFTER ROMANCE

By Lee Savino

The day my stepfather sold me to the Berserkers, I woke at dawn with him leering over me. "Get up." He made to kick me and I scrambled out of my sleep stupor to my feet.

"I need your help with a delivery."

I nodded and glanced at my sleeping mother and siblings. I didn't trust my stepfather around my three younger sisters, but if I was gone with him all day, they'd be safe. I'd taken to carrying a dirk myself. I did not dare kill him; we needed him for food and shelter, but if he attacked me again, I would fight.

My mother's second husband hated me, ever since the last time he'd tried to take me and I had fought back. My mother was gone to market, and when he tried to grab me, something in me snapped. I would not let him touch me again. I fought, kicking and scratching, and finally grabbing an iron pot and scalding him with heated water.

He bellowed and looked as if he wanted to hurt me, but kept his distance. When my mother returned he pretended like nothing was wrong, but his eyes followed me with hatred and cunning.

Out loud he called me ugly and mocking the scar that marred my neck since a wild dog attacked me when I was young. I ignored this and kept my distance. I'd heard the taunts about my hideous face since the wounds had healed into scars, a mass of silver tissue at my neck.

That morning, I wrapped a scarf over my hair and scarred neck and followed my stepfather, carrying his wares down the old road. At first I thought we were headed to the great market, but when we reached the fork in the road and he went an unfamiliar way, I hesitated. Something wasn't right.

"This way, cur." He'd taken to calling me "dog". He'd taunted me, saying the only sounds I could make were grunts like a beast, so I might as well be one. He was right. The attack had taken my voice by damaging my throat.

If I followed him into the forest and he tried to kill me, I wouldn't even be able to cry out.

"There's a rich man who asked for his wares delivered to his door." He marched on without a backward glance and I followed.

I had lived all my life in the kingdom of Alba, but when my father died and my mother remarried, we moved to my stepfather's village in the highlands, at the foot of the great, forbidding mountains. There were stories of evil that lived in the dark crevices of the heights, but I'd never believed them.

I knew enough monsters living in plain sight.

The longer we walked, the lower the sun sank in the sky, the more I knew my stepfather was trying to trick me, that there was no rich man waiting for these wares.

When the path curved, and my stepfather stepped out from behind a boulder to surprise me, I was half ready, but before I could reach for my dirk he struck me so hard I fell.

I woke tied to a tree.

The light was lower, heralding dusk. I struggled silently, frantic gasps escaping from my scarred throat. My stepfather stepped into view and I felt a second of relief at a familiar face, before remembering the evil this man had wrought on my body. Whatever he was planning, it would bode ill for me, and my younger sisters. If I didn't survive, they would eventually share the same fate as mine.

"You're awake," he said. "Just in time for the sale."

I strained but my bonds held fast. As my stepfather approached, I realized that the scarf that I wrapped around my neck to hide my scars had fallen, exposing them. Out of habit, I twitched my head to the side, tucking my bad side towards my shoulder.

My stepfather smirked.

"So ugly," he sneered. "I could never find a husband for you, but I found someone to take you. A group of warriors passing through who saw you, and want to slake their lust on your body. Who knows, if you please them, they may let you live. But I doubt you'll survive these men. They're foreigners, mercenaries, come to fight for the king. Berserkers. If you're lucky your death will be swift when they tear you apart."

I'd heard the tales of berserker warriors, fearsome warriors of old. Ageless, timeless, they'd sailed over the seas to the land, plundering, killing, taking slaves, they fought for our kings, and their own. Nothing could stand in their path when they went into a killing rage.

I fought to keep my fear off my face. Berserker's were a myth, so my stepfather had probably sold me to a band of passing soldiers who would take their pleasure from my flesh before leaving me for dead, or selling me on.

"I could've sold you long ago, if I stripped you bare and put a bag over you head to hide those scars."

His hands pawed at me, and I shied away from his disgusting breath. He slapped me, then tore at my braid, letting my hair spill over my face and shoulders.

Bound as I was, I still could glare at him. I could do nothing to stop the sale, but I hoped my fierce expression told him I'd fight to the death if he tried to force himself on me.

His hand started to wander down towards my breast when a shadow moved on the edge of the clearing. It caught my eye and I startled. My stepfather stepped back as the warriors poured from the trees.

My first thought was that they were not men, but beasts. They prowled forward, dark shapes almost one with the shadows. A few wore animal pelts and held back, lurking on the edge of the woods. Two came forward, wearing the garb of warriors, bristling with weapons. One had dark hair, and the other long, dirty blond with a beard to match.

Their eyes glowed with a terrifying light.

As they approached, the smell of raw meat and blood wafted over us, and my stomach twisted. I was glad my stepfather hadn't fed me all day, or I would've emptied my guts on the ground.

My stepfather's face and tone took on the wheedling expression I'd seen when he was selling in the market.

"Good evening, sirs," he cringed before the largest, the blond with hair streaming down his chest.

They were perfectly silent, but the blond approached, fixing me with strange golden eyes.

Their faces were fair enough, but their hulking forms and the quick, light way they moved made me catch my breath. I had never seen such massive men. Beside them, my stepfather looked like an ugly dwarf.

"This is the one you wanted," my stepfather continued. "She's healthy and strong. She will be a good slave for you."

My body would've shaken with terror, if I were not bound so tightly.

A dark haired warrior stepped up beside the blond and the two exchanged a look.

"You asked for the one with scars." My stepfather took my hair and jerked my head back, exposing the horrible, silvery mass. I shut my eyes, tears squeezing out at the sudden pain and humiliation.

The next thing I knew, my stepfather's grip loosened.

A grunt, and I opened my eyes to see the dark haired warrior standing at my side. My stepfather sprawled on the ground as if he'd been pushed.

The blond leader prodded a boot into my stepfather's side.

"Get up," the blond said, in a voice that was more a growl than a human sound. It curdled my blood. My stepfather scrambled to his feet.

The black haired man cut away the last of my bonds, and I sagged forward. I would've fallen but he caught me easily and set me on my feet, keeping his arms around me. I was not the smallest woman, but he was a giant. Muscles bulged in his arms and chest, but he held me carefully. I stared at him, taking in his raven dark hair and strange gold eyes.

He tucked me closer to his muscled body.

Meanwhile, my stepfather whined. "I just wanted to show you the scars—"

Again that frightening growl from the blond. "You don't touch what is ours."

"I don't want to touch her." My stepfather spat.

Despite myself, I cowered against the man who held me. A stranger I had never met, he was still a safer haven than my stepfather.

"I only wish to make sure you are satisfied, milords. Do you want to sample her?" my stepfather asked in an evil tone. He wanted to see me torn apart.

A growl rumbled under my ear and I lifted my head. Who were these men, these great warriors who had bought and paid for me? The arms around my body were strong and solid, inescapable, but the gold eyes looking down at me were kind. The warrior ran his thumb across the pad of my lips, and his fingers were gentle for such a large, violent looking warrior. Under the scent of blood, he smelled of snow and sharp cold, a clean scent.

He pressed his face against my head, breathing in a deep breath.

The blond was looking at us.

"It's her," the black haired man growled, his voice so guttural. "This is the one."

One of his hands came to cover the side of my face and throat, holding my face to his chest in a protective gesture.

I closed my eyes, relaxing in the solid warmth of the warrior's body.

A clink of gold, and the deed was done. I'd been sold.

Almost immediately, the warrior started pulling me away.

I fought my rising panic, wishing that my stepfather's was not the last familiar face I saw.

"Goodbye, Brenna," my stepfather smirked as the warriors streamed past him, following their blond leader into the forest.

"Wait," the blond stopped. Immediately the warriors grabbed my stepfather. "Her name is Brenna?"

"Yes. But you bought her. Call her what you like."

The dark haired warrior tugged me on. I half followed, half staggered along beside him. My nails bit into my palms so I could keep myself from panicking. Fighting the giant beside me wasn't an option. Neither was trying to outrun him.

The blond joined us, and the two warriors pulled me into the dark grove. Terrible thoughts poured into my mind. I belonged to these men, and now they would rape me, sate themselves with my body, then cut my throat and leave me for the wolves.

My eyes filled with tears, both angry and frightened.

They stopped as one and drew me between them. I shut my eyes in defiance, and the tears leaked out.

As I healed from the attack, I could make some noises, horrible, animal things, but they were so ugly, I stopped making any sounds at all. Sometimes, when alone, I'd sink into the river, open my mouth and try to scream. But no sound came out anymore. My throat had forgotten my voice.

Now the only sound in the grove was my harsh breathing.

I sensed the warriors on either side of me, their massive shapes towering over my fragile body. I was much smaller than them, tiny and petite beside their massive forms.

Right now I tried to remember to breathe and submit to these men. One blow and they could kill me.

My heart beat so hard it was painful. I was ready to die.

But when they touched me they were gentle. A hand brushed back my hair, then stroked my jaw. One steadied me from behind as the other cupped my head and turned my head this way and that. The one behind me gathered my hair behind me. I held my breath as the two massive warriors handled me.

I realized the smell of blood had fallen away, replaced by another scent, an animal musk that was much more pleasant.

A finger ran over my neck, near the scar and I sucked in a breath. The hands dropped away.

Their faces dipped close to mine, and I felt their breath on my skin as if they took deep scents of my hair.

"So good," one of them groaned.

I didn't understand. I was afraid of them taking me but I didn't know why they weren't.

"It's working," one murmured to the other. "The witch was right."

As they dipped their heads and scented me, my heart beat faster in response to their proximity. Something stirred deep inside me. Desire. A few minutes alone with these men and I'd been more intimate with them than any other.

As one they bent their heads to mine, nuzzling close to my neck a tingling spread over my skin.

I felt it then, unbidden, a stirring in my loins. Ever since I had come into womanhood, my desires were strong. Every month I fought the pull to find a man and join with him. I was hideous and destined to be an outcast and alone. But each full moon my body came alive, beset by waves of roiling lust until I felt desperate enough to grab the nearest man and beg him to give me sons.

The heat poured over me until I heard a gasp—one of the warriors jerked back and stepped away.

"She's ready," one growled. Instead of frightening, the sound excited me.

What was happening?

"Not here, brother," the blond rasped.

Without answering, the dark-haired one pulled me on.

For a while we walked, pushing through the forest and forded a stream. The heat in me faded as I followed, weak with hunger and fear, eventually stumbling on exhaustion numbed feet.

The dark-haired warrior stopped, and I flinched, expecting him to bully me into continuing on.

Instead, he guided me to face him. Again his hands came to me, stroking back my hair. I winced when I realized what he was doing: looking at my scar.

Involuntarily my head jerked and he let my chin go, offering me water instead. He held the skin while I drank, and when I'd had my fill he offered me dried meat, feeding me from his hand. I stared into the strange golden eyes, unable to keep the questions off my face: Who are you? What are you going to do with me?

When I was done, he lay a hand on his chest and uttered a guttural sound I didn't understand. He repeated it twice, then lay his hand on my chest.

"Brenna." I could barely make out my name, but I nodded.

A shadow of a smile curved his full lips. Shrugging off the gray pelt he wore, he wrapped it around my shoulders before pulling me back into the circle of his strong arms.

My heart beat faster. The pelt's warmth seeped into my tired body, and the big man held me steady. I still felt frightened, but waited obediently in the dark haired warrior's embrace. I dared not struggle.

The brush around us rippled and the warriors surrounded us. I shrank towards my black-haired captor, but he held me fast, turning me so I faced the warrior who seemed to be their leader.

The blond was so huge, my neck had to tip back to see him. He moved forward and I couldn't help trembling so hard I would've fallen if the dark haired warrior let me go. Every instinct in me screamed that this was a wild man, a beast a dangerous monster and I needed to run.

He reached out and I flinched.

His hand halted.

He swallowed, as if trying to remember how to use his voice.

"Brenna." My name was no more than a soft growl. "We mean you no harm."

I studied him. As big as the warriors were, the blond was one of the largest. He walked lightly, muscles bulging. Long locks of blond hair brushed his broad shoulders. His face was rawboned and half covered in a beard, the defining feature his great gold eyebrows over those amazing eyes.

When his gaze caught mine, his eyes glowed.

His hands touched my face, a thumb stroking my lips. He tilted it to and fro. He pushed my hair away from my neck. I shut my eyes, knowing what he saw, the white weals and gnarled tissue, healed into a disfiguring scar that had taken my voice, and nearly taken my life.

I barely remembered the attack: a large dark shape rushing at me from the shadows, then pain. Lots of pain.

My mother told me I lay near death for days. No one thought I would survive, but I did.

Some believed it would be better if I hadn't. Even though I healed from the attack, the scars marked my face and my life. The boys used to chase me down the street, throwing things. I grew up learning to blend into the shadows. To move silently so I wouldn't draw attention to myself. Later, when my mother married my stepfather, I learned to cower and hide.

Her body is pretty enough, my stepfather had said. *Just put a bag over her head so you can stand it.*

Now my new owner tipped my head this way and that, studying the scar. He nodded, looking satisfied. "The mark of the wolf," he rasped.

A ripple went around the assembled men, and the other warriors pressed closer. The black haired man held me still, hefty arms around my body.

I wished I could ask what the blond warrior meant.

The men surrounded me, staring at my hideous scars.

My blond captor released my jaw and I ducked my head down again in shame. His large, rough hands caught my head again, and raised it, but this time he cupped my face.

I shut my eyes. I couldn't even cry out. This man now owned me. I'd resigned myself to living life with a disfigured face, unwanted and unloved, but I'd never thought I'd become a slave.

"Brenna," The command came in that rasping growl. "Look at me."

Somehow I obeyed and met the leader's steady gaze.

Something in that golden glow mesmerized me, and I felt calmer.

"Do not be afraid." His throat worked for a moment, as if he was trying to remember how to speak. "Is it true you cannot speak?"

I nodded.

"Can you read or write?"

I shook my head. This was the strangest conversation I'd had in my nineteen years.

He looked frustrated, exchanging glances with the warrior who held me.

A voice spoke at my ear, still rough and guttural, but a bit more clearly than before. "We would like to find a way to talk to ye." The speaker turned me to face him, and I flinched as he brought his hand up, but he only examined the scars as the blond had.

By the time he was done, all warriors but the blond had melted away. Dark hair touched my cheek and I winced, realizing there was a bruise on my face from when my stepfather struck me.

The blond crowded closer, a sound rumbling in his great chest, not unlike a growl.

"Brenna," he said. "We will not hurt you. I swear it. No one will ever hurt you again."

The dark haired one took a few locks of my hair in his hand, gripping them lightly and raising them to his face. He breathed in my scent, then looked at me with glowing eyes and said in a clear voice.

"Ye belong to us now."

~

The rest of the night passed in a blur. We walked into the woods, the thick darkness, and went along a path. The warriors went behind and before, I was safe in the middle.

Finally exhaustion took over and I stumbled. Instantly, the dark haired warrior swung me up in his arms, and the group's pace increased. His hand came up, pressing my face to his neck.

I must have slept, for when I woke again, the blond was carrying me. I lifted my head blinking in the starlight and cold night air. The warriors must have walked all night, and were still hiking, following a trail up a mountain. I roused a little and stared into the leaders golden eyes.

"Sleep," he grunted. "Almost home."

I do not know how long I slept, but as I slept I dreamed. The starlight fell away into a deeper darkness. I was in a warm, safe place with two warriors leaning over me, large hands sifting through my hair. One of them pulled out a dirk and sliced away my gown, and then the hands began stroking down my body. Their touches fed my heated desire, and in my dream I longed to pull their bodies over mine, wordlessly begging them to fill me.

Instead, I lay still as they touched me with reverent fingers. I heard them speak, but not out loud. They didn't use words but somehow I understood them.

"The witch was right. She calms the wolf."

A grunt of agreement, then a pause. "I can smell her heat."

"Patience, brother. We have waited this long."

They lay on either side of me, still touching me. In the darkness their eyes glowed.

"Brother," one said in a tone of awe. "The beast rests."

"As does mine."

"It has been so long."

"Too long. But the struggle is over. The beast will sleep again."

SOLD TO THE BERSERKERS

When Brenna's father sells her to a band of passing warriors, her only thought is to survive. She doesn't expect to be claimed by the two fearsome warriors who lead the Berserker clan. Kept in captivity, she is coddled and cared for, treated more like a savior than a slave. Can captivity lead to love? And when she discovers the truth behind the myth of the fearsome warriors, can she accept her place as the Berserkers' true mate?

Author's Note: *Sold to the Berserkers is a standalone, short, MFM ménage romance starring two huge, dominant warriors who make it all about the woman. Read the whole best-selling Berserker saga to see what readers are raving about...*

The Berserker Saga

Sold to the Berserkers

ALSO BY LEE SAVINO

Exiled To the Prison Planet

Draekon Mate

Draekon Fire

Draekon Heart

Draekon Abduction

Draekon Destiny

Draekon Fever

Draekon Rogue

Printed in Great Britain
by Amazon